Presented To

Monongahela Area Library

ANIMAL ACTS

A NOVEL

RHODA LERMAN

HENRY HOLT AND COMPANY

NEW YORK

Henry Holt and Company, Inc.
Publishers since 1866
115 West 18th Street
New York, New York 10011

Henry Holt® is a registered
trademark of Henry Holt and Company, Inc.

Published in Canada by Fitzhenry & Whiteside Ltd.,
195 Allstate Parkway, Markham, Ontario L3R 4T8.

Library of Congress Cataloging-in-Publication Data

Lerman, Rhoda.
Animal acts : a novel / Rhoda Lerman.
p.   cm.
I. Title.
PS3562.E68A82   1994
813'.54—dc20   93-38343
CIP

ISBN 0-8050-1418-7

Henry Holt books are available for special promotions
and premiums. For details contact:
Director, Special Markets.

First Edition—1994

Designed by Kate Nichols

Printed in the United States of America
All first editions are printed on acid-free paper. ∞

1   3   5   7   9   10   8   6   4   2

For Walden Pond Shore Acres Ben, for Marilyn Cole of the Metro Toronto Zoo, and for Rachèl Watkins-Rogers of the San Diego Zoo, who led me so kindly into the animal world.

And for the women and their gorillas who shared stories and dreams with me:

Ann Baker and Sampson	Burnet Park Zoo
Ruth Bowman and Angel	Private ownership
Pat Bumstead and Kikinga	Calgary Zoo
Marilyn Cole and Charles	Metro Toronto Zoo
Patty Kuntzman and Ramar	Philadelphia Zoological Gardens
Mae Noel and Otto	The Chimp Farm, Tarpon Springs, Florida
Pat Sammarco and Otto	Lincoln Park Zoo
Pat Sass and Frank	Lincoln Park Zoo

And for all the people who shared insights and information:

Rob Sutherland, primate keeper, Calgary Zoo
Keith Lloyd, gorilla keeper, Port Lympne, Kent, U.K.
Ron Cohn and Joanne E. Tanner, Gorilla Foundation
Bud Watkins of Watkins Famous Chimp Acts
Carmen Presti, Christy Scarupa, and Charlie the Karate Chimp

For Florida information, I thank Mr. and Mrs. Ken Williamson of the Williamson Cattle Ranch, Okeechobee, Florida; the Okeechobee Historical Society; Scott Sedge of the Kissimmee Prairie Preserve, Audubon Society; Noel Chandler, warden, Audubon Society; Steven Sullivan, U.S. Army Corp of Engineers, Clewiston, Florida; and J. R. Wilcox, chief environmentalist, Florida Power and Light Company.

This book could not have been written without *Gorillas in the Mist*, by Dian Fossey; *The Aquatic Ape*, by Elaine Morgan; *The Year of the Gorilla*, by George Schaller.

Special thanks to Allen Coit Ransome and Randall Van Syoc of Toad Hall Galleries for the commissioning of the cover artwork.

ONE

Whenever I felt I could no longer bear another moment of my marriage I would imagine my husband's funeral, my heels sinking into the zoysia, I flinging a handful of dirt onto his casket as it's lowered into the groin of earth. I wouldn't meet the children's eyes. They would suspect something. For years they'd wanted to ask me, "How do you really feel?" "What are you really thinking?" I would stand beside the grave, lean on his brother's arm, and imagine the things Steven and I hadn't said that needed to be said, things that were too dangerous to say. Oh, Steven, how good we were at jokes, how superb at innuendos, how we laughed. But there was that killing ground for us, wasn't there? That dark and treacherous pool we'd swum about all these years, breaking, now and then, the silvery surface, to fire a barbed arrow into each other's heart, part of us hoping to miss, part of us hoping to hit an old wound. Still we swam together, shackled as we were by our commitment, comfort, laziness, love, certainly hope. Hope was the worst, wasn't it?

The hole in the earth was the hole in my heart and I would weep for the loss although he lay next to me in the four-poster throne of our bed, alive and well, making believe as I did that he slept peacefully.

It was my ultimate test to imagine him dead, to examine then the pulse of my heart, and each time, still, after a quarter of a century of marriage, and many imaginings, I could not bear him gone. I would weep at the thought and forgive him and myself and life and go on swimming in our circle.

Lying in the high-ceilinged room, the moon and its many moons falling on us from each diamond and flower tracery of the leaded glass in the French doors, from each slice of the Palladian fanlight, I saw its golden path along the water, shimmering. A pale blush on the carpet, a puddle of gold at the foot of the bed, a gloss on the dog's velvet head, the puzzle of moon pieces carved the arches of my windows, the cherubs, seashells, and half-Doric columns of the Adams fireplace, the dappled glass of the old windows, the great and serene beauty that was ours. Above the hills beyond the lake the moon held itself steady, collected over the notched pinetops, over us all, calm, still, and unchanging, its fragments lighting our flesh while we hid our secrets in our hearts. The Don't Disturb sign I took from our room at the Mount Kenya Safari Club hung on the doorknob, fluttered in a faint breeze.

I wouldn't meet the children's eyes at the graveside. They'd examine me exquisitely as if my secret self were a key to their own. They will never know my true nature because I don't. But if they did, intuitively, a piece here, a bit there, like the moon, would they tell me? And if they told me, could I bear knowing? How they would watch me wipe my tears. I have given them the gift of my absence so they could struggle for their own presences. My nature held itself from me as the moon, held itself whole over distant hills, and tantalized me with its pieces. It was most what I wanted to complete, the puzzle of my self.

The fireplace inhaled wind. Steven's snores were short, adumbrated, genuine. My limbs relaxed now that he was asleep. He had fallen asleep with *The New Yorker* rising and falling on the shores of his chest. It is our marriage, that magazine, with all its richness of things, its collections of culture, fur coats, pearls, four-star hotels, and the stories, mostly the stories, in which, as in our marriage, nothing happens. Steven rolled away from me in a flap of pages. We've talked about the magazine, almost talking about our lives. "Why would you want anything to happen in a story? Why would you want change?" he'd ask.

Change was the enemy. That's why I had taken the Don't Disturb sign from Kenya. Two fat elephants in plaid aprons sleep, curled up together. But something disturbed. Something out there rattled in the cornstalks, something I feared so deeply I was afraid to sleep on my own balcony at night, reluctant to walk about in my own home in the dark. And I was well aware that that something was, somehow, my self.

Steven owned shares in a national discount chain. The partners organized a trip to Paris. We stayed at the George V and motored one night into the country to a château. White deer wandered in a dry moat. We danced to a band of Frenchmen playing "New York, New York" again and again. Under the flickering candles of the chandeliers we drank the champagne of the château and danced in circles on marble floors. Steven and I were tipsy and dizzy. We found a small cubicle, a little room with a wooden fireplace screen of hunting dogs, pigs, and a truffle harvest. There, in a great amber velvet winged chair, I in his lap, we pressed against each other. A bronze plaque hung above the fireplace. I translated it for Steven. It was the history of the château. "The Fairy Milusen, the protectress of the château, promised to make Raimondin, son of the King of the Bretons, the first nobleman of the realm if he married her, on condition that he never see her on a Saturday, the day of her metamorphosis. His curiosity got the better of him and she flew away from the château in the form of a winged dragon."

Steven lifted me slightly from his lap, tried to focus on my face, finally achieved a steady gaze, a strange and pained gaze, and asked, "Have I ever seen you on a Saturday?"

"No."

I can recall the beat and faint strains of "These vagabond shoes . . ." and Steven coming back into the room where I sat before the fireplace weeping. Very cautiously he said, "That's the last time we drink champagne. We can't handle it." Steven is very smart. I don't know whether he was avoiding the hole in my heart he'd just looked into or hadn't seen it at all. But he'd led me into my heart and I'd seen too much. Who can know me if I dare not know myself?

"Are you sleeping?" Steven asked softly. Our dog, Diggety, sat up.

"Yes," I mumbled, pulling the pillow around my ears. I acknowledged his presence without hearing his words. We had an alphabet of grunts, signs, mutterings, like dolphins, to establish distance, invite or dispel advances.

He ignored my grunt. The mattress lowered. He was up on one elbow, watching me. "What do you really think of me doing it?"

He was reaching into the hole of my heart. He knew what I thought. Hidden in our dark, our ugly bottom fish fat on our secrets, he was thrashing to the surface, wanted me to come up with him. I groaned in complaint, softly.

"You think I'm a fool, don't you?"

"Stee—ven."

"You do, don't you?"

"It's two in the morning."

"What do you really think?"

I sat up, packed the pillows behind me. "Oh, God, Steven, what do I think about what?"

"The Coney Island project."

"Mmm." I forced a yawn. "You're not touching the principal."

"Come on, Linda. Say good or bad and go back to sleep."

I rolled over and buried my face in my pillows, mumbled. "Lacks dignity. A bit . . . oh . . . silly."

"And . . . ?"

"But. A horror house with a resident gorilla. You could dine out on it for months."

"Your husband sounds like a fool."

"Not in the least. No."

"And your name?"

"Linda."

Steven had two-thirds of a J24 sailboat, half a Cessna with his brother, a quarter of a racehorse at Jamaica, time shares here and there, some acreage in Kauai, two lots on Kit Carson Mountain in Colorado, a condo in Coconut Creek, a piece of a rubber stamp factory, a partnership in a high-tech medical firm, the discount chain, this, that, all exterior, all consuming, of no interest to me. He took meetings, flew here and there, invested, had a degree in law, which he didn't practice, and said, rightfully so, "Why should I? We're fine." We didn't touch the principal. We were almost fifty and I didn't know where we were going. I preferred his entrepreneurship to his vision quest period, which I, thinking it would hold answers, had shared. Knowing how to cross a five-hundred-foot abyss on a rope ladder taught us nothing but the bitter taste of the fruit of our fear.

"Does he have teeth?"

"Who?"

Diggety sniffed at my face, my nostrils.

"Your gorilla."

"I suppose."

Diggety, a great-shouldered, noble-headed Newfoundland, was left at home when my son went off to college. Diggety was our keeper. He lay across my chest, sniffed, sought a chemical message, assessed the danger arcing between us.

"Is he loose, Steven?"

"If you ate twelve cabbage heads for supper you'd be loose too." We chuckled and snorted together. Our game is to misunderstand each other. "I hired an old carnie who runs the Ferris wheels to clean his cages. Day cage, night cage. Night cage so you can clean the day cage, vice versa. He knew him. In a zoo. Dino."

"You don't leave him out at night, do you?"

"He's fine."

"The ocean winds . . ."

"He's fine." Steven's voice had a defensive edge. He was not fine. "He's a tough guy, as old as the hills, Linda. He used to ride a tricycle around the stage in Las Vegas. He wore a feather bonnet and beat his chest and rode around the stage."

"Oh, God, Steven."

He rolled over, toward me, waited. "I asked you a question, Linda. What do you think?"

And I rolled away from him but I touched my feet to his. He wanted me to ask him why he's doing it, to get into the meaning of life, our life, what he wants, what I want. I yawned mightily and said as casually as I could, "I think I'll go to Ireland and paint."

Steven lay still, sighed, exhaled, sorted out what I really meant, yawned deeply once, twice, as if he were about to drift off, as if he were innocent. "You sure the house is available?"

"Seems so. Seems no one else is ever there."

He was quiet, trying to imagine the pink stone house, me, painting, walking the coastline, the bicycle and its basket, soda bread, turnips. He seemed to sleep. Diggety was alert, sniffed at my lips. I waited. I touched my arms, rubbed the inside of my neck, elbows, thought about getting old. *The New Yorker* is wrong. Everything changes. There is no stopping it, not our illusions, nor our games, nor weekends at the Stanford Court, nor love, nor adventures with horror houses and show business gorillas. Nothing.

"You could take my gorilla. I only rented him to the end of the summer but I could extend his lease, call Rent-A-Pet, tell Mr. Froelich he's going abroad. . . ." His voice was soft, childlike, as if he weren't really thinking about what he would say, dreamy, his arrow steady in his bow.

"What a marvelous idea, Steven. I'm astonished it hadn't oc-curred to me. He could ride his little tricycle around the village."

"His collar size is forty-four. He'll need clothes for the plane trip at the very least. And you'll be protected. But you must take his tub. He goes no place without his little washtub." Steven was circling the target. I felt him rise on an elbow, his face hovering over mine, his voice even softer. "Linda, how can you stay alone there when you're afraid to go downstairs in this house in the dark?" The arrow trembled, quivered. I felt his pain.

Because, I did not say, John Banks lives with me, sleeps beside me, hides his handgun under the bed, his hunting rifle at the door and is, I think, trained to kill, and when he's gone on this mission or that—clandestine moments which might really have been simply going home to England to see his wife and son—I

7

stay awake at night and sleep during the day. "I stay awake at night and sleep during the day."

"Aah."

I thought about meeting John Banks at the bus station, about the treacly marmalade, the electric teapot which never boiled, the needless discussion we'd begun to have about selling his paintings for him or at the very least buying them from him because someone has said they were awfully good and I'd realized someone was another woman, besides or instead of his wife, and I'd realized I was tired of his strong silence because it was only emotional selfishness. His paintings were barren and I had refused to buy them or hawk them at galleries in New York although I needed them to justify my trip. We split our expenses to the penny. I pointed out last time a charge for roast beef. I don't eat red meat. "This must be yours," I said. "Aah," he said, covering something. I knew he had wined and dined someone else here and she'd cooked a roast and was British because no one else would eat eel pies, for which I also refused to pay.

Steven said, "They call it a dark ride. It's two minutes going around in the pitch dark with seconds of light on monster shapes and lots of noise."

"Sounds like marriage." I was nasty to keep him quiet.

"Cute, Linda. Cute."

"I was trying to be funny."

The closest Steven had ever come to exposing suspicion was asking me why I never painted at home. He had removed one of John Banks's oils from between two books on our library shelves where I'd left it because it wasn't valuable to me or hidden it because it was. It was of dolphins in the harbor. I'm sure Steven was terrified I would answer truthfully. "It's a different part of me that paints, Steven. It's not very good, you know, my painting, not very interesting, just a personal exploration."

He watched my face carefully. I'd gone on too long. "This is simply not like you, Linda. Here. They are . . . oh, heavy-handed, too attentive to detail. This effect you've made on the retaining wall, which is background—it could have been adumbrated, shadowed. It isn't something, as you say, you'd waste your consciousness on. And far too realistic for you, tedious."

Steven had never criticized my paintings or shown any particular interest in art. What we owned, I'd chosen. He understood I painted in Ireland and brought home a dozen or so and did nothing with them. Adumbrated was not his word. He'd taken the paintings to a critic to find out if I'd really painted them.

"I don't speculate," John Banks said. "I paint what I see."

"Then why are these dolphins chartreuse, John? Have you run out of black?"

I had come upon him at the harbor at his easel. He said, "Must I remind you, Linda, if you're going to touch me, don't approach me from behind?"

"Well"—I shoved my oil between its two books—"you didn't notice the chartreuse dolphins."

Steven laughed. "Now, *that's* like you. I bet you ran out of black."

I hugged Steven around the waist. We are sister and brother. "I made them chartreuse because in black they looked more like the *Merrimack* and the *Monitor.*" It was my irrationality and my incompetence he wanted to hear. He smiled down at me. I am a pet. I am small. I am cute. I am second down on the food chain. I have lost the courage of maturity and I'm afraid of the night.

Diggety settled his nose between his paws, sighed deeply. I kept my sigh beneath his. He licked each of my fingers, up and down, between them, pushed my hand over with his nose, licked a mosquito bite on my wrist. Diggety walks upright on his rear legs in the water. When he swims, he paddles overhand with his front paws like a human. No doggy paddle for him. In deep water, he positions himself upright and treads water with his forelegs. Sometimes we stand still together and hold paws/hands as if we were dancing. I think he could learn to walk upright on land. Diggety does what I do. I broke his heart when I went to Ireland.

When I went to Ireland, I paid for the oils and canvases; John Banks painted. I believe he kills people. He's very elegant, commanding, sexually proficient, almost priapic, schooled probably in Oriental bordellos. He is actually conscientious about sex, performing dutifully and powerfully as if he were in competition. I don't know with whom. I don't know his history, nor do I care about his fate. I met him first in a Galway tea shop. I was waiting to be seated when I heard a woman shouting. She stood above a large man sitting in a booth. She shouted and when she was done shouting spat heavily into his dish of trifle. He was big and brutal, with pale sloping eyes, not unlike the eyes of a sad animal. His skin was British pink and flawless. He had flat, even features and wore a perfectly cut vested tweed suit. She was a small weak woman in a porkpie hat and ratty coat. I imagined immediately that she'd had an anarchist son killed by the British. John Banks, certainly his suit, was British. Behind her, from the counter, two flame-faced toughs in turtlenecked fisherman sweaters swung from their stools. John Banks raised an eyebrow at her so regally, so arrogantly, I left my place in line, cutting off as I did the two IRA men and the irate woman, slid into the booth across from him, and said, "Hello, darling," in as flat and loud a Long Island accent as I could muster. The woman shook her head, confused, left. The two toughs stopped, turned their backs, conferred with each other, returned to their counter stools. John Banks looked at his watch.

"Late again, Gwen. Everything tidy?"

"It's the same problem with the oil delivery."

He handed me a menu. "Oxtail soup today."

He held my hand until the waitress approached with tea and a second dish of trifle for him. She took up the first dish. "Sorry, sir. On the house, if you please."

John Banks ignored the trifle in front of him. His hand on mine was cold and sweaty. He obviously was in danger. We sat in a vacuum of noise and movement. The toughs had swung around on their stools once again to watch. "Well?"

"I told you that wall had to go out farther. Now the damned oil dealer refuses to deliver because his truck won't fit into our drive."

He ran his tongue over his teeth. His mouth was dry. "May I remind you, dear girl, you also told me not to bother your rose beds."

I raised my voice. A row would be more convincing than tenderness. "On the contrary, I told you that if you had to disturb my rose beds to widen the driveway, to let me know and I'd tell you where to put them."

The waitress, now swollen and red-faced with embarrassment because everyone was watching, cleared her throat. "Is it all right, sir? Your trifle?"

He ignored her. "Ah, so it's my fault again, is it?"

"I don't suppose it matters whose fault it is. The point is we're going to be cold this winter and I'll be lugging peat because of your bloody fence."

"Find a supplier with a smaller truck," he snapped, and dipped his spoon into the trifle, let the bite sit on his tongue, said, "Very nice," to the poor girl as if she were his wine steward, and carefully laid his spoon beside his plate. She did the beginnings of a curtsy, caught herself, left. The toughs swung back to their teacups, others drifted into their own noises, eyes fell from us.

We had already told each other we could play and that we had long dwelled in the perilous landscape of marriage. He leaned forward, pushed hair from my forehead, murmured, "There." They were very different men. Steven, of course, had a disadvantage. He was my husband.

Under the guise of tenderness, John Banks continued to murmur, "I just want to warn you, that if you ever find the need to touch me, don't approach me from behind." Then he stood, offered me his arm, and we walked out toward the shadows of the city, toward my car, toward my cottage.

I considered the four years of our October rendezvous and found no desire to call John Banks, to return to the cottage. I believed I carried a virus. Both men had grown alike. John Banks and I had the same arguments as Steven and I. There was more invective with John Banks because I had stored up the fury that I wouldn't vent on Steven. In both homes—the small pink stone house on the coast, the Classic Revival on the lake—I had created a problem about can openers. Last year, John Banks and I had just finished his Tuesday menu of mince, turnips, canned peas, and pineapple, and I, cleaning, had dropped the can opener into a kitchen drawer. He chose the food and cooked. I cleaned.

"Linda, dear girl, why don't you put the can opener where it belongs?" He framed the question as if he were genuinely curious. But I'd seen the way he treated the waitress in the tea shop. The British cover up so much with their manners.

I said to John Banks, in his voice, "Really."

"Just think about it, Linda."

"What difference does it make?"

"You know how it irritates me when I can't find what it is I'm looking for."

"Jesus."

"Pardon?" He lifted a high church eyebrow.

"Jesus, John," I dared. "There are only three drawers in the kitchen. All at your fingertips. So it takes a minute more."

"I'm surprised at you, Linda. Just *think* about the can opener, Linda, dear, that's all I ask."

"John, God has given me so many moments of consciousness before he snuffs out my candle. I'm not going to waste any of them thinking about can openers. I'm tired of men who are so antiquely frightened of the universe that they must have their can openers in the correct drawer because they need to control things."

John Banks raised an eyebrow at me in the precise angle of hauteur with which he'd raised it at the woman who'd spat into his trifle. He drummed his fingers on the table. "It's simply logical, Linda."

"Logic," I told him, leaning back against the counter for support, "logic is a flimsy construct of men against the universe. Logic is a cover-up for ignorance. Men cling to logic because of fear."

"And I'd say that's a flimsy female justification for putting the can opener into the wrong drawer." He cocked his head and examined me. "I thought you women had resolved all of that poppycock thirty years ago."

And I cocked my head and examined him while old rages erupted in my arms and legs and climbed toward my mouth. "What makes you think being born with a penis automatically gives you entry into a state of grace?"

"Who said anything about penises?"

"Poppycock."

He tried not to laugh at me. "I see. Very well, then. I shall do the tidy-up and you can go off and be conscious about whatever your God wants you to be conscious of."

Steven said, "Jesus Christ, Linda, just put it someplace I can find it."

I said to Steven, "I have this feeling you're criticizing me."

And because Steven's a nicer man, he said, "Okay, okay. I'll buy my own can opener. Never mind. You can put your can opener any place in the house. But leave mine alone, okay?"

And I bought him a sweatshirt with KITCHEN POLICE emblazoned on it and we laughed and when he found a milk carton in the cupboard or the dirty fork in my purse, we laughed and we were safe.

John Banks and I were not safe. After the tiff with John Banks I did walk off. I went to the harbor and watched the dolphins come in from a sea storm and wrapped myself in wind and longing. Something of me still ran free over old paths in the jungle and drank from strange cold streams dripping from hibiscus cliffs.

Another beach, Tasmania. Steven and I had flown from Sydney to walk and I asked him to let me walk alone. I wanted to think about first man and aboriginal paradise and innocence and beginnings and feel the flutter of the past and feel the beach as they felt, the ocean as they felt. I wanted to be so completely absent of self, I could feel their presence.

"Alone?" Steven turned heel and walked up the beach, I down it.

Even as we increased the distance between us I felt the burden of his hurt burning on my back like a noon sun. There was no opening my consciousness to an ancient flutter because Steven's hurt was so present. Around a bend in the cove I came to a cow sunk into the sand, stuck in the sand. The tide lapped at her hocks and she couldn't move. Her muscles worked like sea waves across her sides and I understood she was in labor, blatting, and the tide . . . I ran up the beach to Steven, hoping we could help her from the sand.

"Come away," he said after we pulled her head, tried to dig around her feet, she bellowing, I weeping. "This isn't our business."

"How can she be so stupid?"

"Domesticated animals are stupid. They'd never get into such a problem in the wild."

"I am a domesticated animal."

John Banks was gone when I returned. Late that night I heard him arranging bedclothes in the living room. "John, I'm very sorry about the can opener."

"Yes."

"I'll make certain I put it back."

"Thank you."

I lay down next to him, touched his thigh.

"I get very irritated when I can't find what I'm looking for."

"Yes. So do I." And I knew it was our last October.

I felt Steven turn to me, wondered if I'd ever called out John Banks's name to him; his name to John Banks. Steven mumbled, "You're really caught between us, aren't you?"

I grunted without meaning, yawned, and rolled to him, put my face on his shoulder, answered softly, half in his shoulder, half in his pillow. "A gorilla, Steven. It's just such an insane idea." I yawned a high and contented yawn from my repertoire of deceit. "Tomorrow I'll go with you and visit him. Then I'll tell you what I think.

Tomorrow." I drifted off. I could not catch my breath. He rolled over, away from under my head, and I lay there on his pillow trying to sound as if I were breathing regularly. Eventually I slipped from the bed, used the bathroom. My legs shook. I steadied myself on the seat with my hands.

"How long have you known, Steven?" I might have said.

And he would have said, sleepily, "Known what?" And I wouldn't have been able to face him in the morning.

"You okay?" he called without alarm. We asked this of each other throughout the day. It meant, I think, Are we okay?

"Uh-huh." I padded into the dressing room, reached for a pile of neatly folded sweatsuits, my antique comb, a handful of cash, underwear.

"I can't remember the last time you walked around the house at night. Something's wrong."

"My back. I'm looking for the Motrin." I turned lights on wherever I passed. I was terrified of the night but more of confronting Steven. We were not okay.

"I'll be happy to find it for you." He was too alert, his words too clear. Diggety's nose was at my knees.

"I'll be back in a minute, Steven." But I couldn't find the keys to the Lincoln in my purse or in my coat pockets.

"Linda?"

"I'll be up in a minute."

"I don't like you wandering around at night."

"I think it's downstairs or in my bag on the car seat. You sleep. I'll be up in a moment." In the kitchen, I ran water, flushed the maid's toilet, slipped out the back door. I couldn't find my Lincoln keys or his Porsche keys. I grabbed my fanny pack from the seat of the Lincoln. The only vehicle we always left the keys in was the old Suburban in the barn.

I pulled my sweats over my nightgown, shivered in the hard cool air of early spring, slipped on Steven's oversize ski jacket, which was festooned with lift tickets from Vail, Aspen, Gstaad, Angel Fire. I felt a quarter, a matchbook, a feather sprung from the down lining. Oh, Steven, our lives, our lives. I looked back at my home, at the fluted Tuscan columns melting in the moonlight, the hundred-year-old pines breathing gently above me, the sky, a fortune-teller's crystal. I had arranged tonight's stars, pinned each one in its place. Lying naked on John Banks's lap, across him, on the sofa, John Banks fully dressed, I'd foretold this moment. I remembered the tweed of his vest scratching a nipple as I turned to him. I had pinned the stars into their places and I had to leave because I could not bear the pain I'd prepared for my husband's dear heart. Who am I to have played so lightly with another's soul? Really. Meager-souled and faint of heart, where shall I go? Halfway houses and retreats and pad around softly with the monks who lay in their cells dreaming of a life of luxury and passion like my own? And shall I be one of them, walking the earth sky-robed and mad? Who am I and how dare I go out into the night alone?

T W O

A cloud of fog clothed our land, hid the moon. Fear gathered, sifted, and settled over the familiar. The familiar became the unknown. I inched across my lawn. The cry of a hawk swept before me, drew me down a corkscrew dirt road, over fallen branches, last century's watering trough, the cracked stone filled with long grasses. I crossed a ditch onto the sedge of pasture and struck out toward the barn. My feet were heavy with fear, my breath laden. I imagined the next tree, the drainage gullies, the fences. I felt the soft assuring press of our sheep against my legs. But then a pheasant burst from a thicket and both of us screamed in the same key of terror, my scream too much like the hawk's. Glossy black-berries hung against the bleached and shattered shingles of the toolshed. I leaned over a rusted plow and gathered my courage. It was a small thing, my courage.

Lights burned in the kitchen and in the upstairs bedroom. Steven was awake, looking for me. Steven, I'm leaving you, Steven. Even as I lie to you, betray you, I love you. My house is already abandoned, already packed away in the cotton batting of memory like a delicate Christmas ornament.

Clinging to each tree as it presented itself, I moved tree by tree, into the pines, under the black walnuts, up through the apple orchard deep with blossom. Diggety appeared from the fog and stood beside an apple tree, appeared as if I'd snapped my fingers and created him full size. He lowered his head and stared at me. "Go home. Go home," I hissed. He whined. I hissed. "Go home. Go home. Go." He wanted me to go home also. With a firm and gentle mouth over my wrist he pulled at me. He was Steven's sorrow in dog skins. I felt his pain. He curled around my ankles, thrust his head between my legs. He was as lonely as I. Under the soft tapestry of apple boughs, I bent over to him and whispered his name. "Hi, Diggety." He danced at his name, rubbed against me, pawed me. I whispered again, for I had spoken to his soul and lit it. "Hi, Diggety." He forgave me. Frenzied, he bounded at my side, leaped at me, his paws on my shoulders, asked me, his tongue all over my face. And I was struck not only by the weight of his joy but by the wrench of separation. "Someday, Diggety, we'll all be together again. Someday. When I come back." I put my hand in his mouth and let him lead me to the barn.

The Suburban waited inside the barn. Its keys lay on the seat. But Diggety was at the Suburban growling a message, his leash hanging from his mouth. If I were to put Diggety into a stay, he'd stay at the barn forever and Steven might not find him for days. I could only command him to stay at our house. I let him into the Suburban. He laid his great head in my lap, licked my hand. With my headlights off I drove to the house and shoved Diggety from the seat onto the driveway, commanded him to stay. He would. It was too cruel. I wept. He was my sorrow also. He stood on the front porch with his leash in his mouth, ready to go. "I must, Diggety. I must. I'm sorry." Diggety would forgive me. Steven would not.

I released the brake and let the Suburban roll down the curve of my crystal ball, through the stands of pines, through the gates, to the great ribbon of highway. Veiled in exhaust and the red wash of pollution at the edges of the horizon, I lost myself. I had run away from home. I had no idea where to go.

And so I entered the night. I had never, in my entire life, been alone in the night, in the real and terrible night, and I mourned now for myself, but still I went forward, away from Steven, away from my home, away from my life, and I didn't know which way. An exile of conscience, an exile of consciousness, where would I go?

The night winds rushed at me, propelled me along the reluctant road. My lights probed nothingness. I didn't know left from right or right from wrong and my eyes were filled with tears for Diggety because I dared not cry for myself. Behind the metal divider, I heard the crackle of the garden's winterkill, of windwhipped willow branches, black raspberry limbs, the sweep of pine needles. Metal hit metal, rattled as I swayed on turns. The sour smell of rotting greens drifted into the cab and I realized, knee deep in metaphor, that I had run away from home with the week's garbage. I was grateful for the interim direction and turned toward the landfill. My hands trembled on the wheel.

Oh, Steven, don't I, don't we, cling to the leitmotifs, the small legitimacies of our lives? We give to Save the Whales; we do not give to United Way. We eat pumpernickel bagels on Sundays, fish at the Chowder House on Friday nights. We wear primary colors or white and beige. We have rights and wrongs. Even as I betray our marriage bed, break up our home, I cannot bring myself to leave our garbage along the roadside. Over Quarry Road, along Beesaw Ridge Road, through the stands of pines, the left turn at the roofless barn, once and then again at the sawmill. The fog lifted. My headlights swept a landscape gone strange and I shivered. A pickup truck was behind me, lumbered past me, suspicious. Only animals and thieves are about in the night. I stroked the zipper of Steven's jacket, wished I were inside him, watched for signs to tell me Wrong Way. Turn back, Linda. Turn back. At the burned Victorian house, I turned again. Its cupola had lost its sides. The moon's face drifted between the framework, followed me, drew me.

What will I tell you this time, Steven? That I am a puzzle and there are pieces missing which I alone must find? That I left because I am seeking my fully realized self? That I am tired of the carapace of your logic? That I want to sleep under the stars, on the grass? That I want to go off to paint? That I am a spoiled three-year-old child? That I want to walk the beach alone? I remembered the labored groans of the drowning cow and heard your voice echoing.

"*Linda, honey, where the hell is the can opener now? Who really painted these pictures? Linda, don't leave me. Whatever you do, whatever you've done, don't leave me. You belong here. In this drawer.*"

"*Oh, God, Steven, forget the missing can opener. It's you, after all, isn't it, who have put your dear and caring heart in the wrong place?*"

"*And you, Linda?*" *He sat beside me in the Suburban.* "*With your wandering heart and your Irish sojourns. What about you, Linda? Keeping things in one place may have been my way to keep you in one place. What do you make of that?*" We would not say these things to each other.

Instead, when I return, Steven and I will chuckle and snort over the utter wealth of my running away with the garbage. "There you are, Linda," he'll say at the door. "Thank God." And then later, after he's poured me a snifter of brandy, after I've explained and explained, he'll say—his finger pressed on my lips, forget, forget—leading me by the hand up the stairs to the safety of our bed, "And so, our heroine, having made a great mess of her marriage, through this seeking of some elusive self, left to wander the earth, not sky-robed but garbage-clad." And that's all he'll say. He will not speak of John Banks. The surface of our pool will close over my shame, our wound, and be still and unchanging, more dreadful.

I probed the landfill with my flashlight: a flapping flag, broken chairs, sofas on end, a doorless refrigerator, the fan of pine needles, staccato of cricket and frog. The tiny black porcelain feet of old stoves scratched at the air. The only nightmares were my own. Around the grottoes, gullies, and drumlins of trash a chain link fence rose high and formidable. I backed the Suburban up to the gates, turned off the engine, stepped into the landfill night.

Just beyond the padlocked gates, the green corrugated sides of a trash compactor rippled in moonlight. Outside the fence, next to the gate, someone had arranged a yellow silk sectional. It had the smell of dying: sour milk, mildew.

I heard Steven. "What is it about you that needs to be alone, that you are willing to destroy all we've built together?"

I sat cautiously and straight-backed in the sofa's silken curve, pushed Coors cans aside, breathed carefully, counted my breaths, exhaled and inhaled the vapors of dry apples, the corrupted fish market stink of old women's parts, old men's fleshless thighs, all oddly reassuring.

. . .

Ignoring the pain, the cow drowning in her sea of fear, my arms around my self, my fingernails pressed into my forearms, with the forceps of necessity, I brought forth my child of courage into the world.

Steven is downstairs in his bathrobe looking for me, looking outside, whistling for Diggety, treading the space where the Suburban had been. "The dump, Linda? Pretty déclassé, isn't it?" He is trying not to be critical, to keep the situation light. He is desperate for me to come home. "You want to go hang over an abyss in Utah again? I mean, as vision quests go, the dump is somewhat less than uplifting. Yes? Oh, Linda, I don't care what you've done. I don't care where you've been. I want you back. Do you understand?"

I dug in the sofa's sides for the artifacts of another life: a garter stay, peanuts, a wooden match, a pill. The things of the landfill were in the wrong place. They had, as I had, left their homes and were changing from useful to absurd, struggling away from form and existence. In the moonlight, wives became tramps, tin cans silver, bottles liquid, stoves dogs.

"What does one thing have to do with the other?" Steven is going to be logical.

"Everything, everything. But the connection is too dangerous for you to make and I, frightened as I am, skirt around it. I sit here in a great rift between things as they are and things as they might be, between the landscape of logic and the landscape of longing. Perhaps the missing piece of my puzzle is change itself. Here, you see, Steven, everything is being transformed."

"To garbage, Linda."

"I know. I have to work that out, don't I?"

"I'll say."

John Banks sits at the far end of the sofa. He holds a book of mine in his lap and riffles the gilt-edged pages. "Foolish of you, Linda. You should have found the keys to a decent vehicle or waited another day. Dear girl, acting on impulse may be cute and rebellious and perhaps sexually satisfying, but it isn't functional. And why leave? Why couldn't we just go on?"

"Because I'm tired of going on just to go on. Because I'm looking for my face."

"I see."

"And I'm afraid of the night."

"Which of course has been my good fortune, dear girl, if not yours."

"Not mine. I thought orgasm was an escape route but I still fear the night."

Even so, I wrapped his memory around my shoulders to comfort me. Insects swarmed in the mercury light, drank from the light until their bodies were light, extended, lengthened, became strokes and streaks of sperm on the canvas of the air turned thick with moisture. The clarity of night was gone. Thunder rumbled distantly, lightning flushed far away behind low hills. The terrier tongue of fear licked my face, mouth, eyes, ears. My nightmares danced before me. Everything took a new shape, loomed dangerously. Everything not seen, not heard, not smelled, that is what I feared the most. I was poised on the edge of my landscape of longing, afraid. Can it be that what I want the most, the freedom of the unknown, of the irrational, is what I fear the most?

On one of our Octobers, John Banks was to arrive in Dublin and I was to meet him with the car. I had the date wrong, not intentionally. I've had other dates wrong. Confused over the international dateline, I've kept Steven waiting in Anchorage, and I've waited for him in Frankfurt. When I was to have met John Banks in Dublin, I had instead spent the night in Galway at a lovely bed and breakfast, wandered in the parks and on the streets all the next day, ate a fresh salmon tea, had my hair rinsed auburn, bought lace handkerchiefs, a marvelous nightgown, postcards, and a rare gilt-edged book entitled *History of the Picts.* I had bought it for the frontispiece—a lithograph of druids burning animal sacrifices in a great wickerwork cage. I drove home to hear John Banks's cold and furious voice on the phone. He'd been waiting overnight in Dublin, finally took a bus to Clifden, was now waiting for me at the pub. I sped to Clifden. I hadn't seen him in a year. His face was oddly handsome but without information.

"I thought," I said softly, "that you were coming on the eighteenth."

"Today is the nineteenth."

"I'm terribly sorry. Terribly. I've lost three days."

He said nothing.

At the house he sat fully dressed on the sofa and told me to undress.

"John!" I protested.

"Why don't you begin with your hose."

I did because he sat there leafing the gold edges of my *History of the Picts,* riffling through them with his thumb. I was scared and excited. When I was naked, he told me, still leafing the pages, still sitting on the sofa, to go on my hands and knees to the floor. There, after long moments, he mounted me. I thought of young nuns sunbathing on dry grass, yellowing blades scratching behind their knees. I thought about their soft pussy-willow thighs and wondered what they daydreamed there on the dry grass. I thought of old nuns eating Egg McMuffins on a riverboat in the Mississippi morning fog, black and cloudy, great birds on little limbs, the boat swaying in the river tide as they clung together and hid from their dreams. When he was done he asked me what day it was and what day he'd been expected.

"The eighteenth."

"And today is?"

"The nineteenth."

"Very good."

Standing at the bathroom sink, he washed himself. "I'd like very much to go back to Clifden and get a pie."

"Well?" he asked at the pub. I watched him sip his Smithwick, watched his mouth, hated him.

"Despicable. Animal, low, despicable. Animal." I thought of the wickerwork cage aflame and the animals within it.

"Sliding into the tar pit on a slimy sea of desire, are you?"

I stabbed at my veggie pie but couldn't bring myself to eat.

"You enjoyed it, Linda. I could feel you."

"I don't like you, John. Not at all."

"But that isn't why we're here, is it, Linda?"

"Shut up, John. Just shut up. And stop smiling. Most of all, stop smiling."

On the way home I asked finally, "What was that really all about, John?"

I shall never forget the levity of his answer. "Why, Linda, I thought you'd understood. It was about putting things in the right place."

I made my bed on the sofa and lay in a stiff fury until I became so frantic with loneliness, I climbed into bed with him and clung to his back until morning.

At the beach the next day, John Banks drew a diamond watch from his pocket, slipped it on my wrist. "It isn't new," he said without apology. "So if you want to exchange it—"

"Is it antique, then?"

"No. It simply isn't new."

"It's very lovely and very expensive, John."

"I suppose your husband gives you things like this."

"Sometimes, on important occasions."

"I'm not your husband nor will I ever be. You understand that, don't you?"

"Of course. Is this an occasion?"

"A fortuitous set of circumstances. I don't believe I've ever given you a gift, have I?"

"No, you really haven't. I'm very pleased."

Later I asked if the person it belonged to was someone he had been assigned to kill.

He looked at me squarely and said, "It has a calendar, you see."

The rest of the world might be in the right place at the right time. I was not. John Banks thought I was morally wounded in some way. "John," I asked after I'd decided to forget what he'd done to me, "how does one ever really know what the right place is?"

"One knows." John Banks belonged to the order in which personal worth is determined by universal intention, otherwise known as grace. Then he cupped my chin in his hand and asked me, "Have you ever heard of the noon wife, Linda? She is a demon who visits the fields at noon when the laborers doze. She asks them questions. If they don't answer, she tickles them to death or they vanish in a whirlwind. You are the noon wife."

Years ago when the children were still in junior high, I traveled by train to Buffalo to see a Hiroshige woodblock exhibit. Steven had offered to go with me, to drive me. I explained I needed some time alone. The car I chose was filled with tourists who called each other "Sister" and "Brother." I sat next to Sister Elizabeth, who held a stack of passports on her lap but slipped them into a carryall when she saw me looking at them. I assumed the earnest little group was going on to Canada. I was wearing a butterscotch suede coat lined with red fox and a suede skirt to match. I remember playing tic-tac-toe on my suede knees. The brothers and sisters wore layers and layers of thin clothing under very short, very old coats. They were small, thin, fine-boned, with intense, slightly dark, feline faces, large cheap crosses on their chests, and an excess of good nature. I thought perhaps they were Filipinos, Mormons. They changed seats often, fetched each other food from the dining car, balancing Cokes and coffee in thin cardboard boxes as they swayed with the car. Ignoring me entirely, which was fine because I had taken the trip to be alone, they leaned over me to offer Sister Elizabeth grapes and Toblerone bars. Just before Buffalo the train slowed down at a siding. Sister Elizabeth leaped up, tiny pointy breasts breaking at my chin. "Look!" Brothers and sisters crowded at the window and leaned toward the right side of the train to snap photos of a crumbling brick warehouse, its roof and third floor gone, windows agape, piles of old red bricks around it. With complete authority Sister Elizabeth announced, "The Spanish must have bombed it." A wall of steel dropped between us.

I didn't understand why her ignorance so depressed me. I felt a terrible alienation, as if knowing a truth set me apart, a small stick figure in a vast, unmarked landscape, with no right places. Perhaps, I thought, my marriage with Steven was an unspoken agreement to see the same things incorrectly, to carry matching maps. Dearest Steven, if you think the world works this way, perhaps it does. Doesn't it? Don't ask. Truth is too lonely. The sisters and brothers traveled the same path I traveled and they had it all wrong. I rubbed out the foolish marks on my rich suede knees. There are no true maps. We all carry our own Mappi Mundis, worn and skewed, our views of the world, and they are all false. No one has really seen the territory. We are separated from it, banished from the Garden, yearning at the gates. There is no right place.

John, you are wrong. Steven, we've wasted our lives trying to create one. We cannot get back in. We are all lost. We are all on dark rides.

I never saw the Hiroshige exhibit. I wasn't ready for yet another landscape because my ground was loosening beneath me. I checked instead into the Marriott, into a suite on the concierge floor, sat in the hot tub, tried to steady myself until I could go home the next day. In the late afternoon, I took a cab to a Bali outlet store to buy underwear, ordered room service that night, and watched "Police Woman Centerfold" on pay TV until I fell asleep. The story of that odd Amtrak contingent of Don Quixotes crossing America was a good one. Sister Elizabeth who had it all wrong became a family joke. If anything were lost, damaged, rearranged, the Spanish, we assured each other, must have bombed it. But it wasn't my joke. I never told Steven that I hid in the hotel room, wept in the hot tub, hadn't gone to the exhibit.

Steven has joined us at the far end of the sofa. "Aren't you aware, Linda, that you are our Sister Elizabeth? That it is you who leave a vast loneliness between us? That you have chosen your own beach and walk alone on it?"

One of them says, "Your dalliance with the irrational is your way of feeling superior, thumbing your nose at the rest of us who carry this world on their backs." How is it that Steven sounds like John Banks? It is John Banks; Steven would never have claimed to carry the world on his back.

Headlights swept over me, passed. I stretched out on the sofa, hid my face in the old fish smell of my grandmother's thighs and the White Lilac talcum between her breasts, and left both men. Tingling as I was with the absolute and startling consciousness of complete aloneness, I was at last able to close my eyes and breathe steadily. Like a ghost hovering, I floated into my house, into the attic, into the servants' quarters, far back behind the new partitions to the crumbled walls of the old gypsum insulation. I float over the gypsum. In it, the slenderest of reeds keep the heat of the house. I imagined the wickerwork of reed as our psychic cage. I imagined our thin sweet song drifting in its filigree of dream and illusion and unfinished rooms. I saw among the reeds, now and then, my face— bright, round, inquisitive, trusting, open, young, so young—there in a quivering window frame, flitting from one room to another, like the moon in the ruined cupola, asking me something from its land- scape of longing, its wicker of sacrifice. I listened. It was all familiar. It was my original face, the woman I was going to be, the girl that I was, from the time when everything was possible. What had hap- pened to my bloom between then and now that, grown, I've pressed myself between my own pages and am so small against the night?

"Steven," I explained, "it may be that the reason I've left you is, having achieved a perfect ending, I needed to break free of it. Perhaps that's why I chose my Octobers with John Banks who makes swift and certain endings of people's lives. Perhaps, I felt, if John Banks, the author of endings, entered me, I might create other endings for myself, many endings, confuse the gods, delay them long enough so I might look full at my face although looking may be an act in the nature of death."

I heard something. I opened my eyes. Faint light rose behind the compactor. The air was moist, cooler. Something rattled near me, something moved, a door latch clicked. I heard the crack of another hinge and springs. The guard opening the padlock? The sound came from my Suburban as its door swung open. I saw a white flash of light. "Steven?" I whispered, for a man was lowering himself from the back of the Suburban. "Steven, this isn't funny. Steven?"

I heard steps on the ground, too many, double time and a drag. "If this is your idea of a joke, Steven . . ." And Steven hooted, a cross between an owl hoot and a puppy bark, soft, mellow, ques- tioning hoots.

"You jerk, Steven. You pure, unadulterated jerk. This isn't funny anymore."

In the softening of the night, in the opal light of the day's first moment, I saw the shape of a gorilla, humped and huge, startling, beautiful, eternal, a monstrous phallocentric shape moving clumsily through the slender birches, a great psychopomp rounding up souls and leading them to dump death, a mythic creature waiting for me at the edge of the trees, lumbering sideways, his legs shorter than his arms, knuckle walking, dragging his length of linked chain like a bride, pornographic. I was swept by his attraction. I wanted to be with him, to ask him questions. Or was it my husband in a rented gorilla suit? One of them stood still, upright, faced my direction, hooted. There was something familiar about the question in the hoots, something faint and desperate, poignant, something I'd heard before.

"Oh, Steven, you jerk." Of course it was Steven in a rented suit, carrying a plastic washtub. I laughed and turned away. "Oh, no. I don't believe you." It was too absurd. "Oh, no," I said again and again as if I were the fool on "Candid Camera." I turned away, and turning away, one hand over my eyes, I laughed, embarrassed at being fooled, and when I dared pull my thumb over my flashlight and turn it on, dared to look, I looked into deep glowing ancient garnet eyes that were and were not human eyes. They were too deep, too old. Did I imagine them? For a moment I allowed myself to wonder if it were really Steven's gorilla and not Steven, which of course was what Steven wanted me to think, and I waited for him to rip off the mask.

Often Steven would call me from his carphone, tell me he'd be home in forty-five minutes, ask if I needed him to pick up something at the grocery store. He would take my list, repeat it carefully, ask sizes and brands, ask if I got the mail, and ten seconds later would walk in the door, mail in hand. We would both collapse with laughter each time. And sometimes he actually was forty-five minutes away and did stop at the grocery store to fill my list. So it could have been Steven in a gorilla suit. And it could not have been Steven in a gorilla suit. It could have been my imagination or it could have been Steven's rented gorilla. Impossible. Gorillas don't unlock cages and open Suburban doors.

He moved closer to me, loping, a Quasimodo dragging his chain and his tub. I won't hurt you, I won't hurt you, I heard. It was Steven's joke to hunch his back, drop his tongue out of his mouth, limp after me around the house.

It was not Steven. It was too accurate a gorilla to be Steven. He moved closer, a primitive rising, moved on his knuckles, sideways, awkward, something strange about his movement. It was not animal-liquid. He wasn't four-footed or two-footed; neither animal nor man. But he was us. That I knew. He was more us than not. He leaned on his knuckles, swung his great head into the night, sniffed mightily, trying to locate himself, this place, this danger—a monitor lizard in the grass, a leopard on the roof of the compactor building, a troop of baboons in the refrigerators, the fish smells of woman. His stomach rolled out a warfare in minor keys. His head was a great mantilla of bone surrounding a compressed face. It rose from his shoulders to a domed peak. He had no neck. I thought of mountain ranges and escarpments, huge lithic shapes made flesh, animal as landscape, ancient and eternal. As if the senses were latecomers to the bedrock of bone, his ears were small leathery flowers of flesh, his eyes drill holes under the overhang of forehead, his nostrils the size of half-dollars. "Steven? Steven, say something."

Steven is downstairs in his bathrobe. He sees the space where the Suburban was and he is laughing and not laughing. Or he is here with me in his foolish suit.

"Oh, Steven. Oh God, Steven. How could you? How could you?" Of course it's Steven. He's come to take me home. It isn't Steven.

. . .

John Banks speaks to me. "This, my dear child, is the rational universe split asunder; this is the wilderness beyond the garden where nothing is in its right place. Dear child, logic isn't a cover-up for ignorance. Logic is a cover-up for this. It's all we have, the only weapon we have. If you have so little logic, for God's sake, Linda, stay in the right place."

"Don't be silly, John. A gorilla can't unlock a cage, open the doors of the Suburban."

Hackles rose on the back of my neck. Before the mercury lamp the great shadow swelled and swam on the side of the compactor. I had called up the beast, called him up from a deep limbic fear. An odd child, like myself, he struggled up from my pool and became . . . flesh and fur.

Steven is waiting for me. He has rinsed his mouth with Listerine. He is downstairs in his blue seersucker bathrobe and he sees I've taken my fanny pack, my checkbook, my credit cards, the Suburban.

"Why did you let him sleep in the Suburban?"

"I didn't think you'd take it. I didn't think you'd leave."

"I couldn't find the keys to the Lincoln."

"That's why you left? Because you couldn't find the keys to the Lincoln?"

"No. Yes. In a way, Steven. But he shouldn't be in the cold. Spring nights are cold. I am cold now. He should have been in a warm place. He's a tropical animal. He's in the wrong place, Steven."

"And what about you? What are you doing in the dump at three in the morning?"

"Steven, get him away from me. Steven!" My courage died stillborn before the bristling black presence, before its watermelon mouth, teeth struck white by my flashlight, the ragged sleeve of fur shielding its eyes. This is why I can't go out into the night alone; this is why I am afraid to walk downstairs in my own home: the known becomes the unknown and swallows me. As if he were real, he sought the gate, shook the padlock, squeezed it open, moved up the fence away from me. The fence vibrated, chimed at his touch as he tested it. When he was at the farthest reach of the fencing, I picked up a chair leg with a nail in its foot. I kept before me the fish smell of my grandmother's thighs, the White Lilac talcum between her breasts. She sweeps the catalpa pods from the picnic table with her forearm, spreads her Ouija board, takes the cup from her pocket, clears her throat gently, waits for me to play with her at her board, to write down the garbled messages from her saint, a strange and hairy wild man brought up from the rivers of myth into the church. My bare feet rest on her lamb's-wool slippers. My fingers ride lightly on the cup as it moves on the board and I write the strange messages from the dead in her notebook. My grandmother whispers above me. "Come to me, my Il Peluseo. Come, my Santa Nofrio. I cannot find my keys. Come, tell me where my keys are. Come. Come." And the cup moves about on her Ouija board. "Come, my saint, come." He was covered with hair, she told me, a wild man of the forest, her saint. That smell, this smell: her legs, her old woman fish smell sleeping in the sofa. "Help me." I whisper to my grandmother's saint, "Help me find the child who had no fear. Help me find myself."

He hooted again. His hoots built into roars, folded into each other, uroburo octaves and series of octaves, swallowing each other, swelling, until the landfill and my heart echoed with a long drumming series of piercing jungle screams, the language of trees, of beast hearts, fury. I had pinned these stars in their places.

The gorilla had almost circled the square of the landfill. I knew what was familiar in his hooting. He asked the same poignant questions that drift in my reed house. Now I heard the words. My words. "Where are you? Who am I? Where are you going? What am I supposed to do? Don't leave me. I am afraid of the night. I am in the wrong place."

He had rounded the landfill fence, lumbering, hunched, hunchbacked, arms akimbo, desperate. He ran to the Suburban. He ran to me. I did not smell Listerine. I smelled a goat and garlic musk of fear. It was not Steven. Steven was home in his blue seersucker bathrobe. I was in the landfill with his gorilla.

"Linda, I don't like you wandering around at night."

"I'll be up in a minute, Steven."

"Linda?"

I sprinted toward the Suburban, keys ready. I was inside the safety of the cab. The ignition grunted, grunted, would not turn over. The windows would not roll up without power. I locked the doors, pressed the gas again, turned the key again, and, in the rearview mirror, watched him grow larger and larger, closer and closer. Caution: Objects in this mirror are closer than they seem. And then, inexorably, he stopped at the open doors of the Suburban and hoisted himself up. The Suburban sank. I heard him grunt, wheeze, cough. I heard him slip the latches closed, I heard him pull the Suburban doors closed. I heard another set of hinges and locks as he closed his cage. I heard the faint scratch as he moved the winterkill aside. I heard him settle back against the divider. I felt his body press the metal against my back. And then, for no reason at all, the engine turned over. The ego may be considered a multimodal image whose umbilical cord has snapped. The self has withdrawn inward, displaced from the world. I tore up earth with my tires and drove toward my husband's Horror House. I didn't know what else to do.

T H R E E

In the small hours of Coney Island morning, the sun squatted on the horizon, gaining strength, glorifying broken glass and mica chips in the heaved pavement of Surf Avenue. This time I wasn't fooled. Not after my night in the garbage dump, where fantasy became being beyond being and was, at that moment, in the back of my van banging on its sides. "Where am I? Where am I?" the gorilla cried out. For himself, for me. Waves rolled onto the beach. The wind arranged bouquets of paper cups, newspaper, napkins, flipped them across the parking lot, around my ankles, abandoned them in corners. Two garbage cans jousted, spilled themselves, rolled off. Gulls screamed over a hot-dog roll green with neon relish. From beneath the boardwalk, I sniffed the sharp brine of ocean, new pickles, young sex, old bums. Above me, the subway rattled on steep wooden trestles. A guard slept, snored, spread-eagle on a picnic table, a pink blowup plastic pillow under his head.

I used his language. "Dino around?"

"Huh? Dino? Dino's in the Horror House. Left on Surf, right on Bowery. Old Caddy, green door." He embraced his pillow, a fat woman thigh, turned on his side.

Don Quixote, with Sancho Panza in the backseat, I tilted with the rusted skeletons of roller coasters, whirlybirds, Ferris wheels, sky jumps, thunderbolts, parachute rides. A plastic kiddieland had sprung up nearer the boardwalk. In the surviving cluster of the old midway, games and rides were updated with freshly painted *Star Wars* monsters, G-stringed girls riding Jurassic dinosaurs. I suspected Steven's Horror House would be near. Tunnel of Love, Funhouse, Horror House. I knocked on its wind-bellied barn doors. A wooden vulture sat astride the roof, a snake dropping from his beak, bloody claws clutching two skulls. Oh, Steven, my lovely Steven. You too are in the wrong place, aren't you? Both of us reaching out into strange universes, seeking something that we're not, something that we might actually already be or become or have been. We are so confused, aren't we, gathering possibilities, trying to fold them all into our little black holes. I'm sorry, Steven. I'm sorry we aren't enough for each other. I'm sorry we aren't enough for ourselves.

If the garbage was metaphor for my life, there was Steven's metaphor: his mirror home of rotten wood and rusted beams. I knocked a second time. My alarm vibrated in the knock. The vulture nodded. I pushed the doors.

Vertical lights sliced through the warped siding. Sand followed me in, hissed in dark corners. Someone slept under a faded Mexican blanket in an open grip car.

"Dino?"

Startled by the light, Dino stirred in the cage of dusty beams, sat up, smoothed his hair.

"I'm Mrs. Morris. I have a problem." The lines, the lines. When Steven and I talk about this absurdity, we will laugh at the lines. They will become precious to us, private jokes. "I have a problem."

"Right." He threw a lever forward and sent up a cloud of exhaust. The grip car ground toward me, past leering masks, ghosts in dirty sheets, nets of cotton wadding, fluorescent skulls, disappeared. A white rubber mermaid wiggled her hips. Lights flashed. Sirens, bells, whistles, evil laughter. I saw a burst of giant, of devil's head. The car broke through torn rubber curtains, more light, dark, light, bells, screams, buzzers. A mechanical arm swung a stuffed and toothless gorilla out over the track. A rubber skeleton flapped unconvincingly. Dino's car ran away from me into a dark room. I heard John Banks's voice within me, still calm, still distant: *This dark ride, Linda, it is like your life, is it not? Long moments of dark and confusion, then swift and sudden moments of illumination, often more terrifying than the dark.* The grip car returned, stopped at my knees. Stuffing popped from the split leather seats.

I smiled cordially. "Mr. Morris . . ."

Dino waved me off. "Process of elimination." He climbed from the grip car, dragged a pair of crutches after himself, hopped beside the tracks to the double doors that swung open at the end of the ride, relieved himself behind them. I heard his water splash on cement. He called me to a bridge table. "Bum ankle," he explained in a raspy alcoholic voice, and invited me to sit next to his Caddy, his beach chair, a chipped Thermos, an open box of sugar doughnuts.

I took a deep, steadying breath. I was so out of context. My legs shook. "Mr. Morris is in Cleveland. The neighbors . . ." We had no neighbors.

"I told Mr. M. you can't bring him into a neighborhood. Not that no-good gorilla." Powdered sugar drifted on the dark stubble of his beard. His mouth was a march of silver teeth, yellow teeth, gaping spaces. His face was flat, folded, high-cheeked, Slavic. His eyes were tough and wounded. I desperately needed him to take the gorilla from the van so I could leave.

"Okay, you old cheese, you want some fresh air, huh?" He opened the doors to the van.

The gorilla, answering him, slammed a great arm against the cage, shuffled across his cage, scratched under his armpit, shook his hand in agitation, beat his chest.

"Yeah, yeah. I got better things to do than tickle you. Come on."

The gorilla shoved black fingers under the lower frame of the cage, begging. His hand was the size of a telephone directory, his face that of a car window, his head a bread box. He walked forward clumsily on his knuckles. I felt the lure of him, the lure of my beginnings, the secrets of the Garden, the mysteries of existence. He was gorilla and Gorilla, mortal and immortal. I was irrational in his presence. I wanted to talk to him. I wanted to touch him. I wanted him to touch me. The upturned hand was a gesture so human, so ours, I could not believe it of the gorilla. Dino brushed his teeth over a drinking fountain, gargled, spat vigorously. To hide my desperation, I forced myself to become mildly conversational. "It looks as if he's actually begging."

Through a mouth full of spit and toothpaste, Dino answered me. "Born begging."

"Does that mean then that mankind learned the begging gesture from them?" I was so convivial, so patronizing, so self-conscious, I could not bear myself.

Dino shrugged. He didn't want to discuss the origins of man any more than I. He rolled up newspapers and hay from the day cage next to the ticket booth, stuffed every awful thing in a plastic bag, into a garbage can.

"What's his name?"

Dino shrugged again.

"When he was in the circus?"

Dino ignored my question. "Okay, old man."

The gorilla glanced at me sideways, backhanded the cage. He is almost I as I am almost he, not less, perhaps more. We have known each other longer, I suspect, than we have not known each other. I hoped he might discover me, recognize something original, something compassionate, even extraordinary. He didn't. He glanced indifferently at me, dismissed me by turning his silver back. His contempt diminished me.

"He opens his own cage, Dino," I called to Dino's back. "He actually opens his locks and the doors."

"Sure. When he wants to. Right now he doesn't want to." Again, as commentary, the gorilla slammed his arm against the back of the cage. The sides of my van buckled. I giggled. I didn't intend to giggle.

"Scared you, huh? Likes to scare people. Used to vomit into his hand just to hear the girls scream." Dino turned to me. "Stand over in the ticket booth. He throws poop."

The gorilla made an agitated sign with his hand, as if he were shaking water from it, stared at the coffee Dino poured from his Thermos. "See? That means hurry up. Gimme the coffee. Yeah. Yeah."

Through the bars, Dino passed him his cup half-full of coffee. The gorilla drank it with both hands, cradled it, held it out for more. Dino filled it from the Thermos.

I heard Steven. *"Come, darling. You can drive home, Linda, leave the van in the driveway, climb into bed, and make believe this never happened. I will never mention it to you. You see, Linda, you're not crazy and I'm not crazy but we are doing crazy things because families are crazy and we are a family. Never forget that. We are a family. Linda, listen to me."*

I tried not to listen, to remember why I was there, that I must leave.

Dino offered me the open doughnut box. The gorilla made a sound deep in his throat, begged for more coffee. Dino put his hand out. The gorilla placed the cup into it. Dino filled it. The gorilla drank, crushed the cup, returned it to Dino's outstretched hand. Dino looked at his watch. The gorilla looked at his wrist where a watch might have been. "See that? We're family, we go back." He pressed his index and second fingers together; with a snap of his wrist he presented them to me vertically to show me what he really meant. "Family. See?" I did not see. "He's upset. No sense moving him when he's upset." Dino offered me his chair again. I shook my head. Steven would be coming soon. I could not face Steven. I began to suspect Dino's delays were deliberate.

Dino broke off a piece of doughnut, held it up for the gorilla to see, to want, smacked his lips, teased the gorilla. The gorilla's eyes were solemn, sweet, deep dark espresso pools of want and agitation as he gestured with his hand for the doughnut. I was struck by the intensity of the gesture, the vigor of the language between Dino and the gorilla. It was the same intricate, intimate pattern of grunts and movements between Steven and myself, warnings and invitations. I mimicked the gorilla's "hurry up" signal, shook my hand rapidly. Not surprisingly, Dino responded to my gesture.

"Okay." Dino placed both palms on the bridge table, pushed himself up. "Okay, let's get you off the truck and into your day cage so this here lady can go on home." He banged a kneecap into place, organized his crutches under his armpits, hopped to the cage, leaned on the crutches, spread his arms as if inviting an embrace, sang in a broken voice, sang a silly "Old MacDonald Had a Farm." The gorilla nodded his head to "E-I-E-I-O."

"See that? They understand more than they let on. I know guys who swear these bastards don't talk because if they talked, we'd put them to work."

Dino teased me as well. I was also his prisoner. It was highly likely that Steven told him I was coming, that I was to be kept at the Horror House until Steven arrived. I took out my compact, powdered my nose, put on lipstick. I felt the gorilla watching me, but as soon as I turned he had looked away. Then he reached outside his cage, found a cigarette butt on the ground, and rubbed it across his strange thin lips as if he were also putting on lipstick. I was somewhat acknowledged. I had penetrated something.

Dino slipped the doughnut I'd refused over the tip of his crutch and waved it at the cage bars. "Look at me. Look at me. Come on. Look at me and I'll give you the doughnut. Who's boss, huh? Who's boss?"

The gorilla dropped the cigarette/lipstick, rolled his lips back to cobblestone teeth, a roadkill mouth, growled. Dino laughed. "Think you're tough, do ya? You ain't got no fangs. We got your fangs, baby. See that, Mrs. Morris? That's a challenge. You mind your manners, you old fleabag."

Dino hopped in front of the cage on one crutch and waved his doughnut-tipped crutch at the gorilla. The gorilla hopped from one leg to another, almost in rhythm, Dino's mirror, tried to grab the doughnut, the crutch, Dino. Dino was a brute.

"Smart-ass bastard," Dino continued to tell me, although I knew he was speaking to the gorilla and had forgotten me. "C'mon, I've got something for you, dummy. C'mon. What goes around comes around, huh? Well, I talk Mr. M. into having a real gorilla to bring the kids in and I told him I'd take the risks, he takes the bucks. These punks watch murder from the front porch and gang rapes in the park. They got a gang here, the Homicides. They work

for me. 'Least I pay them off. Nothing scares them except this guy."
Dino jabbed the gorilla with the crutch. "Well, they say don't get
involved with them gorillas. That was my mistake. When he was a
little tyke I took him home with me from the zoo. He used to
groom me, always looking for lice. I never had lice, but he never
stopped looking for them. I used to rub his chest so he could sleep.
In my bed. Never messed it once. Didn't like me snoring. Used to
kiss my lips to stop me from snoring. Used to cock his head and I'd
be a chicken or a pig and he'd growl real soft. Hey, kid, and on this
farm? Listen, we'll make some dough, we'll buy a little farm in
Carolina, you and me, hey, 'E-I-E-I-O.' "

The gorilla sat still, his face relaxed, held his arms over his head,
cocked his head to listen, said a soft "Uh-uh," a belching sound.

"Dino," I called him from wherever he was.

"C'mon, I've got something for you. C'mon, look at me. C'mon."

"Dino," I reminded him. The gorilla was fast, sly. The moment
Dino turned his head toward me, he grabbed the doughnut, rolled it
in the hay and dirt at his feet, tossed it, coated, at Dino.

"That's to eat, you pig. I was giving it to you." The gorilla
growled softly, threw himself off the back of his cage, threw his
washtub to the back of the cage, slammed it, shuffled across to the
other side, swung off that side, posed at the front, head turned from
me, on his haunches, snorted through his nose or adenoids. It was a
sound I could make, an intake snort. I made it. It tickled the upper
palate of my mouth, went up my nose. It was Steven's snore. The
gorilla looked steadily almost in my direction, snapped his chin up
sharply at my presence. I felt his anger. Dino took another doughnut, turned his head to talk to me. The gorilla grabbed the second
doughnut.

"Yeah, yeah. I'll take that doughnut. I said, gimme the doughnut, bummiker. They don't grow on no trees."

"Dino, I really must get going."

"Gimme that. You already messed yours. Look at me. Give me that doughnut. Look at me, goddamnit, look at me." Everything had reversed. It was Dino now who stretched out his hand, the gorilla who teased him. Mimicry? Intentionality? Is the gorilla aware that he is doing to Dino what Dino had done to him? Is this his joke?

Dino prodded him with his crutch, swung at the doughnut. "Okay, that's enough. I want the doughnut."

With subterranean growls and rumbles, the gorilla held the doughnut over his head, grappled with the crutch, pulled it into the cage, shoved it out into Dino's stomach.

Dino grunted, doubled over, danced away. "You wanna play rough? Is that what you want? God damn you." The gorilla slipped the doughnut over the tip of the crutch, brandished it in very much the same motions Dino had tormented him with the first doughnut, rolled back his lips to his cobblestone teeth, to the roadkill red mouth. Dino steadied himself against the cage, shoved his second crutch into the cage, pinned the armrest against the gorilla's neck. Size forty-four. I remembered Steven telling me that. I could not imagine the little man would win, and I cried out at the stupidity, "Let him go, Dino. Let him go." Don't fight, children. Share. Share. Don't fight.

"You get on the floor, Mrs. Get on the floor so he don't see you. I'm going to get him out of that cage or else." He stiff-armed the crutch, shoved it hard. The gorilla barked sharp barks, angry. "You're a mean bastard, Moses, and you've always been a mean bastard."

The gorilla heard the gong of his name, the pain of his history with humans, snapped his chin at Dino, barked twice, short angry barks, warnings, saw something he had seen before, alert, stiff, his eyes suddenly hard and glittering, steady.

"Dino . . ."

He couldn't hear me. How many times have I seen this locked

combat between my sons and my husband—a standoff over car keys, lawn mowing, anything, as if their lives were at stake. It was not a woman's world. Dino and the gorilla knew of no one else but each other. They were family. They did go back. I was witness to a blood feud, not a training drill. The gorilla reached out with his immense hand, pinned Dino at the neck. I could not tell if his act were pure mimicry, justice, or anger. They stood locked, pressing at each other's throats. Hit 'em hard. Grab the ball. May the best man win. Don't fight, children. Share. Share. No fighting, no biting. How many times to no avail? Only the men. My daughter always withdrew, wrote her hostility in her diary, hid it.

I knelt on the floor of the ticket booth. Moses. I suspected something odd. I suspected sequence. The gorilla mimicked sequence in order to understand Dino, imitated Dino's act to understand Dino's intentions. If I put on lipstick as the lady does, I can feel her feelings, her motions, her intentions toward me. If I clutch his neck as he holds mine, I can perhaps understand. I must understand. I could almost hear him trying to understand, but his name rang in his brain and he remembered. Moses. What did it mean to him? What awful urgency did it carry? I imitated the sequence. I wrapped my fingers around my own throat. I tightened the fingers. They turned cold. I felt what Dino felt, what Moses felt, the precious precision of my pulse, gluttonous, powerful, banging against my fingers. His name is Moses. And I am the princess in "Rumpelstiltskin," turning my gold to straw, and, indeed, Dino the dwarf stamped his feet, dropped the crutch, staggered in a strange and diminishing semicircle, sank to the ground. I flattened myself against the ticket house wall, pressed along to the door, felt for the phone. Call Steven. Call Steven now. But the phone rang. I picked it up, grunted anonymously.

"Dino, it's Steve Morris. Listen, is my wife there? . . . Dino? You okay, Dino? . . . Who is this? Dino?"

I pressed the button and cut Steven off, cradled the phone. I spoke to the empty phone wires. My message was tangled in the feet of birds.

"I'm not crazy, Steven. I'm not sick. I'm afraid of the universe."

"I know. I'll take care of you, Linda. I promise. Trust me."

"I feel safe with you as if I'm curled up in your tweedy pocket and you slip your fingers in now and then to stroke my hair and scratch my back."

"You are safe."

"But then I feel I shall strangle on the lint and go blind in the loom of your tweed. You understand, don't you?"

"I try to."

"I must go out alone."

John Banks stood under the vulture, his hands on his hips. His hips so slim, angry and slim, hard, I could feel again the punch of his hipbones, the suck of flesh as we pulled apart. "Linda, take the gorilla back to the rental place. Get in the truck now and drive to the rental place and leave him there. And then get on with your life. You are sinking into a solipsistic sea of anthropomorphism. This is an ugly cantankerous wild beast who is not only dumb but considerably more stupid than you can imagine, volatile and dangerous. Get rid of him and get on with your life and don't get hung up on your foolish husband's antivivisectionist childishness. You Americans. Go."

"I hate the way you talk, John Banks. Really hate it."

The phone rang again under my fingers. "Linda, is this you? . . . Linda?"

Eye level at the cage window of the ticket counter, I watched Steven's gorilla open his cage, drop to the ground, hoot softly at Dino. Growling, he tickled him under the armpits. Dino didn't stir. The gorilla made a "hurry up, tickle me" sign, waited, lifted Dino's wrist, listened to his watch, followed the dial with a finger, lifted his own gorilla wrist, listened to his non-watch, left. I heard ocean waves crashing, the faint drag of chain as he left. Gulls filled in the empty air. I didn't think I could make a run for my van. He returned. Moses—I granted him the dignity of his name—Moses knelt over Dino, ran his hands gently over all of his body, turned him over, stroked him again, searched carefully his poor starched and sunken face, with one hesitant finger his hair, Michelangelo's God reaching a finger out to man. And, separating the greasy tousles of Dino's hair, an old friend, hunted for lice. I had a girlfriend who was raped in her apartment. She called the police, called a cab, went to the hospital, came home, called her mother, two days later had a heart attack. She told me she hadn't had time to be frightened. I watched, frozen, fascinated. Moses pulled a straw from a cold drink cup, poked Dino, sniffed the straw, withdrew, stood upright, passed his hand over his own face, from one side down across his mouth and cupped his chin. It was Jack Benny's now-what gesture. Little wonder we all responded to it. Having thus considered something, he dropped to his fours and ran off. Dino should have stirred, shook his head, said, "Where am I?" Moses returned with another Coke container, a coffee cup, another coffee cup, some under his arm, one in his mouth. He placed them around Dino. What was he doing? Dino had given him a coffee cup. It was precious to Dino. Does it follow in gorilla context that coffee cups are the coin of the realm and so he has, apologizing, creating a sequence, brought coffee cups to Dino because he has assumed that coffee cups are the coins of Dino's realm? More. Napkins, beer cans, cups, containers, a frenzied gathering of the cardboard garden's blooms. With great care he plastered Dino's belly with three soggy French fries in a jagged line. Medicine? Burial goods? Ornaments?

I too wanted to touch Dino, ask, "Are you okay, Dino? Dwarf man, old goat man with sugar on your beard, are you okay?" Dragging the chain, busy, intense, Moses returned with the entire wire garbage can, poured out the contents, spread them over Dino. He sat silent and still. Is this ritual become instinctive? Instinct become ritual? Is this Moses' creative act in response to the moment, a new set of sequences, a new series of maps to imprint in his biogram? He bowed and touched his forehead to Dino's forehead. Women have done that to me in Tibet. It is a respectful greeting, homage. Then he touched Dino's mouth and smelled his own fingers, smelled deeply for the honey of death. Then touched him all over, poked his belly, chest, arm, hands, eyes, harder and harder until, somehow finished—I could not bring myself to say satisfied—Dino piled with coffee cups, the gorilla rested on his haunches and considered, with an ancient weariness, what was before him.

I had seen something profoundly moving, extraordinary. I had been to another universe, a parallel time, almost familiar. Moses, I asked, what have you done? Do you know what a terrible thing you've done, Moses? Were you mimicking Dino? Monkey see, monkey do, and went too far? Did you think, if you do this to me, Dino, I shall have to do the same to you? Did you kill him intentionally, maliciously, fully aware, remembering the crack of the chain on your back? What is it, Moses? Did you remember and, remembering, kill him? Or did you say, simply, innocently, "Feel what you are doing to my neck, Dino. Please, Dino, under-stand you are giving me pain. In my gorilla context, if you do this, I shall have to do this." And you gently placed your fingers around Dino's neck to warn him, but Dino, again, didn't listen, didn't hear you? Is that what I've seen? And then, remorseful, you buried him in coffee cups? How can I say remorseful? How can I impose any of what I feel and what I know on what you feel and know? Steven bought me a copy of Samuel Johnson's dictionary. In it the defini-tion for murder reads, "killing that is done privately." War, done publicly, is not a crime. My clandestine John Banks is more likely a murderer than Moses. I could not imagine that the gorilla had a concept of crime or not crime. I imagined that he had a right and a wrong, a creature with such dignity must, but it was his right and wrong, not ours. Although perhaps it was something like ours. Perhaps I had watched a moral act, a righteous act. Even though Dino was dead, I wasn't certain he'd been murdered.

Magnificent, Moses stood upright, his chest huge, sprung forward. He howled. He fisted his hands and beat the drum of his chest and boomed in my own blood. He screamed. The scream grew, multiplied. Remorse? Triumph? I heard him. He said I am. His sound filled my chest. Coney Island became jungle. He slashed at lamppost trees, ripped up wire vines, rolled the drinking fountain boulder from its base. Water gushed and then there was a stillness. We sat, both of us, in the eye of his storm. I was frozen, waited for him to come for me. And then a final scream invoked all the others. I recognized it, for I was a gut string reverberating to it: it was grief. It filled me. I waited for him to come for me, but the display was over.

"Steven. Steven." I wept into the phone. "Steven, I know his name. His name is Moses. Three lines of soggy French fries on Dino's chest. And coffee cups."

"Just stay there. I'm on my way. Stay there."

Moses squeezed packets of ketchup into his palm, onto Dino's chest, finger-painted bright circles, a Zen artist drawing death, an old friend putting Dino to sleep. There was no question that I knew this: he rubbed his chest so Dino could sleep. Knowing this, a door opened to a path to the heart of the universe.

Knowing this, I opened the ticket booth window and said very softly, "Moses, get in your cage." He swung around, looked over his shoulder, swiveled on his haunches, looked at me and immediately away. "Go on, Moses, cage."

He tilted his head to the right, cocked it like a dog or a deaf man: Language goes in here. I listen to language with this side.

Three lines of soggy French fries on Dino's chest in a circle of red blood. Moses rubbed Dino's chest in circles.

"Moses, please get in your cage. I mean it. This is the first day of my life and I don't need any trouble from you."

He looked back over his shoulder once at Dino in the circle of cups and Coke containers. He looked at me directly, jerked his chin at me, offensive as I was, challenged me, defiantly, trying to place me in his hierarchy, in a sequence.

"Please," I said. "Now, Moses. Cage."

He watched me with his steady gaze, waiting. I made his "hurry up" sign with my hand, shook it again and again for emphasis. He yawned and, with a great exhausted sigh, hoisted himself into my van, into his cage, pulled his tub over his head. I was placed. I was mildly significant, had some authority, knew the sequences. He settled back into the cage, huddled, chewed on cabbage leaves, peeked at me with sly, blinking glances, would not make eye contact.

"Now lock it, Moses." I shook my hand at him again. "Hurry. Hurry."

Again, he cocked his head to the right, listened to my words. My words are tools, tiny stone tools that cut through to his brain, etch something onto his memory, a map of meaning. It was my gesture which moved him. He seemed, I thought, comforted, relieved that I spoke his language and he was in his safe place. I had always thought of a cage as a prison; he might have thought of it as a nest. I had entered his pattern making. He belched his soft sound. "Uh-uh," I belched back.

I walked very slowly into the Horror House, returned with the Mexican blanket to lay it over Dino, and as I did, with the hunger of curiosity, which may be my fatal flaw, I looked at him closely. Sometimes I have leaned over John Banks in bed and examined his face, unseen. Even deeply asleep John Banks has stirred under my attention. It is intensely intimate—a zero experience—to see another human being sleeping and infinitely intimate to see him, to touch him, to touch his death, for I leaned over and touched Dino's cheek and then his hand and I was shattered by my sorrow for this gamey little stranger whom I never knew and would never miss. I was shattered because I felt a loss that was original, tribal, and as human as I have ever felt because, for all his lack, he was one of us. Death is so lonely. For the living. Perhaps for the dead. I crossed the crutches over his body, pulled the blanket over his face. I knew the gorilla watched and understood what I had done at least as well as I understood what he had done.

I found the bag of hay and newspaper. With Moses' droppings I laid out a new map going the wrong way. It was the first map I'd ever made. I was Sister Elizabeth.

The larger a creature's territory, the greater his brain. Evolving, we have endlessly, increasingly complicated maps to make. And then we go to the moon. Wandering from the garden, we make our way and make our maps and our brains expand, biograms, inputs, synapses. Farther and farther we go from the garden until we are lost, until the cord snaps, and we turn inward and attack ourselves. But all our maps begin there at the still silent point of Paradise and we dream of unraveling the knots and twists and turns we have taken and finding each other on the path, going home together.

As if I were sowing seed, I tossed the droppings toward Brighton Beach, threw the bag on the front seat, left the rest of its giveaway getaway contents in front of the Brighton Athletic Club on the corner, and then turned around and drove away from the ocean toward Flatbush Avenue, toward, as the sign on his cage informed me, Henry Froelich, Rent-A-Pet, Flatbush Avenue, Brooklyn, N.Y., U.S.A.

FOUR

Let's imagine, I say to the gorilla behind me, for I felt the heat of his being on the nape of my neck, let's imagine going to my husband's funeral. My voice alone was real. I clung to it, let it fill the emptiness. Let's imagine, in one way or another, we've both killed our keepers.

Imagine we have traveled very far, feel faint and disoriented. I don't know where we've come from. Malaga? Key West? I'm wearing a white suit and a turban. You're wearing 4XL Buffalo Bills sweatpants, a 44 collar shirt, a flowered tie. My suit seems old but very well cut. The sky is a perfect delft blue. A charcoal storm boils far in the west. The family stands under a white tent, Steven's wife close to his grave, my children around her in attitudes of devotion and concern, I under a larch tree at the fringe of Steven's partners, his friends, our friends, you above me, rustling in the tapestry of the tiny cones of the larch. There is a whispering of its soft needles. You cough a soft cough to let me know you're with me. Steven's new wife leans on Steven's brother's arm. She is small, a size four or six, fragile in a stunning two-piece tunic of black linen designed for a tall, willowy woman. She wants to be larger than she is. She wants power. She wears a large black straw hat, veiled. Now and then she lifts the veil and daubs at her tears with a lace . . . goddamnit, my lace handkerchief from Galway. I suspect she wears my nightgowns and my jewelry and my silk blouses, which she must belt, for I am inches taller and wider. My daughter glances at me once, narrows her eyes, pierces me with the chemistry of hatred: bitter, sharp, metallic, like a piece of aluminum foil caught in my back teeth. She jerks her chin up, says to me, "You did this to him. You killed him," all silently, but I understand as she turns back to the new widow. Either for comfort or to comfort. My sons turn their backs and do not see me. They seem to have wives now, small and sweet, in black and white silk, all size four, terrifically tailored, with sun-streaked blond hair pulled back in knots and gold loop earrings and tennis-muscled legs. They look prosperous.

If she'd had money before she'd met Steven, she would have thrown out everything of mine. Instead, coming to him with little, she takes much. My things become her things. He met her at a singles club. I know the story. It is all lies and wishful thinking. I've heard it from many women. Her girlfriends insisted she go this one time (she's gone twice a week for years) and she went and there was Steven and she wasn't interested (lie) but he pursued her and pursued her (probably) and when he called and asked her for dinner she made reservations in the most expensive restaurant (true). She found him extremely undesirable (lie) but dinner's dinner. Then they fell inexplicably in love (I'm not certain). Steven was looking for me at the singles clubs. Instead he found this . . . Melanie, yes, Melanie . . . who was divorced, ran a florist shop and a catering business, and never lost a can opener in her life. Melanie wants power, she wants to be larger in all ways, which is why she is overpowered by her hat and her tunic suit. She has a tiny, full body, a doll body and face. I imagine her face without the veil. It is cute and pouty, flat-cheeked from the side but frontally doglike and overshot. Her jaw exposes her ambition. She has done well. Now she has the principal and my Irish lace and neither of us has Steven.

They married immediately and moved my bed from its niche between our closets over toward the windows facing the lake. People who don't lose can openers or pieces of their souls don't need to watch the moon and consider destiny and the meaning of life. Facing the wall, they slept in our bed together. She threw out my country rose Pierre Deux sheets, dust ruffles, shams, ordered Adrienne Vittadini, matching sets in hard geometrics of black and white. The hatred, regret, and envy I feel are so palpable, my throat closes as she throws the first handful of dirt on my husband's grave.

My older son steadies my youngest by the sleeve of his suit, bends to him, says, "Don't look now, but she's here." I see my young son's back stiffen. I remember that stiffening when he had his first haircut, when Steven took away the car keys. It is half pride, half fear. Now, as he blocks my very being with his strong back, every bone rings with contempt. Is there no longing left for the soft float of quilt as I cover their curved and sleeping shoulders, the feather kiss on their foreheads that became part of their child dreams? They tighten the knot around the new wife, look steadfastly forward, a twitch of jaw. They are warriors against change, against the evil woman who killed their father and ruined their home, on whom they had counted, on whom they could no longer count. "She's here." I have become she, object and abject. I stand under the tree of evil, in my veils of shame and anonymity, seeking self-knowledge. I am my own apple and I have made other lives rotten. I lean against the wind-warped tree and wish a new man stood beside me, supporting me, pursuing me, handsome, angular, somewhat effete in his grace, slim-ankled and lean, long-fingered with stern cheekbones and soft lips and . . .

No, I reprimand myself. I've done that. But I have no one to steady me, no one to comfort me, to hide behind. It is my choice. Does one need to spend a life enveloped by others just for these moments, just in case? How much of life must be spent to save up sympathy for a moment of loss? In a cartoon voice—she has blown up too many helium balloons at birthday parties she's catered—Melanie turns to the onlookers and says, "Of those who knew and loved Steven, we welcome you to step forward and share with us your best memories." Some pull folded notes from breast pockets, clear their throats. Deeply uncomfortable, they speak to the blind grave, fight weeping, gulp. One partner remembers the ski trip when his angry teenage son left the cottage at midnight. Steven put on his cross-country skis, found the boy, talked him into returning. He speaks of Steven's kindness and sympathy but does not mention I was there with Steven, brandy and bologna sandwiches in my knapsack. Nor does he mention that it was I who convinced the boy to return. Nor is it next mentioned by the next speaker, everyone weeping and coughing and blowing their noses, when Steven built a cage to trap the raccoon in the attic and someone . . . "Listen, it was I. I was someone." Someone put on a raccoon coat and squealed in the dark from the landing as Steven struggled backward, dragging the cage up the stairs. How he loved animals. How he loved a good joke. How Steven was scared to death but we all laughed. A favorite joke, a great story, a sense of humor. His partner in the airplane tells how Steven paid for his daughter's wedding when the partner had a cash flow problem. I hadn't known that. I step forward, stand at the graveside, look down at the auburn gleam of Steven's mahogany box. Faces freeze as they see me taking my place to speak. My daughter whispers to the new wife, "Do you want me to stop her?"

"No," she says magnanimously. Given similar circumstances, I would not be as magnanimous. However it might be, she suspects, as I have in the past, often, that I'll bury myself with my tongue. "Let her be."

Some smile in discomfort; some grimace. I whisper but my voice is too loud, could fell trees. "Oh, Steven," I begin, not sharing, "why didn't you wait for me, Steven? You knew I'd come back. I have so many jokes to tell you, Steven. Who can I tell my jokes to now?" I weep and stop myself, pull myself up. "Did you hear about the man who dropped dead on the sidewalk? Broke his glasses and everything?" I tell the assembled mourners about the soap slivers. "Few of you know," I begin again, "that while Steven was ultimately generous . . ." I swallow my sorrow, begin again. "Steven," I say, my chin lifted, my eyes on my children's bent heads, startled that my youngest son has a small bald spot among his curls. They wait for another salvo to their hearts. I cannot hurt them. "Steven saved slivers of soap. He could not bear to throw out the little slivers."

My family, his partners, her family, are traumatized by my story and their own good manners.

"Often, no matter how many times I reminded her, our maid threw out his slivers and replaced them with a new fresh bar of soap. Steven, after all, was a wealthy man."

My son groans. "Mom, please."

My older son comforts his brother. "It's all right. It's all right."

I mean them no harm. I never meant them any harm. I wish them love, life, laughter, light. "One morning Steven woke up early and I heard him shouting and then he stood at the foot of the bed shouting, 'Your goddamn maid threw out my soap again. I want my soap. Where's my soap?'

"I dragged myself from sleep. 'What do you want me to do, Steven?'

" 'Call her up. Find out where she threw the soap.'

"I groaned then just as my son groans now. 'Steven, sweetheart, it's six in the morning.'

" 'Get me her number. I'll call her.'

"So I grappled with the Rolodex, scratched a number on a pad, handed it to him. In the half-light he dialed the number. His lips were set tight. I wondered if he could be dangerous. I wondered what prompted such an outburst. Someone said, 'Hello? Hello? Hello?' on the line. He held the phone away, covered it with his hand, whispered in confusion, 'This is my mother's number.'

" 'I know.' I laid back down, pulled the covers over my shoulder. 'This may be your mother's fault after all.' " I hear a murmur of appreciation from my daughter. If it hasn't already been, her life from now on will be my fault. She will never have her own face.

Steven's brother has stepped forward, stands before me. "What's the point, Linda?" He is as angry about my memories as Steven was about the soap.

"There is no point, Jeff. I just needed to talk about him." Then I say to everyone, "Steven would understand. You see, when Diggety won the dog show and he came home with a bag of Dad's Dog Food and a pot of mums, Steven was the only one I knew who understood how funny it was. . . . Oh, Steven, mums and Dad's. Remember?"

I return to my tree, weeping. The new widow stage-whispers patronizingly as I pass her, "Thank you for sharing with us, Linda."

"The point is," I warn her, "things can be in the wrong place. And it's very frightening. Steven knew that."

And I lean against the larch tree and hear above me the dry

rustle of the needles. I hear your soft hoot and a chuckle. I imagine my husband's new wife, the looks on the faces of my family, as you, gorilla, swing down and stand beside me, pat me on the head, put your arm around me, look in my eyes with calm and understanding, the eyes of an angel. On your fours, doglike, your head at my waist, your fur cilia, underwater in the wind, we walk away. I leave with you and wish to bury my face in the silver tips of your back and weep until I am dry. I leave the imaginary funeral and the new widow wearing my underwear.

Back in the shaking van, Moses banged on its thin walls and screamed. "Where is my soap?" he screamed. "Where is the can opener? Where am I? Are we here?"

"It's all right. You're all right," I called back to him.

"It's all right," I called back to Steven, rolled over, touched his warm shoulder, his forehead, his cheek. In his sleep he kissed my finger and turned into my body, asked, "Where is my soap? Where am I? Where are we really going?"

"Oh, Steven, all this time I thought you knew."

I had felt the chilling winds of the unknown slipping under our comforters, squeezing between the caulk in the siding of our house. The unknown is out there, always. Where am I? is a terrible question with its layers of dissociation, of lostness, of exile, of the yearning to get back inside the garden, to break down the gates, to go home. We are both fugitives, Moses. We are both in the wrong place. Steven understood and I understood. *"You're okay," I whispered to Steven. "You're okay."* And I imagined for miles that I lay beside him waiting for the dawn because he doesn't like me wandering about in the night.

The other piece of the story I didn't tell Steven about my Buffalo trip occurred on the train going home. At each stop passengers stepped off into the night. At each stop I thought about death. By eleven my car was empty except for a fat Amish couple in their strange funereal costumes with rear ends like billboards. It did not help to look away, out the window, for the night was white with blizzard wherever the train lights prodded the pudding of landscape. I could see no lines of streetlights, no soft yellow lit windows, no drift of station lamps as we hurtled past. We were noplace. The screws of fear turned and tightened in my chest. Tracking laughter and light, I carried my things to the dining car. Four workmen played cards, beer cans stacked in rows. The black steward leaned against the counter, on his elbows, flicked snake-lid eyes at my furs, suedes, strawberry hair, nodded mildly. I sat with my back to the men. They were loud and drunk, muscular and fattening fast, grimy.

One yelled, "I bet you think we're drunk."

I didn't turn around, tried not to let the steward see me smiling.

They roared at each other. "No sense of humor, huh?"

I turned to them, offered a tight little nun's smile, turned away. Speechless with laughter, roaring, they thumped the table with their fists. "Hey, barkeep, that's my wife, so whatever she says don't believe her."

I imagined they were bricklayers for the dust on their bodies or iron workers for their lithe and powerful Indian arms. The steward walked by me, flicked his eyes, spoke softly to them. They grew quiet for a moment. I heard the slap of cards, grunts of restrained laughter. One walked past me to the men's room. He was coarse and solid, dusty with grime, hair in a ponytail, feet grounded in hard-toed safety shoes. When he came back, buckling his belt, he stopped by my seat. "No harm, huh?"

"No harm."

The train swayed, throwing his thigh against my shoulder, so I asked him, "Where are we? Do you know where we are?"

He leaned over me, surrounded me, looked out my frosted window. I wanted to press against him, hide in him.

"You'll be okay." He had read me. He pushed off down the aisle. I could hear his bulk drop onto a soft seat, heard him grunt. I closed my eyes and imagined standing with him between the cars, swaying against him, my bare feet on the hard toes of his safety shoes. I woke to men running forward past me, the steward wiping circles in the window with a bar towel, walkie-talkies buzzing, and the train slowing to a stop, stopping in utter darkness, not a place, and the crew yelling to each other as they ran to the rear of the cars, yelling into their headphones. Lights swept the countryside.

"Fucking train's lost."

The men held their cards. One of them snapped his fingers. "Anyone else on this track, we're meatloaf." The snap of his fingers was as loud as a crack of bone. I wanted him to sit next to me, hold me.

The steward looked at his watch, swore, said nothing. The train whistle blew urgently, alarmed, alarming as we backed up slowly. Over my shoulder, I dared to ask again. "Where are we?" I meant, where am I?

"Near Colonie."

"Maybe."

"Maybe?"

"He's backing up on the wrong track in a blizzard, hoping he'll come out where he went off." All of us in the same place, holding different maps. I wished for Sister Elizabeth who did not know she did not know. I knew.

How I yearned to curse the storm with them, lean against them, sit on their laps, drink their beer, laugh, be angry because we were lost and the train had shunted onto the wrong track and was backing up blindly. I pulled my coat over me, tried to close my eyes, tried not to cry, not to think of the man with the ponytail holding me between the cars, holding me against his chest, me whimpering, "Where are we? Where am I?"

"I think, Linda," John says, as if he were preaching in a modest country church in the Cotswolds, projecting his arrogant benevolence, "it is within the framework of a death wish. Something in you must be driven to go off in the night with an animal-slash-stranger as a witch would. I should think someday you will return clubfooted or, as Cinderella, lose your foot-slash-slipper. The flaw in your script is that there will be no Prince Charming waiting to marry you and keep you from your flights, from your own true nature. You cannot depend on any of us for that much longer, certainly not as you lose your looks."

"Jesus, John. You make me feel so lonely."

"Then you should stay at home with your prince while you can and give up your flights."

"You've turned this into a confession scene. I had no intention . . ." In the same intuitive way he knew if he pressed under my arm I would come, he had guessed my myth, had seen my dragon nature.

"Linda . . ." His voice grew deeper. *"Dear girl."* He orchestrated his voice to indicate his feelings. A deepening voice was a sign of affection. There were few other signs. *"Your stories frighten me. They are fairy tales of witches, seeking devils."*

"I thought my Amtrak adventure would excite you. I should never have told you. Why is it you see your adventures as normal and mine abnormal?"

"I'm out to get laid, my dear child; you want to satisfy your curiosity. Far more dangerous."

"John . . ."

"Of course at a deeper, darker level you are seeking the other in order to find yourself, which is not in itself unattractive or uninteresting. But your curiosity, my love, that, I venture, is your fatal flaw. Curiosity."

He pronounced the word as if it meant dysentery. "As in what killed the cat, I suppose?"

"Don't get snarky. I'm offering you some perceptions, that's all. You see, you are drawn outward by your curiosity, but drawn inward by your fear of the dark corners. Curious and afraid. I find that very tender."

"I'm afraid of the universe."

"Yes, yes, and you also yearn for its mysteries and its comfort."

"Not bad, John. You may not be nice, but you are certainly smart."

"And you are not dull, dear girl. At any rate, Linda, your story does excite me," he said, reaching for me. "It does excite me."

Afterward I said, "You really set up walls, don't you?"

"Walls?"

"To keep love out."

"Linda . . ." His voice deepened again. "I find you irresistible. You are very very precious to me but I do not feel I am in love with you. If I were to tell you, if only for the benefit of your own personal emotional triumph, that I love you, I am not certain I would mean it. At all."

"That's what I mean, walls."

"If you had wanted a man without walls, you would have chosen one. A man with walls allows you to keep your marriage quite intact, doesn't it? Don't complain. You've chosen me well."

I thought about the workman and his safety-toed shoes until the train pulled into my station and the steward held my bag for me, helped me out. I protested, not wanting to step into the night alone, "But the station is closed."

The steward said, eyes flicking back to the men, "No one's getting off here. You're okay."

The door of my car was caked with ice and I could not force the key into the hole. There was not another car, sound, person, in the parking lot, nothing lit in the distance, the snow still filling the air with its dead silence. Using my house keys, I chopped away until I saw him standing in front of my car, his athletic bag on my hood. My hand trembled.

He watched me as I worked at the car door. "You belong in Hollywood with that coat, that hair."

I could not ask where he was going. I would not offer him a ride. "Just leave. Okay?" I don't know where the words came from. "Just leave. Do you see how much work I have to do? Do you have any idea how far I have to drive?"

He blinked, hiccuped, lifted his bag, walked away into the snow. I remember my voice softening as he left, the steady steam of my dragon breath following him. I knew I would not be able to drive. I did not want him to leave me alone in the night.

"Hey, hey. Come back."

His hands were rough-skinned and callused, his belly warm. He called me sister on the reclined seat, and when I was in a hurry and worried he was too drunk, he said, "Okay, sister, okay." And after I asked him to make certain my car started, which he did, then he walked away, slipped into the storm. A little warmth in the night, two animals in the wilderness, rubbing against each other, me lost in my fear, he in his safety shoes and his neolithic simplicity, giving each other a moment of comfort. I always wondered how he got home, how I got home. How I dared go home.

On the way home Steven sat beside me. "Why. Just tell me why." It was not a question.

"I liked his shoes. He was wearing safety shoes."

"Safety shoes or vagabond shoes. What do you want?"

"I needed comfort."

"You could have been killed."

"I was more afraid of being alone, of being lost."

"You really have a problem, Linda."

"*Of course I have a problem. With the universe. I'm afraid of the universe. Do you want me to see a shrink?*"

"*Are you kidding? He'd have you on the couch in five minutes flat and I'd still have to pay for it.*"

"*On the contrary, Steven. I would have him on the couch.*"

"*Yes. I understand that. I don't understand how you can be so powerful and yet be so afraid.*"

"*Perhaps what I'm afraid of is being so powerful, of realizing my full power, how many of you I'll hurt when I do.*"

"*Bathe before you come to bed.*"

"*Of course. I'll tell you I have to take a bath to relax and I will be clean when I lie down beside you under our comforter.*"

"*Poor Linda. You're a woman of many rooms. When I enter one, you slip into another.*"

"*Poor Steven, poor dear wonderful Steven.*"

I made believe Steven had a ponytail for a few wild nights that rather surprised Steven. I had no desire to find my erstwhile rapist, only to think about him, to use him to glue my marriage together. "No harm. No harm, Steven." We are brother and sister, Steven and I, lost in our lives. Once we walked together and held hands. That helped. But then a woman of rooms met a man of walls and her house became a horror. I didn't dwell on this for the pleasure it gave. It gave me none.

FIVE

On Flatbush Avenue I sat in gridlock, my engine turned off, my husband's gorilla banging on the sides of the van. Lit by a dusty morning sun, the handsome dome of the Dime Savings rose above me. Beneath it fin de siècle fungus spread outward across the bridge into America. I stepped from my van and walked forward between vehicles. A Haifa cab was parked in a loading zone, a Queens Dairy truck double-parked next to the cab. A city bus had failed to maneuver through the narrow neck of pavement. "Listen, Moses, this is the most I can do for you. It's the most I can do for myself. You're not in my plans. You can't count on me. Ask my family. I'm sorry. I'm sorry I got you into this. I'm sorry about Dino. I just don't want to be in the way when they shoot you. It's that rough. Maybe this Rent-A-Pet person can help you. I can't. This is the most I can do. I'm sorry. Believe me."

We were stalled ten minutes, fifteen, probably backed up to the bridge. Under the protective shadow of the dome, the uneasy light lifted bits of cornice and frieze, gargoyle and pediment. Old Brooklyn was smeared now with grime, its windows blinded, its graceful entrances ragged with storefronts and weak neons, Bottomless Breakfasts ninety-nine cents, discount, discount, steam, exhaust, brown depression, anger. Enough traffic was backed up so there would be no unwinding of the tangle, no backing off, and from the rear, more of early morning Brooklyn traffic impacted. No one knew where the cabbie and the milkman were, if indeed they even were. Moses' jungle howls and hoots were indistinguishable from the bang of hood, pound of horn, shouts of the drivers. In front of me a man in a suit and a raincoat sat on his hood and with two fists beat out a tinny rhythm of what began to sound like "Three Blind Mice."

"Those are not nice guys out there, Moses. They go crazy losing five minutes in traffic. Imagine what they'd do if they lost a gorilla. I've never seen an animal become a man. I have seen men become animals. All you want, you poor soul, is to be left alone and be a gorilla. You must be worth a lot. And now you're going to be a dangerous animal and they'll be justified in killing you because you've killed. I can't get involved. Steven, who is so clever, as if he were protecting me from you, will somehow weave, complicate my crime of wifely waywardness into your crime of murder so that his decisions will be based on his fact that we've both killed our keepers. I know Steven. I could turn around now and take you home and yell, 'Steven, Steven, I have your gorilla. He killed Dino. Help me, Steven, help me.' But I won't do that to you. Or to me. I'll take you back to the Rent-A-Pet and give you a chance, not much of one, but a chance. Take you back and they can sell you again. I'm sorry. It's all I can do."

Twenty minutes. A dusky dreadlocked boy aimed a stack of roped newspapers from the back of a truck to the sidewalk, but the papers landed on the roof of a dark green Jaguar with an MD license plate. The doctor in Italian sharkskin exploded from his car, barreled to the truck, arm raised, shouting, "You fucka, you fucka!" The truck's rear doors closed from inside, the driver rolled up his window, didn't hear him, see him. The doctor banged on the window, kicked the side of the truck, returned to his dented roof, tossed the newspapers in the gutter, breaking the rope, spreading the papers. He brushed his lapels, pressed his portable phone against his cheek like a baby blanket, talked to his lawyer with animation. An old woman, thin and bent as a paper clip, stooped to read the headlines, looked around, took a paper, struggled to the stairs of the subway entrance on the corner. I would be old, penniless, alone. I wanted to call Steven.

"And what brings you to Brooklyn?" I hear John Banks inquire politely as he bows toward the subway entrance.

"Shame. Shame before my husband," I answer.

Banks beckons, sweeps the ground with his arm, inviting me away. "Just leave the van, Linda. Just walk away."

"My life is a solo. I let no one intrude. I am misplaced. In the land and with these people, I pay a terrible price of solo and sorrow, a terrible necessary sorrow. I am my own creation. I can depend on no one." I didn't know if I or the gorilla spoke. It could have been either of us.

I twisted between the cars and trucks and walked quickly toward the subway entrance, touched the railing to descend, stopped, turned because I could still hear the creature's hoots. "Where am I? Don't leave me. What will I do without you?" It was either Steven or the gorilla or my soul calling. I heard the questions in my heart, the way one hears one's child's cry. I bought a string of figs, a *Times,* a pound of Jordan almonds from a grocery store that had just rolled up its metal chain-link wall, returned to the van. It was not a commitment, this returning. It was just a matter of minutes before I found the Rent-A-Pet and returned the gorilla, barely used. Then I could call Steven or go on. Or call Steven and tell him I was going on. I bent to the Jaguar, rested my dazzling diamond, my marriage price, on its open window. The doctor jumped, then relaxed, for I smiled, displayed a fifty-dollar bill, asked if I might use his phone. He took the bill and passed the phone out the window. "Send and end," he instructed. I turned my back to him and called Steven.

"It isn't that simple, Steven."

"It is, when two people love each other. . . ."

"That's simple. What I'm talking about isn't simple."

Steven heard something in my voice, didn't answer. Was there a sound of psychic flesh tearing? A silken sound? Of soul's blood rushing to the raw wound? "I'm leaving for a little while."

He hesitated too long to answer. Steven was calculating. He should have shouted, "Don't!" Instead he said, "So?"

The doctor was studiously involved with his fingernails, not missing a word. Steven's voice was loud enough for him to hear.

"I have to decide what to do, Steven."

"Yes."

"What do you mean, Steven, by 'yes'?"

"I'm not certain. What did I do wrong?"

"It's not you, Steven."

"I wasn't good enough. I bored you."

"Steven!"

"I didn't listen to you. I didn't provide for you. Tell me what I didn't do."

"You forgot to add, 'that he does.' What didn't you do that he does. There is nothing. There is nothing you didn't do, nothing that he does. This is about me. Not either of you."

"Either of who?"

I could not tell him or the doctor that I had looked at the puzzle of the moon and the puzzle of myself and found a piece missing. "I'll be back, okay?"

"I don't know."

We'd both broken the surface of our pool and thrashed about looking for blood. I retreated. "Just make believe I've gone to the Golden Door. For a week, let me go. Let me work this out."

"If you have the gorilla, your life is in danger."

"My life, not ours. It's different. Please, Steven."

"You have money, your checkbook, your gas cards, road maps?"

"I'm okay, Steven. Stop organizing me."

"Your passport?"

"Don't be cute."

"It's Saturday, isn't it? I looked at you and you turned into a winged dragon. Just how far are you going to take this, Linda?" He shifted from sorrow to hostility so quickly, I was breathless.

"I'll call, Steven. Every night."

And then he took aim. It was sooner than I'd expected. "Don't."

"Don't?"

"Don't call."

I handed the phone to the doctor. Nothing in his face stirred, but he offered me my fifty. I waved it off. "It's okay. We do this a couple of times a day."

"You should get back in your car. With that ring, around here."

I climbed back into the cab of my truck, pulled the door shut, listened to the gorilla hooting softly. It was a heartbreaking cry. I would not get involved.

• • •

I have sat at cocktail parties, at dinner tables, and said things like "If the body really renews itself every seven years, why do we die from worn-out organs?"

Once, the man on my right, an Indian dentist who had just graduated from the University of Michigan and built a two-million-dollar medical complex on the main highway, answered me. "Gravity," he said very softly. "Some of us are not meant for gravity. We were not designed for gravity," he whispered to me again as I slipped on my coat. Steven had gone into the snow for the car.

"Gravity?" I was stunned.

"It shortens life. The earth is so hard. Perhaps we do not belong here."

Steven stood at the open door, smiling, keys in hand.

"We are misplaced, so we die."

"I must speak to you about this," I murmured.

He smiled, rejected me, kissed my hand elaborately. "No, no. A pleasure."

I was misplaced.

When they hear I've left, Steven's friends will call and ask, "Are you okay?" They will not ask, "Have you heard from Linda?"

Nor will Steven be ready to say, "The kids think she drove off into the sunset with that fleabag gorilla I rented for the summer."

"That's ridiculous," they will not dare respond.

"I know," he'll want to say. "But they did vanish at the same time. She had him with her in the van and she did buy a string of figs for him the next morning in Brooklyn. And Linda hates figs."

"You're sure you're okay, Steve?"

"Yeah, sure." Instead they'll make lunch/fishing/flying/golf dates and treat Steven more gently than they had, also will not invest in any more projects with him.

Flatbush Avenue was still in gridlock. The noise of horns magnified, coalesced, rose as the drivers, all of them together, honked, in the same beat. The din pressed on me, squeezed my courage dry.

At last a black traffic cop walked slowly into the heart of the gridlock, through the encampment of bellows and blasts. She looked forward, eyes on a fixed point like a warrior, did not respond to the shouts. She knuckle-rapped hoods, slapped roofs as she passed. Each horn fell silent. I watched hungrily. She was without fear. She was small, fat, black, Jemima-breasted. Her uniform gray skirt rode up in back and showed a lacy pink slip, outlined a behind that had perfected a vast food storage system six million years ago in dry times across the Nubian desert, that swung independently between the vehicles. She was so unimpressive, so unimpressed, the men didn't know what weapon to use. When she hit Moses' roof, he slammed back like a child in the womb. She examined the interior of the dairy truck, the Haifa cab, wrote on a pad of paper, wrote and wrote, until, as if she'd come upon the correct combination for the Lottery, the cabbie and the truck driver sprinted from the Bottomless Breakfast ninety-nine cents. One held a half piece of toast. She tore paper from her pad and posted it on the dashboards of the cab and the milk truck, all without anger. Drivers gunned engines.

The cab pulled away, the dairy truck, the bus moved. The policewoman nodded at me, and I rolled forward to Rent-A-Pet, but it had become a kosher pizza falafel restaurant. A young bearded man swept the sidewalk.

I cruised up and down the street, wondered if I had the numbers right. The night of sleeplessness was a dead plumb weight behind my eyes. Finally, having driven past him three times, I pulled up to the curb of the falafel shop, leaned out the window, and asked the bearded man: "Froelich? Henry Froelich?"

He wouldn't look up at me. Someone sat behind a Yiddish paper on a beach chair. The young man said, "Moved." The reader, a small and wrinkled version of the sweeper, folded his beach chair under his arm and shuffled into the dark recesses of the restaurant.

"But I have a—"

"Moved," he snapped at me, and swept faster. I was garbage. "Left the country moved."

I contained myself. I thought of the black traffic cop and I spoke softly to his bent back. "Surely someone has taken over his business?" I stepped to the sidewalk.

He shrugged without turning. I pushed my hair off my face so that my very large wedding ring caught light. His eyes followed my hand. Uptown maybe six carats, pear-shaped, clear, blue, downtown. Hah. "You see, I'm supposed to return the gorilla . . . for my husband." I had a ring, a husband, money, legitimacy. "The gorilla," I projected the word to the back of the restaurant.

The newspaper rattled, the feet shuffled toward me, Henry Froelich called, "Tell her to pull around the back. Open the gates."

"Okay, lady," the son told me sullenly. "Take a left at the corner. Watch for the gates."

John Banks clears his throat, crosses his legs. He is wearing gleaming boots.

Steven stands up in shadows. I see a flash of ring, his white teeth. "I only want to take care of you."

A metal curtain rolled up electronically. Mesh gates swung open to an old-world alley of stoops, kitchen gardens, a crab apple tree, piles of trash, here and there a beach chair, a kitchen table, a trellis, a curling grapevine. A rubber tire hung from a tree. I was in the right place. The son waved me into a slot. The gate closed. Its state-of-the-art curtain rolled down behind me, locked into a track. A red dot flashed above it. I left the engine on as an empty gesture of power.

"Turn it off. We're switching trucks."

"Now just a moment—"

"My father says so."

I turned off the engine. "Come." The old man beckoned me with his folded newspaper. "Come. Come."

I sat at an ice-cream table in the back of the restaurant. I'd paused in my plunge, caught a rock hold on my way down, but something within me gave way and I wept tears, gulping and heaving. The men backed away from my display. "Get your mother." The father offered me a box of tissues, a glass of pineapple juice, a glass straw. I remembered having measles and drinking from a glass straw.

"I have to get him out of the country fast. My friend in Tarpon Springs has a zoo. She deals. She'll buy him from me, sell him to another country, and ship him out before anyone knows where he went. So I need you to take him to Tarpon Springs. You'll take the refrigerator truck. You get ten grand on delivery. Deliver him and I never saw you. I'll get rid of your Suburban. From then you're free. I'm offering you a deal works two ways, you and me. Maybe even for poor Moses."

"Why should I do this?"

"Why shouldn't you? You got more than enough money? You got someplace else to go?"

"I said get your mother."

I didn't like the lascivious son. Neither did his father. I knew the son was calculating what a woman has to do for a man to get such a diamond, uptown or downtown. Yesterday I could have liked or disliked a person. Today I had to decide if he'd help me or hurt me. It was a vast difference, a new positioning, and with it I could judge the depth of my fear.

The son returned with a jeweler's magnifying glass. "She's coming." He was afraid of his father.

"You're going too fast for me, Mr. Froelich," I protested.

"You're not in a hurry?" He called to his son, "You, pack and go with her."

"No." I caught my breath. I didn't know if they were benefactors or criminals or both. Nevertheless I said no sharply.

"No? I'm offering protection, a driver."

"No." Somehow I knew I could say no. "I don't like the way he looks at me."

"See?" He dismissed him with a wave of his hand. "So, we're agreed, good. After you sleep, we'll talk details. You drive him down, deliver him in one piece, alive, bring back the money, and I'll give you back your wedding ring."

"I didn't—"

The son returned from the alley. "Seventy-eight thousand miles, lousy brakes, the gorilla's wheezing." There was something small and bitter about the son. His feet were too large for his body, as if he'd been sick as a child and his growth was stunted. Somewhere under the mustache, there was the slightest impression of a harelip operation. He was clearly the dregs of their cup of joy.

"Moses," the father told me, "he only has one lung. Why did you let him catch cold? Your husband knows how valuable he is. The faster he gets to Florida, the better off he is."

"What if he dies on the way and I never get the money? What if someone shoots him, or takes him? Then I'm out a ring."

"I want you to go upstairs and take a nice nap. You have a long trip ahead of you, a long night behind you. So rest. Mrs. Froelich will watch over you."

"I don't want to go to Florida. I don't want the gorilla."

"Of course you don't. Who would? But for now, do me a favor and go upstairs?"

"Why can't I just leave the gorilla here? He's yours."

"Here? Where here? You got a rogue gorilla. Animal Control will shoot him, confiscate him. This will be their first stop. But you're okay, don't worry. You'll have a nice nap while we get the truck fixed up. Ben, you'll take it to the make-over shop. Go out by the Chink. Second light, yellow building. Jimmy. Ask for Jimmy. Tell him for me." He turned to me, shook a pill bottle up and down. "Restoril, six hours, no side effects. Terrific stuff. I gave you one. Listen, I'm not a thief. I deal quick, sometimes dirty, but I don't steal. With me, you're safe, understand. I need you to take the gorilla to Florida. Now they think Moses is dangerous. Now they think he should be shot. And, you'll forgive me for mentioning it, but isn't there a mister involved here who could also follow you?"

"He wouldn't."

"A gorilla's a gorilla. You never know about men." He pursed his lips together, wondered, I knew, if he should tell me something, decided to. "Who do you think called Animal Control? Who called me and told me you were coming? Who's got problems with insurance? Who's responsible?"

Damnit, Steven, just damnit. "What did he say?" I was on a dark ride. It wouldn't end. One terror begot, contained the next. Steven wasn't protecting me from the gorilla; he was protecting himself. I was the outlaw. "He said you were very upset and you had the gorilla and he also called Animal Control, for which I could wring his neck. I warned your husband about using Dino. I warned him. Your husband should learn to listen better."

The son examined my ring in his jeweler's glass, nodded at his father. "It's worth a gorilla. Uptown, you could add the truck."

"I'll think about it."

"Of course, your head will be clearer."

I could no longer penetrate his logic, judge my position, my choices. A woman in black with a terrible wig and thick glasses led me upstairs, continued Froelich's conversation as if they were one person. "This way you're gone for a week, you have a chance to think about your marriage. If you want to go home, you'll have plenty of money. He'll pay you extra when you get back, or send it to you. Five, ten thousand . . . and you're done. Listen, he pulls fast ones but he doesn't steal. We own the gorilla. He's killed a man. Animal Control, FDA, someone, will confiscate him unless we get him out of the country. We lose all our money. Mr. Froelich's friend in Tarpon Springs has a zoo. She'll sell Moses to Japan, to Germany, out of the country, ship him out."

"What will they do with Moses if they confiscate him?"

She had swollen lobster eyes. She looked at me too hard. "Kill him. Or give him AIDS. Or put shunts in his brain. Or cut away half of it. If you don't take him, he'll die or suffer for years. If you don't take him, we'll lose a fortune. Think about it. It's so simple for you, so hard for us." She led me to the recesses of the second floor. The rooms were velvet-draped, doilied, polished, dark. Elaborate grape-and-vine plaster outlined the fixtures and ceilings. A china cupboard was filled with silver religious objects, platters, goblets, incense boxes, candelabras. She opened a door to a fastidiously clean bedroom, lined with Hebrew books, some covered in silver and studded with turquoise stones. The books relieved me. Mrs. Froelich called me with one finger, pointed to the window over the courtyard. "This you gotta see." I had the impression she spent most of her days in this room, listening and waiting. We stood at the window, her hand on my shoulder.

The gorilla and Froelich sat drinking milk at a bridge table, both grunting softly at each other, "Uh-uh." "Uh-uh."

"Half 'n Half," she whispered. Waiting, listening, and whispering. "He loves Half 'n Half."

"You'll be okay," Froelich said to the gorilla. "You'll go to Tarpon Springs. You'll be okay. I'll fix you up good. Don't worry." Moses lowered his head and looked at him from under heavy brows. "Trust me, you'll be okay."

The gorilla poked himself in the armpit, made a hurry up sign to Froelich. Froelich reached over and scratched his chest, down the sides of his rib cage. The gorilla opened his mouth, hooted.

"Hurry," Mrs. Froelich whispered. "Hurry, tickle me."

I thought for a moment she was speaking to me. A door opened down the alley. Moses jerked his head in the direction of the door, barked once. A muscular man in a butcher apron stepped out, scratched himself, picked brown leaves from a trellis above his head, saw the gorilla. "Look who's back. Hey, Froelich, how many sandwiches you get from him?"

"What a way to talk, Pinsky. He understands."

Moses stood. "Sit, Moses. Stay right there and finish your milk. You got a long trip. You hear about the butcher who backed up into the fan and got a little behind in his business?"

They laughed. The gorilla chuckled. "He laughs," Mrs. Froelich explained. "He can't cry, but his eyes fill up when you yell at him."

"Oh, that's so sweet."

"He's very sweet. He's the gentlest creature I've ever known."

I thought she might have been including her family.

"Hey, piece of cheese," the butcher called. "I got something for you."

"You want me to close the window?"

"I want to watch the gorilla." I wanted the gorilla to come inside and curl up under the featherbed with me. I wanted to hide in his chest, my fingers deep in his fur.

"Can he eat some meatloaf?" Pinsky called.

"Sure. Moses, do a trick. He wants to feed you."

The gorilla stood up from the table, ran across the alley. As he ran he kicked out a back foot, an extra step, a Jackie Gleason movement. He was huge and light on his feet. All his strength was in his upper half. At the far end of the alley he stopped in the shade, considered, I supposed, another trick, looked at his wrist as if he were wearing a watch, examined the rubber tire hanging from a tree, ran to it, crashed into it, propelled himself from it like a jai alai player, toward the butcher. The butcher swung a cleaver in front of his chest. Moses stopped, stood on four feet, pulled in his shoulders, folded his hands under at the wrists, somehow made his long arms almost the same length as his short legs, stacked himself into proportion so that the top line of his back was straight, drew himself up and large, until he looked like a giant black silver-backed toy, a proud giant creature, everything a designer from FAO Schwarz could want, and when he had adjusted himself, he turned his head bashfully away from the butcher and posed before him. In silhouette, I saw his delicate eyelashes. He batted them, somewhere between flirtation and bashfulness. I could feel his gentleness.

The butcher threw a piece of meatloaf on the ground. Moses picked it up, held it to the light, brushed the dirt from it, sniffed carefully, delicately, chewed it slowly, picked crumbs from his chest and belly.

"You couldn't spare a little more, Pinsky? He's a big guy. Hey, piece of cheese, you want another piece?"

The gorilla stuck his fingers in his ears and screeched.

"That's telephone," Froelich called. "Show him belly dance."

He stood upright, raised his hands to his head, did a bump and grind. I hated it. I hated him doing tricks. "Now show him to make dirty. Get the paper. Not here, Moses. Over by the Chinaman." Froelich pointed to the back of the laundry. "By the laundry. Make dirty. Don't forget your paper."

The gorilla pivoted, ran back for the newspaper Froelich held out for him, ran to the piles of plastic baskets behind the laundry, spread his paper.

"Throw it away, in the can. Good, good. Watch out for the guy in the apron, Moses. He kills animals."

The gorilla dropped his wrapped mess into the Chinaman's garbage can. Pinsky threw him the remainder of the meatloaf.

"Hey, big spender."

"Ahh," Pinsky said, tying his apron on, "it was rotten anyway."

I felt the pain of the insult in my own gut.

Froelich swatted the air with his hand, dismissed Pinsky, who had already left. "Come on, Moses. Come sit down. Let's talk about butchers."

Moses rested his elbows on the table, looked expectantly into Henry Froelich's face. They knew each other well.

"See that?" Mrs. Froelich nudged my elbow. "He won't look into your eyes until he knows you. Looking direct is a challenge . . . until he knows you. Remember that, don't look in his eyes."

"He seems very intelligent."

"Who can judge if he's intelligent when we don't know what he knows?" She led me from the window by my hand. "If you do go, at least you'll know what to do. If you don't go, you don't know what to do. Where else can you go?" I imagined a gun in her apron.

I sat on the edge of the bed next to a Princess phone and a pink and gold ceramic unicorn. It had been a girl's room. "You have a daughter, Mrs. Froelich?"

"No."

There is pain everywhere. I'd call Steven when she left the room. But she didn't leave. I felt the first chill of sleep come over me. My limbs were numb, floated. Why should I call Steven?

I slipped into silken sheets. It would be all right to be here, to sleep. When I woke up I'd be able to consider Froelich's offer rationally. Now it seemed that it was given by God: surrogate father and mother, the pineapple juice of my childhood, the first healing on my wounded path, and I was tempted to flow with what was offered. Perhaps it wasn't a dark ride. Perhaps when I woke up I would know what to do. Then I could say no. I could even say yes and leave the truck at the corner, take the subway to Penn Station, buy tickets anywhere. I owed them nothing. I owed the gorilla nothing. I'd like to live near the ocean. Key West. I covered my hand, covered my finger where my ring should have been. Mrs. Froelich laid a featherbed over me, over my shoulders, tucked me in under the chin, kissed my forehead lightly, whispered, "You want more juice?"

"Tapioca."

"I'll make some for when you wake up." She pulled an orange leatherette bucket chair up to the bed and sat. I heard pages turn. "You have children?" Her eyes were close to mine, something crystalline locked behind lobster eyes in goldfish bowl glasses, something terrible and trapped.

"Grown, three. You?"

She touched my cheek, felt the skin. "I'm forty-one," she offered, her hand on her own cheek.

"I'm fifty. Good cream. Retin-A."

"Such different worlds. I'm as far from you as the gorilla is from my husband. So distant."

"Parallel," I murmured politely.

She grunted, disagreeing, turned pages, said softly, "Marriage is either written in heaven or it's not. If it's written in heaven, it can survive. I'm telling you. Don't worry about the ring. If you want it back, you'll get it back."

"I don't want the gorilla. I just want to leave."

"Where are you going, sweetheart?" she asked. "Where are you going? Where can you run from life that you'll be safe?"

"What if the gorilla dies? What if Animal Control kills it? Then you have my ring and I have nothing."

She grunted, shrugged. "Let me tell you again. We own Moses. He's worth a lot of money. If he's confiscated, they kill him. We lose a lot of money. We can sell him fast to a woman in Tarpon Springs, who'll sell him and get him out of the country. We need you to take him there fast, very fast. You've got nothing better to do. We know you've left your husband. He called here and asked us to stop you. Also, if you care, your husband is responsible for Moses because he's under contract with us, like renting a car. So he could get sued. Now if you take two or three days and go south, we get our money, your husband doesn't get sued, you'll make a little money, and you'll have time to think about what you want to do. The rest—insurance, your ring, your Suburban—you'll have to talk with Mr. Froelich."

"I don't want Moses to suffer."

She nodded. "He shouldn't suffer. He's a good boy. It's up to you."

I heard John Banks. "We're not finished," he intoned, stentorian. "We're not finished." But it was not John's voice I heard below. It was almost the same, the same district, the same school, the same urgency in my groin, the same necessity that shrinks and pulls in, that may be fear or invitation, a vacuum.

Mrs. Froelich leaned against the closed door of the bedroom and listened, cracked it open slowly. "Duncan," she whispered, "Animal control." She placed her finger over her mouth. I heard the clipped Brit voice. "He'll want to kill Moses."

"All this time, Cholly, I thought you chased exotic animals, not women. Shame on you. But now you'll excuse me. It's time for my prayers. Ben, make him up a little gift arrangement. He likes lox."

"And when did you become religious, Henry?"

"The day I met you . . . that God could make such a miracle."

"Henry, I know it's your gorilla. And it's a rogue and it has to be put down, whatever it's worth."

"What do you want from me? I don't have it."

"I'll close you up again, Henry. You won't do business in this borough as long as you live. I'll get you. That gorilla kills someone else you'll end up in jail, you'll pay."

"You got me. You got me already. You closed me up. You killed my animals."

"I had to put the sick ones down, Henry. You know that. But this one, let us not forget, this one's killed a man. And I'm going to find him and kill him."

I imagined Froelich running his fingers through his beard. "A man kills a gorilla, it's called hunting. A gorilla kills a man, it's murder. Nice."

I imagined Duncan striking a match on his boot sole, lighting a British cigarette, wondered if he knows/knew John Banks, wondered at coincidences and accidents and pinning the stars in place. Of course Steven called Animal Control. My wife, the van, the killer gorilla, Dino. He was using that as an excuse to have someone else find me. "The scene of the murder was Coney Island," Duncan told Froelich. "His windpipe was crushed." There had not been enough time for him to have seen Dino; he'd talked with

Steven, who had, I could only guess, talked to the guard and sent him over to the Horror House.

"Oh. Coney Island. That explains it. You didn't say Coney Island." Froelich was so sarcastic, so insolent, I liked him. "In Coney Island, that's entertainment." He laughed at his joke, sucked the laughter in.

"No human being could have crushed—"

"Coney Island you got gangs. You got real animals." He directed his wisdom to his son. "See, Ben? A gang animal kills a man, the city sends him to a shrink, apologizes for his environment, sends him to school. A gorilla don't get a chance to explain. How about his environment? No one asks him why. No one sends him to school. If I was Moses, I would have killed Dino myself. Dino's the animal, not Moses. Gorillas don't kill for gold chains, my friend, don't stomp faces in. So go chase your gorilla and make the streets of our city safe for women and children. My best wishes to you and yours. Ben, give him some coffee and bagels and plenty of cream cheese. You like lox, Mr. Duncan, if I remember. Make it up, Ben. Nothing's too good for Mr. Duncan. No charge. Nova. Jelly, tomato slices. Don't give him the cheesy mixed fruit. The marmalade. The herring spread."

S I X

By the time I'd eaten my tapioca, the refrigerator truck had returned, its sides decorated with an overkill of orange and black uncials: "Caribbean Specialties, Montrose, New York. We cater, we deliver." And a sun and palm tree logo. Froelich proudly showed me the inside, the cage, a cooler of sandwiches and Yoo-Hoos for me, crates of cabbages and bushels of apples for the gorilla, a pile of clean blankets for both of us, and a tote bag filled with mace and Reese's Peanut Butter Cups studded with knockout drugs for emergencies, Fisherman's Friend tablets for the smells. "She uses Fisherman's Friend to peel onions. She can peel for hours, she doesn't cry." He looked at his wife. She looked away. "She doesn't cry when she peels onions." There was something terribly sad, defeated, between them. The wrong child had died. "So you'll use them. And the tranquilizers if you have to. You shouldn't have to. Moses can't get out. You don't have to let him out at all. You'll be fine. You'll be fine." He spoke to me in the same tone he'd assured the gorilla. We were both his fools.

"I don't think I can do this, Mr. Froelich. I am so afraid."

"Afraid don't pay off, girlie. Careful. Smart. If he were loose, yes, because he doesn't know you and you don't know him and he could break you or ignore you."

The son chuckled a dirty chuckle. "Or fall in love with you."

Froelich gave him a withering look. Something moral about Froelich invited trust. "All you have to do is drive the truck. Drive the truck. He's chained to the floor. He'll take care of himself. He has a pile of papers if he messes, food, water. But he stops eating when he travels, a gentleman."

"But he can open the . . ."

"A combination lock? They don't read, *maidele.* So drive, keep him warm because he only has one lung. If you think someone's following you, get lost. Go another way. Wait a day." Froelich unfolded a torn and yellow AAA Triptik, underlined in pink, with arrows, X's, circles, a route, I knew, he'd sent animals on before, something covert and illegal. I was to be in Tarpon Springs in two days, which meant the first night I would sleep at Froelich's X, a golf course outside Harrisburg, and the next in a state park on a barrier island above Savannah, and the following morning, I was to cross Florida to Tarpon Springs.

"You drop the gorilla, collect the cash, and drive on. The gorilla is not your problem. If you make him your problem, that's your problem. Just keep him warm. When you stop to eat, park in noisy places, near traffic, away from other cars." He pointed to an X. "Terrific French fries. Bernie's. If you need anything, Bernie knows me. Two nights, *maidele.* Nothing." He patted the back of my hand. "You got cash? Don't use cards. Here." He pushed a handful of hundreds into my pocket. I thought he might have taken a feel of hip. I wasn't sure.

"Mr. Froelich, I have the distinct feeling you've done this before and it is highly illegal."

"And you should be happy you're receiving the benefit of my experience. When you pull out drive around the block very slowly, just like you did when you were looking for me, not like you're in a hurry. But on the highway, speed. The punks going fifty-five have the cocaine in the trunk. Sleep in the truck. If you decide not to come back, you keep the cash and I'll keep the ring. Either way, you'll be fine."

Mrs. Froelich returned with a white, flattened, frizzy wig, worse than the one she wore. She lifted my hair gently, wrapped it in a knot, pinned the knot into place with three-inch silver bobby pins that could remove eyes. Then she pinned the wig in place with more bobby pins, patted my backside, pinched my cheek.

Froelich grunted at my appearance, gave me six green rubber alligators in a plastic bag. "He's afraid of alligators. Just shake one at him. Listen, *maidele*. Listen carefully. The gorilla, he is what he is. Be afraid of your husband."

There was something cosmic and incoherent: a paradox. I could trust the gorilla to be a gorilla. I could not trust my husband to be a man. "And should I be afraid of *you?*" I dared.

He sighed at my innocence, sighed so deeply I knew he'd been innocent once himself.

The son hung back, smirked jealousy. If his jealousy was genuine, his parents' sincerity could also have been genuine, or all of them could be excellent cons. Her touch, I knew, was real. I nodded at the son, kissed his mother on her cheek. She sniffled and hugged me as if I meant something to her. I could not judge. I'm still not certain. But Mrs. Froelich's point was well made. Where else was I going?

"Go, go." She held a crumpled handkerchief to her mouth.

It was afternoon coffee break time on the street. A demolition truck and a police car were double-parked in front of the Bottomless Breakfast, and again I couldn't get through. In my rearview window I spotted Steven in his Porsche, weaving wildly through the big trucks. I expected him to drive over hoods, under axles. Weeping, wiping his eyes with his sleeves. Steven, my heart. I felt the concrete of my life hardening and closing around my feet. I could see Melanie in front of my underwear drawer, my jewelry box, packing my books in boxes to donate to the library sale.

The policewoman waved me forward. She stood in front of Steven's long sleek rich hood, blocking him, and I pulled out. "Where do you get your courage?" I wanted to ask her. "Where do you get your strength?"

Near the Jersey shore I stopped at a noisy intersection, waited for the light to change, rested my head on the hard rubber of the steering wheel. I could not drive any longer. In a diner, not Bernie's, I ate a chicken cutlet layered in sauce and mozzarella, read a real estate magazine, and tried to picture myself in a four-bedroom glass-walled Bermuda hideaway, but all I could see was Steven at home in our Classic Revival, walking from room to room, absorbed, wrapped in his seersucker bathrobe, smoking his pipe, considering, his mahogany mules slapping softly on the carpets to the rhythm of his ifs and thens and therefores, knee deep in his landscape of logic, brokenhearted and furious.

"Linda. Linda. Linda. All right." He turns and walks counterclockwise toward the music room.

"On the other hand," he starts up again, changes directions. He stops at the dining room door. He walks into the kitchen, sits at the table, holds his head. The rational mind knows only what it contains. "All right, start with Banks." I knew Steven knew who John Banks was. I knew he had my paintings examined to see if I'd really done them. I was certain Steven had acquired a full dossier on John Banks and knew more about him than I knew. Steven leaves the kitchen, walks to the bedroom. He passes a telephone. Musing, he picks it up once, twice, puts it down, lights his pipe. Steven sits on the edge of the bed, rehearses. "I beg you, Banks, help me find her and save her, for you, for me, for her. Help her." Steven suddenly suspects I really have gone to Ireland after all. He calls the AT&T operator to find out what time it is in England. It is beyond him to imagine that John Banks feels nothing for me. Steven expects, man to man, John Banks will honor his request. He dials John Banks's home phone, which is in the dossier. A sleepy child answers. Steven hangs up. He calls again.

I called him from the pay phone at the diner. "Steven?"

"Where the hell are you?"

"Steven, if I had told you something was missing from our marriage, you would have torn up the earth to find it. If I had said I don't know why, sweetheart, I just have to go, you would have flayed your skin until you found a reason. It was despicable to leave you this way. I am ashamed."

"You should be."

"Steven, did you call John Banks?" It was the first time I'd spoken John Banks's name to him.

He waited too long to answer. "No."

Aristotle wrote that all the transformations undergone by physical bodies here on earth trace their origin to the local motion of the imperishable beings that constitute the fixed stars. But I have fixed the stars myself, pinned them carefully into place. I hung up and leaned against the phone booth wall, caught my breath, and called again. "Steven, did you really call John Banks?"

"Don't blame any of this on me, Linda. You've started this ball rolling."

"Does that mean someone is looking for me?"

"How should I know?"

"Steven, there is something undercover about John Banks."

"I'll say."

I ignored the innuendo. "He may be . . . like an agent."

"I believe it was you who involved Banks, sweetheart, not I."

At a 76 truckers' stop, I pulled up near the rear of an eighteen-wheeler with its engine running so that the gorilla's sound would be muffled, so my actions would be lost in the steam. I opened the doors of the truck and looked at him. Who was it who had to open the box from which the demons flew? *"Ah, my sweet Pandora child. Curiosity, Linda, may be your fatal flaw."* I shoved John Banks behind me, looked into the cage. Moses looked away from me. His face and chest were leather. His body covered with deep black fur, except for his back, which was gloriously whitened, silver in its wealth. He balanced himself, posed for me as he had for Pinsky the butcher, proud, sweet, powerful. He knew he was magnificent.

"Perhaps I too am your butcher, Moses. In this universe into which you've plunged, everyone is your butcher. We are all each other's butcher. Look, listen. I don't know what to say to you. You are a magnificent creature, an extraordinary thing, a miracle of the universe for which we must thank God, but I don't know personally what to do with you. You have a problem. I have a problem, but they don't match. I can't figure out any mode of self-interested altruism for us. And you have after all killed a man. It seems to me to have been a righteous act. But it won't be to anyone else. How can I convey to you that I wish you no harm?"

A trucker walked by, slowed down, looked at me, shook his
head once, hitched his jeans. I had no idea I'd been speaking out
loud in singsong. I pulled myself up into the truck, pulled the
doors closed, checked the cage lock to reassure myself. There was a
kickplate disposal in the floor, five-gallon gas cans filled with
water. The gorilla moved to the far side of his cage, posed again, his
face stretched so far away from me it was nearly horizontal with the
top of his cage, studiously showing me that he wasn't looking at
me. I too looked away from him, saw him peripherally. Once I
caught him looking at me. I dropped my voice and spoke secrets to
him. "Have you ever been to Amboseli? Below Mount Kenya?
Surely you've been to Mount Kenya and chewed on bamboo
leaves." As I spoke I saw a horizon, a vast smoking valley between
two sharp ridges, dry salt beds. I did not remember that view at
Amboseli. "Well, at any rate, Moses, below Mount Kenya I
watched a cheetah in the Amboseli. I watched her track, spring,
leap, kill an impala. I watched her three cubs feed on its bowels and
while I had thought I would be ill with the steaming bowels and
the bloody jam on the cubs' jowls, I was not. Somehow, I rejoiced
in the necessity, the triumph, of her act. So I am not horrified at the
killing. On the other hand, I don't want to be in the way when they
shoot you. Clearly that is your destiny here in our weave of jungle."

He dropped his head for a moment when I stopped speaking,
snapped it away when he saw my eyes. But we had looked at each
other for a split second. In that split second of absolute candor and
curiosity, we had seen each other. I felt his being like a hot wind
passing through me. "Even so," I assured myself, "he's booked for
Tarpon Springs. Even so." I jumped from the truck, closed the
doors tightly, checked, rechecked them, left for Harrisburg to the
state park marked on Mr. Froelich's map. Still, as I drove, I saw
that vast smoking valley, the sharp cliffs, the shimmering salt
beds. I did not know where it was, although we'd flown over the

Rift Valley, ballooned over the Masai Mara, but I could not place the smoking valley. It seemed as if it were something the gorilla was showing me, not a place I had seen.

Dusk fell into an orchid sky. I approached Harrisburg, Gettysburg. My lights illumined historical signs, but I could only glimpse the first few words. "Here. Civil. Scene of battle."

I called Steven. I was in Pennsylvania someplace where General Lee had been, in front of the diner of a 1940s motel, a compound of separate wooden units, Philly special scrawled in chalk on the window: Green peppers and onions $4.00. Behind the diner's dirty glass window, a grizzled man struggled to chew a sandwich. A redhorn rooster and two solemn hens foraged in the parking lot. The phone was low, next to a bench. I sat on the bench and dialed our number and rehearsed.

"I'm not certain where I am, Steven, somewhere in Pennsylvania. It doesn't matter. What matters is I'm not there." Trucks and trailers swept dust over me. It was not my neighborhood. The phone rang five times and a short. I heard Steven's voice. "Thank you for calling. Linda and I are out of the country. Please leave a message. We will return your call as soon as possible."

I hung up, but I could not leave the bench. Out of the country. England. Ireland. He thinks I have gone to John Banks. So Steven will soon sit someplace with John Banks. Where would Steven find him? I've never wanted to know about John Banks. The details could only be mundane no matter how brilliant his thriller-killer career. I needed to keep him in fantasy, strange, unpredictable, other. Which is why the issue of the can opener storage aroused such hostility. I couldn't imagine the Banks home. Does he live a moderate and seedy life or a charming country life with pickets and rambling roses and moors rolling out beyond him?

John Banks's face freezes. "Yes?" Is he to be killed here in his office? But John Banks has seen danger before, jealous husbands before. "Of course,

you must be Linda's husband and something is wrong. Please. Please sit."
He fills the spaces. There is no room for Steven to accuse or confront.

"Where is she?" Steven blurts.

John Banks is honestly surprised to be so accused. He spreads his hands
over his desk. "I assure you, Steve, not here." The familiar. He is good, this
John Banks. He presses a button and requires brandy, which is delivered
almost immediately by an effete boy. There is a gun-size lump under a
dinner napkin. "This is terrible," he murmurs as he pours. Steven has to
lean forward. "I have heard nothing from Linda in months. We are very
very over. If she's in trouble, why, you must return as soon as possible. I can
get you to Heathrow. I'll have a car immediately. Of course." John Banks
offers Steven the brandy.

Steven believes him. His manner changes. His face falls. He had hoped
for a standoff, a shouting confrontation about shame and betrayal, about
who is the better man, who will make her happy. He was utterly un-
prepared for John Banks's distance and amazement. Steven is charmed,
takes the brandy glass. John Banks, thoughtful, rolls the liqueur around
in the bottom of his brandy glass. "Since I have most likely contributed to
this problem, I will be very happy to help you. A matter of honor. Or
dishonor." He drinks. Steven drinks. They drink to dishonor. Steven is
utterly out of his league.

"She used very bad judgment. Where there is conflict, character will
always overcome judgment. Steve . . ." John Banks leans forward. "This is
typical of a deeply narcissistic personality. She has been thwarted and she
had to act out, do something wild and rebellious. The question before us is,
how can we help her, how can we bring her back to herself?"

John Banks is someone else. It is he but not he the undercover
operator. I have a sudden and choice intuition that John is and has
always been a psychiatrist, that the man I knew was his own fantasy.

Steven will not allow himself to imagine us in bed. Raw brick walls,
leather-top desk, wool chairs the color of brick, studded with brass. Steven
imagines us in bed, John Banks's hands cupping my breasts. He pushes his

hair back from his forehead and erases the image. His hands shake with fury and exhaustion, and I am sorry, for it is I who have painted the black circles under his eyes and drawn his mouth down and I see one shoelace on his buckskins is broken and knotted, which means he doesn't care for himself or he is relaying to the world that he needs care because his heart is black with spite, blue with grief. He hurts.

John Banks's office is still. Steven walks to the arched windows, flattens his hands against the cold wet glass, spreads his fingers, says, "There is another circumstance, somewhat complicating the situation." He turns slowly to John Banks, who is reclined on his chair, who leans backward, stares into the amber of the brandy glass. "Linda has left with . . . a . . . a . . ."

Steven turns toward the traffic again. "Through a series of peculiar circumstances, and, I believe, a minimum of choice, she has left some-how . . . somehow with a gorilla. And now that I know she is not here, has not contacted you . . ." Steven leaves the window, begins again. "You see . . ." He sits down. The chair rocks independently. "If Linda has not flown here to you, she is still with the gorilla, which . . ."

"Is that a nickname?"

"What?"

"Another man?" John Banks is gentle with Steven. Or patronizing or both. I can't tell even as I imagine it.

"I'm afraid not. It, uh, has to do with a small and regrettable business venture. I rented it and she left with it in a van in which it was caged overnight. I frankly don't know what happened to her or will happen to her."

"My God! You can't be serious."

"I'm afraid so."

"Let me assure you, Steven, she is a bright and resourceful woman."

"She dreams."

John Banks rubbed his chin. "Yes, and that curiosity of hers."

"Yes, yes, curious."

"So she's with the gorilla, is she?" John Banks stands at the window now. "A male?"

Steven nods his head.

"Neutered?"

"I doubt it. They're too valuable. No fangs, though. He's circus trained. Sometimes he obeys commands."

"I'm going back with you."

"You?"

"Hire me. Hire me to find her. You couldn't find anyone better, could you? Except yourself, of course, but I am far more objective."

"You didn't love her?"

"Linda?" John Banks throws an arm around Steven. Steven shrinks. "You Americans." John Banks chuckles, shakes his head. "We were the ones who tossed the Puritans out of England. You still see marriage as a sacred institution, although you have no qualms about weapon sales. We don't see it that way. I believe that when your wife is looking for the meaning of the universe, she escapes to the mythopoetic. And when she's looking for the meaning of marriage, I believe she goes outside the marriage to find it. That she had an affair with me only meant she felt her marriage was very important."

Steven flushes, examines his fingernails, pulls his jacket down by the lapels. It is a good jacket. Too casual for today, for John Banks. "If I were to hire you, John, it would be with the condition that we will at no time discuss my marriage."

"Only insofar, Steven, as information about your marriage might contribute to finding your wife."

"It is now the end of March. Let us say we contract for mid-April?" John Banks gives directions to his assistant, who has brought in a traveling coat, an umbrella, and a suitcase. "It is ironic and just," John Banks says as he helps Steven on with his coat, "that the level of intimacy I've had with your wife will now be used by you to save your marriage." The assistant hands him travel vouchers. They leave.

It is possible. Is John Banks a psychiatrist with a second life or an agent with a background of psychiatry? Is John Banks his own fantasy as well as mine? What was he doing in Ireland?

From the open spread of highway, I turned onto a narrow road and entered the forest. Forests are all accident, all possibility, anything can come from them. As shapeless as the forest was, Froelich's map was precise. I passed a summer theater, its windows still boarded up against the winter, a Victorian railroad dining car on blocks, now a restaurant with red velvet curtains and stenciled glass windows. The dining car going nowhere was not a good sign for me. I faltered, unnerved, my hands slippery on the wheel. Avoid signs, I warned myself, avoid metaphor, avoid meaning, follow the map. I had reached the cuffs of my courage and they unraveled at my fingertips. At the entrance to the golf course, a cobblestone gatehouse, I removed barricades, replaced them, drove down another road cut through the forest.

"Wilderness," Cotton Mather told the Puritans, "the wilderness is an insult to God." Map the forest and bring it into Order. Kill the wildman, the bewitched wives, the ripping beasts. Make it safe for God and Man. Was it possible, I thought at that minute, with my courage gone and the tightening of paranoia in the back of my throat, that Steven would have me followed, chased, caught, in much the same way the determined Animal Control person would hunt the gorilla? I would be taken home. Rogue wives and rogue gorillas. Moses would be shot. They would hunt me because I had become the hag, the hagazoousa who sits on the fence between forest and garden, evil and good, dark and light. Outlaw, I had turned my back on the harmless kitchen garden and faced, now, the forest.

S E V E N

The road narrowed, pressed in on me, darkened. At the end of the road, tall broadsides of pines opened to the golf course. Hunch-backed bushes, wrapped in burlap, leaped at my headlights. I entered the colony of golf club homes facing the golf course, circled like wagon trains, their backs hard up against the danger of the intruder forest.

The houses were dark-shingled, shuttered, substantial, with the obligatory screened porches, boats and golf carts wrapped in electric blue tarps, split-rail fences, picnic tables upright against pine trees, porch furniture draped in clear plastic. The largest house was L-shaped. Its vertical half swung deep into the woods. I would be well hidden. I pulled between the house and the garage, nosing up to a fallow garden, tomato stakes draped with dead vines. Comforted by the sound of the engine, I was reluctant to turn it off. When I did, the silence paralyzed me.

Moses panted, hooted, "Where am I? Where am I?" echoing my own fear. I pried my fingers from the steering wheel and forced myself from the truck.

It was almost a thing itself, the silence of the woods, filling the twisted darkness, not an emptiness. And I had become the wanderer, huddled in the shadows of the forest and casting rhymes into its thicknesses. But the thicknesses would take no shape, had no shape, did, didn't. The moon rode high and distant, would not help. The fear of capture swallowed the fear of night and would soon swallow me. I pulled bags of pine mulch from the garage and built up the front of the truck's engine until the truck lost its truck shape. I found a tarp over an outboard and, with much tugging and sweating, threw it over my construction. Then, although I have not lifted anything in years, something filled me—survival? panic? being? —and I was able to pull two picnic tables from their pine trees, drag them over the gravel drive, lean them against the truck.

Ascending on the thin thread of my accomplishment, I opened the back door of the van, called in softly, "You okay, Moses? Another night, you'll be in Tarpon Springs." He coughed a low croupy cough. "You'll be with other apes, maybe a gorilla. Perhaps they'll let you mate. You'll be fine in Tarpon Springs. Fine. It's warm there. They have palm trees and bugs and lovely flowers."

I heard his soft shuffle, the drag of chain across the metal floor of his cage. "Look, about Dino. From your point of view, you had to do it. Right? Your ifs and thens aren't the same as our ifs and thens. Your ifs are detached from our thens. I understand your confusion. Here you are with your cabbages and apples and your washtub house. There is no other context between us but food and you are safe only in your cage, rocking like an autistic child deaf to our sounds. Well, I'm not the sort of person you can count on. Ask my family. I'm launching myself into the unknown. But you are just too much unknown for me. I'll take you to Tarpon Springs and after that . . . well, after that . . . I'm sorry."

He moved to the center of the cage, sat on his haunches, his head twisted and lifted away from me. I wondered if my whispering had drawn him closer.

"I know what it is to be so lonely. My truth makes me lonely. Do you think death is lonelier than truth? Your truth makes you lonely in our landscape, an alien. You make little paths in the new territory, small deals and trusts with the natives, with me. You won't hurt me; I won't hurt you. At dawn you get fresh water and a clean cage. We have a deal, don't we? You won't hurt me; I won't hurt you. You can make sense of that much."

He sniffed at me, strong sharp sniffs.

"It's got to be horrible for you, Moses," I whispered, "riding blind and chained. How do you stand it? What inner peace do you have?"

He grunted at me, pant-hooted softly, kindly, I imagined. I thought that he liked whispering. "I know the feeling, trying to figure out the contexts, to map the territory, to cling, as I did all my life, to the desperate sequences of things, to cling to order, anybody's order, no matter how poorly you fit into it. I can imagine your little collection, your pathetic little collection, like my own, of our ifs and thens. How you've struggled to put it together about us. They look at their wrists and then they do things. I'll look at my wrist and then I'll do something. If I do this, will they do that? If I do that will they do this? What do they want? Will they hurt me? How do I get food and water? I cannot imagine your confusion. I cannot imagine your fear."

He moved closer to me as if sympathy drew him. I turned the light onto his great blue-black face. He grunted something between a hiccup and a question, stood on his knuckles, his shoulders rising above his head, dropped his head, and looked up at me from under his lithic brow, looked directly into my eyes, a hot, profound, dark, golden ferocity as if he were commanding me to stand still and listen.

I had the strangest sensation that he was probing about in the deep channels of my brain, mapping me, delineating my parameters, my boundaries, my limitations, my possibilities, exploring my head for fertile ground to plant a seed. I wondered if he was trying to show me the smoking valley and the cliffs and the shimmery salt beds again. He dropped his head farther, stretched toward me as if he were about to speak to me, but at that moment I saw his forearm was naked, that he had torn the hair from his skin in a long swath. I flashed a light into his cage to make certain. The light passed over his arm. It was naked, human, plucked clean. How strange that in terror he was turning human. The arm looked like my arm, duskier. My arm.

Once when my son had a growth removed from his back and I had to change the dressing, I had looked inside him, into the same stuff as I would fry up with green peppers and onions. Faint with revulsion, great chills rolling in my blood, I had to grip the shower stall to steady myself just as I had to grip the cage bars when I looked on the strange dusky flesh of terror on Moses' arm.

The naked ape arm was somehow between animal and human, as my son's flesh was somewhere between person and food. A corruption of boundaries, from flesh to meat, from animal to human, a corruption of things as they are, before they become, if they become, what they might next be. I was looking at my own fear because I had cast aside one order and had no other. I was corrupted. I was not far from the garbage dump on Beesaw Road. Moses and I were both fugitives, inutterably vulnerable, out of place, self-destructing. "I'm sorry, Moses. It will be over soon. I'll drive fast."

I offered him a tuna sandwich from Froelich's cooler. He sniffed it, turned his head away, closed his eyes, shuffled back into the corner of his cage, pulled his tub over his head, dismissed me with a grunt. I was weak and of no use. I thought of my own naked flesh and wondered if at some geologic end of the world, flood, fire, or brimstone, having suffered beyond endurance and found neither shade nor mercy, we tore our hair out in sheer terror, just as Moses had, and raced into the sea. I covered my eyes with my hands and wept salty-sea tears, for him, for myself, even for all of us, weeping for the pain we inflict on each other, the pain we inflict upon ourselves.

"He's not a problem," Froelich warned, "unless you make him a problem." So I pulled myself up and turned off the light, muttered something like "Just a few days more, Moses. Try not to do that. Try." Moses cried softly. "Don't do it, Moses," I whispered to him. "Leave your arm alone. Sleep. You're okay," I lied. I crawled into the front seat, the seat belt shoved against my hipbone and armpit, my stomach laboring with nausea at the thought of that human arm, Moses' pain and confusion pressing psychically against me, penetrating. I did not have to imagine his fear. I had seen it. If this was my grandmother's forest creature, her wild man who had come to help me find myself, he was as lost as I.

In his sleep he belched long rumbling belches, the thunder of distant quakes, uneasy continents, new moraines. I drifted in and out of sleep. He brought to me an image of a steaming and turquoise waterfall, of brilliant vines, pale orchids, blue ferns, rainbows on fire, and the great sad blue-black face filling the green jungle air. I did not know what Moses had shown me or why, but I knew the cool sharp smell of the falling water and the dark golden depths of pool, a deep pool as dark and profound as his eyes, and the pool said to me, "Listen. Stand still and listen."

"Listen . . ." Mrs. Froelich waves a finger. "He listens." I pulled Mrs. Froelich's blanket over my head. "How can we judge their intelligence when we don't know what they know?"

Moses hiccuped, coughed softly at me, questioning me. "Shhh. Shhh." On and on, past midnight, Moses coughed his croupy cough, rocked, then snored, coughed. As fatigued as I was, I had expected to sleep but the moment my eyes closed, I'd spring awake and look out the window, gasping for air, my hands icy. I've walked down the hall in my home at night, expecting, waiting, for a strong hand to grab my upper arm. I would force the idea from my head, but still I could feel the hand on my arm, the quick hard pressure in the dark. The hand around my arm was so real, I was too frightened to reach into a dark bedroom to turn on a wall switch. And I could not stay away from the idea. I would consciously open the moment, imagine the hand, loose the notch of reality one more turn. I knew, someday, if I were to let my imagination free, there would really be a hand there someday. And so I heard or imagined the tarp slip from the truck, the heavy thud and drag of picnic benches across wet leaves.

Eventually I must have slept because something woke me up. Somewhere I heard the word *Don* whispered softly, but dream and time flowed into each other, indistinguishable. Something in me, something amniotic, primal, atropic, stretched out, penetrated the dark twists around me. I closed my eyes in order to hear more precisely. What was it out there that alerted me? I heard nothing, but I sensed a presence, a shift of darkness. A deer? The gorilla loose? A crackle of underbrush? Footsteps? The leaves were too damp, the pine needles too soft. Still standing before the waterfall, had I dreamt the whir of flamingo wings, the leopard's pounce, the crack of pig skull in the crocodile's jaws? A whispered "Shit"? Was it my own dream of someone following, someone whispering, "Don!" My own voice whispering, "Be careful"? It may have been my own voice, a soft expletive in sleep, or it may have been a hunter in the woods, my hunter. Or a pair of thieves among the empty houses. Whoever, someone was near. I lifted slowly on one elbow and saw a strip of light wavering in the trees. In the sideview mirror I watched it move horizontally, disembodied, and I sorted through every category imaginable, paused, passed the wavy line of ketchup blood on Dino's chest, reached at last the silver metallic stripe of a running suit, chest high. I imagined the shape of a man in the running suit, moving from the golf course toward my hiding place.

"Don," a man called in a stage whisper. Had he said Don or John? Had he said John? Was John Banks out there in the woods?

"You go that way. Meet me at that clubhouse in ten minutes."

"Steven, you see what you've done. Do you understand? If you were in this truck and you heard women's voices, your blood wouldn't turn to ice water, your limbs to cork. You don't understand what you've done, setting this man on me, what it is to be a woman. We are a different species, man and woman, you and I."

"It isn't as if you had no part in this, Linda."

"If John Banks were to find me, I, not Moses, would be his trophy. He would make an ashtray from my severed hand and give my Movado to his next woman."

"What did you see in him?"

. . .

I rubbed my eyes. I saw nothing out the window.

John Banks said, *"You have no choice, dear girl. Think the way they think. Be logical. What weapon have you against them? The canister of mace? Ah-ha, the marvelous little rubber alligators? You're utterly defenseless. Leave the truck. Leave the gorilla. Leave. You are in the wrong place, Linda. Do you hear me?"*

I could hear Mr. Froelich. "The gorilla is what he is; be afraid of your husband." I left the engine running to keep Moses warm. I would call Froelich as soon as I could and tell him where the truck was. That much I could do for poor Moses.

Muscle by muscle, bone by bone, trembling, I let myself down from the truck, pressed my belly against the ground, squirmed along the undercarriage to the far side of the truck, thanked the leaves for being wet, moved to the side door. Every sound I heard was my hunter and every brush of twig was my hunter. Sometimes he took John Banks's shape, sometimes no shape, but he was out there, lethal, clever, strong, looking for me. It was very possible I was about to be hurt. Moses pant-hooted, built his noise up to higher and faster hoots, to a piercing rocketry of hoots, to a crescendo in the Pennsylvania woods. He had given us away completely. I knew enough about him already to know he screamed because I was leaving him alone. I worked my way around the tomato stakes. I had no idea what direction to take. The farther I removed myself from Moses' screams, the safer I was. Or was I?

At the end of the garden, I entered the woods and had only accomplished a dozen or more yards when I felt open ground under me. I made out a clearing, a corridor running left and right through the woods. I didn't know which way to turn, so I turned to logic. If it were a fire lane, I had a fifty percent chance of hitting the highway or a lonely fire tower. But if it were an old lumber road it would . . . lead nowhere. Logic is limited. The rational mind can only contain what it knows. Imagination becomes the bridge between the known and the unknown, so I imagined a strong, sweet truck driver in a plaid shirt driving a lumber truck, holding out a Thermos of steaming coffee. I poured myself into the night and raced toward him. Leaving the truck was incredibly stupid. I should have driven past the men, through them, over them.

What I had struck was neither lumber road nor fire lane but the soft cinders and rotten cross ties of an old railroad bed. I ran, shining the flashlight at my feet. Within a few yards, I picked up the even placement of the ties and ran on. Moses had stopped screaming. I was either out of hearing distance or he had resigned himself to yet another betrayal.

I had indeed taken the turn toward the highway. Telephone poles quivered above me and I spotted faint headlights far ahead. I was not cunning enough to know if the railroad bed were escape for me or access to me. I crossed a plank bridge; powerful waters rushed far below. The planks bellied and clattered under my weight until I reached the soft cinders. Then I could hear no other sound but the intrauterine boom of blood. It wasn't until I was well past the bridge that I heard the planks rumble behind me as if the dining car, candles lit and red velvet curtains adrift, had come to life and careened along the memory of its old tracks. I did not fear. I was fear.

John Banks was right about my fatal curiosity. I swung my flashlight behind me to see my hunter and, so doing, tripped on a cross tie and fell forward into cinders, but I had already seen the great blue-black face, his mahogany tuft of hair erect on his head, his face furrowed, distorted, dragging his chain behind him, crouched, running on all fours, the corrupted arm naked, behind, beside me. As he passed me he hit my arm with the back of his hand, then ran around me, hit my arm again, ran around and around me, hitting my arm with the back of his hand each time he passed me. At first I braced myself for the blow, then I tried to roll into the vegetation, then I climbed to my knees. How many times he circled me and hit my arm, I don't know.

I screamed at him, "Moses, what do you want? What are you doing?"

He stopped, stood upright above me, shook his arms at the wrists like a swimmer before a dive, looked at his non-watch, did not hit me, looked down at me, considered, it seemed, something, bit his lips, upper and lower. I braced myself for the death blow, the stink of his fear filling my lungs, his face distorted, blocking the first hopeful light of morning. I closed my eyes. I felt him tap my chest delicately the way he'd touched Dino. I felt the probe of his finger near my leg. He hooted softly at me. Then, awkward and upright, he moved slowly away from me in the direction we'd come. His was a different movement now, an exaggerated effort, a charade, a Simon Says, halfway between a strut and a walk. He had traveled twenty or thirty feet down the tracks when he turned, dropped, broke into his nervous and ungainly gorilla gait, ran to me, hit my arm again, circled me, stood upright, strut-walked his monster toddle as if he were struggling to show something to a very dull-witted child. He shook his hand, "Hurry, hurry."

"What do you want?" I screamed at his back. "What do you want from me?"

As he turned and dropped to his feet, ready to run at me again, I lifted myself painfully, my arm pounding, stood and walked toward him in the same exaggerated strut-walk he had shown me. His face smoothed, his crest flattened. He ran along the tracks in the direction we'd come from. Having no other defense, I allowed myself to listen to him and heard him, I'm certain, accurately, because indeed he ran ahead of me, circled me again without hitting me this time, herded me back away from the highway, dropped, and led me precisely down the railroad bed, through the trees, to the garden behind the truck.

He'd ripped his neck chain from the floor as if it were floss, squeezed the combination lock until it burst. With a grinding wheeze and spasms of coughing, he pulled himself up into the truck, shuffled to the cage, closed its door, sat on his haunches, rocked. Whatever he'd done and why he'd done it, bringing me back to the truck had been an excruciating and necessary effort for him. I too pulled myself into the truck, shifted its heavy gears, barreled across the garden, snapped stakes, spilled picnic benches and tarps, bumped over the soft old ties. I drove along a creek, past a ruined mill and, finally, onto the highway.

There on the smooth and quiet macadam, I was able to hear another engine fall and rise as it maneuvered the curves and windings of the golf course road. But they, John, Don, him, whoever, were far behind me. I was alive, and somehow, to a certain heavy-handed degree, I could trust the gorilla. I didn't think he wanted to help me. I thought perhaps he wanted to go someplace and had an idea I would take him there. My arm was swelling. I remembered very little of the drive. I remembered the pulse of pain in my arm, the fever of fear, but most of all the image of that turquoise waterfall spreading like a mirage on the highway again and again as I drove. Later, approaching the northern border of Georgia, riveted with the pain in my arm, I realized Moses wanted me to take him to the waterfall. And as soon as I thought it, I knew it was absolutely true.

EIGHT

The smoking sulfur air of Brunswick's factories behind me, I drove into Georgia lowlands, swamp, past a marker about Sidney Lanier's poetry, along an uneasy causeway through quivering salt marshes, and finally, at the inland waterway, over a graceful suspension bridge to Froelich's second X. Jekyll Island. Two columns of coral rock topped with pretentious European heraldics framed the entrance to the island. A hospitality with a vengeance lady, more garden club than park employee, greeted me from a piney information booth, took two dollars, gave me a recreational facility map, a road map, a geology of the Pleistocene barrier island map. I asked where the coffee shop was. She reprimanded me with the reverential hush of a museum docent. "In the historic district, on the pavilion at the wharf, in Millionaires' Row," gave me another brochure, and asked if I-all were with the Stonecutters of America or the Duplicate Bridge Tournament or making a delivery.

"Bridge," I answered, that having been the most immediate of my experiences. Releasing a little puff of lavender-scented powder from her underarm, she directed me toward a corridor of great oaks draped with Spanish moss. At the end of the corridor, across from the wharf, a resplendent turn-of-the-century wedding cake hotel rose from a hill of formal gardens. Beyond it were a few dozen less but nonetheless grand summer cottages built by, I read in my brochures, the Morgans, the Goulds, the Rockefellers, et al., who at one time owned the island and built immense cottages so much like my own that I felt the constriction of raw and rootless sorrow in my throat. A couple played croquet on the hotel's lawn and I wanted to be them, to play croquet with Steven, lie with him in a grand four-poster in a shuttered room with a ceiling fan.

Across from the hotel, on the waterway, Doric columns as thoroughly incongruous as the heraldry on the island's gateway supported the moss-rotten roof of the pavilion. Under it Stavros's served Key Lime Pie and Catch of the Day in a Hoagie. And Stavros himself, quite obviously, stretched out on an armchair on the pavilion, a tape machine playing Greek music, a white hand-kerchief over his eyes. He was an enormous man with small features, bright red suspenders, thin limbs, a mountainous aproned belly over which a kitten played. He snapped his suspenders to the music. The kitten jumped and leaped from the arms of the chair onto the belly and off again. In a steady hum of engines and soft voices, in a rich cloud of diesel, bilge water, fried clams, fresh coffee, men loaded trawlers for the night's work. Two boys bailing a rowboat watched me sideways, whistled "Dixie" for my Yankee benefit. The fishermen were gypsy-dark and thin-boned, tragic, that odd dark liver-eyed mien of the old South. They were the drivel of the seventeenth century, islanders who looked like Turks, like Indians, like the boy found frozen in the Arctic, men who followed the fish around the southern coastal waters. They came from shipwrecks and bastard sons. Their voices were gentle, measured, comforting, like Froelich's. So I ordered a Coke and clams in a hoagie from a larded dark-eyed girl with an intricate French braid and a faint mustache, wife or daughter of Stavros, leaned against the railing, watched in the water for alligators and great white hunters, watched the fishermen tying knots in piles of net, thought about lying next to the one without the shirt, with a big wooden cross swinging between square brown nipples on his chest and a bandanna tied at his throat, enjoyed the small warmth watching him gave me. Stavros raised his handkerchief, snapped his suspenders, watched him far more intently, watched with a hunger I recognized but hadn't felt in many years. Each time the bridge opened for high-masted boats, the pelicans patiently left the railings and slid along ribbons of air onto pilings.

"You gotta come uptide. I swing around uptide, drop the anchor."

"Bay of Fundy got forty-footers." The shirtless one was probably Greek. Certainly the owner of the coffee shop was. "They don't go noplace."

"This guy tell me how to do it."

"You gotta come uptide."

Stavros nailed the kitten, pushed it onto his shoulder against his neck. The kitten slept. A new man ran down the wharf, hit Stavros on the foot in greeting, received a grunt. Stavros opened an eye, caught me watching him, sat up suddenly. I could not imagine what he'd seen in my face, but he was too swiftly alert. "Hey, Tommy. Hey, you. Let's dance. Hey, you with the bandanna on your neck. Time to dance." The shirtless boy left the boat, climbed onto the pavilion. I wanted to leave, but other men had stopped work, formed a circle, clapped to the music. I would be too conspicuous. The croquet players wandered over from the lawn of the hotel. Stavros pulled the tape, turned it over, tossed off his apron. His shirt rode above his belly, his pants below, but for all the fat he was nimble. Handkerchief up in the air, belly shaking, propelling him, Stavros threw his arm around Tommy and they danced as gracefully as women. Stavros's grin spread across his face. The waitress/daughter/wife clapped in time. Stavros danced near me, too near, offered me the handkerchief, beckoned me to join him, and I did, the boy on one end, Stavros in the middle, I with the handkerchief, the kitten riding Stavros's shoulder. Stavros whispered to me, the dancing smile still on his face. "You need help?"

"Me?" My voice cracked.

"This guy looking for you. He's got your picture."

From Steven? I shrugged my shoulders under Stavros's firm hand.

"Stavros help, strong."

"Yes, strong," I agreed. "Thank you. I'm fine."

"Mean guy."

I smiled my dippy smile and shrugged again. John Banks? Someone from Animal Control? Some agent of some agency out to confiscate the gorilla? But how would they know I'd come here? Froelich wouldn't have told him. And he couldn't possibly have my picture. John Banks would have my picture, but it was too soon for John Banks and he wouldn't have known I'd come here. Unless Froelich told Steven? And Steven hired a private detective? My head swam.

"And Tommy, strong. And Diana, strong." He jerked his head to the waitress.

"Yes. Thank you."

"They made guy go back." He pointed to the bridge. "Out there."

"Threw him off the island," Tommy added.

Who threw him off? The civic mouse guarding the gate? Park rangers? A young couple with tow-headed children returned their rented bikes to the dock. The daughter erased the chalkboard, pulled down the blinds. Stavros wiped his forehead with his handkerchief, nodded at me, shook his head in a yes, shook his finger at me. "You remember."

"Okay, Stavros. Okay." I perspired more with outrage than effort. "Thank you."

"You want some pie, some pita maybe, some coffee?"

"No, I'm fine. Thank you for your concern. Thank you." I could not get away fast enough. Herons lifted from the marshes to find roosts in the oaks. The fishermen boarded the boats. Tommy looked back over his shoulder at me as he left, grinned so intimately, I realized I had become one of them, rootless, in trouble, a refugee myself, vulnerable. I belonged with the croquet players, with the bike renters, at the hotel, not the help. The fear of my rootlessness and danger rising, constricting, I turned away from Millionaires' Row toward the park beyond the Holiday Inn.

Froelich's second X was an oceanside picnic ground in a hammock of lopsided, wind-worn live oak and saw palmetto. The park area was separated from the Holiday Inn by a split rail fence and three Dumpsters. I pulled in behind a concrete block outhouse/shower that would serve well as a blind for my truck and a bunker for me.

The park was empty. Beyond the oaks were cord grass dunes, beyond them a marked channel, beyond the channel open sea. I watched the fins of three sharks knife through the water. There is always terror at the edge of paradise. I thought how different the forest was and how alike, the unknown hidden, rising here and there, terrifying. I thought of our marriage pool and the monsters living beneath the calm surface and I thought I had to wash up, brush my hair, climb the fence to the Holiday Inn for a hot shower, a decent meal, a telephone, a reality check. Moses slept with his tub over his head. I stretched all six alligators in front of his cage, locked the outside doors. He backhanded the truck's side, once. A warning, a greeting, an acknowledgment? "Okay, you big cheese. I hear you. I'll be back. You're fine. Okay?"

It was Happy Hour at the Holiday Inn. I called Steven from a pay phone. "Did you give someone my photograph?"

"No. Did you?" He hung up.

"I don't know, Steven. I don't know," I said to the dead phone.

The lobby, bursting with mauve and silver sofas and armchairs, O'Keeffe prints matching the furniture, dried-flower arrangements matching the prints, looked as if the first ten pages of the Spiegel catalog had come to life. The Stonecutters of America were decked out in the next ten pages in the new resort outfits of mid/ mod America: sparkling white sneakers, gold chains, bright and white washable, no-iron, youthful. I was the only event in the room that didn't match. Everything beyond me and Moses and the truck were madmen in a parallel universe, so I slipped into the boutique, bought a matching set of hot pink cotton slacks and shirt flocked with flocked flamingos strutting across the hills and valley of my chest, changed in the ladies' room, which also matched everything else, and whispered to my ragged image, "Hello. I'm traveling with a gorilla. My life is in constant danger. Before this my soul was in constant danger. I've run away from home. I've left my husband, who no longer seems to be what he seemed to be, and I have given up my life and someone is chasing me. He's waiting for me on the other side of the bridge." Rosalie Tata's Stonecutters of America Hello pin floated in a puddle of water on the countertop. I pinned her to my flamingos, picked up a spare key for her room overlooking the pool, called Steven.

"Yes," he snapped. It wasn't even a question.

"Steven?"

"Where are you?"

"I just want you to know I'm okay."

"You? The last thing in the world you are is okay. You are dysfunctional, mentally incompetent, out of your rabbit-ass mind. Your sons, by the way, want me to give you a message. If you don't come home, they will consider you dead."

"Nice. Somehow I would have expected more."

"So did we. I hear you have the gorilla."

From whom had he heard?

"He's going to kill you, rip you apart like he killed Dino."

I heard mentally incompetent. I heard lawyers. He had had his mother declared mentally incompetent, which she actually had been, so he could handle her money. He knew the routine. "You've done this to yourself, Linda."

"That's true, Steven. That's very true." I had learned how not to ignite smoldering fires. I was excessively agreeable. "So who would have my picture?"

"I gave no one your picture. Don't blame me for what happens."

"What did you have planned?" I asked pleasantly.

"I don't think what I have planned requires your input."

"Steven, we needn't be adversarial. Someone has my picture and is looking for me. With guns."

"Where are you, Linda? Where is the gorilla?"

Steven was not going to help me.

"That's the ultimate problem, isn't it? Where's the can opener, where's the gorilla, where's my wife? Where is anything? Where are we? You have to accept this question and know there is no real answer. There is no map we can really trust."

"Linda." His voice was needle mean, infuriating. "We needn't be cryptic, need we?"

Housekeeping knocked on the door, said she had the extra pillows we'd ordered. "Someone's following me, Steven."

"Not me."

I accepted an armload of pillows for the Tatas, locked the door on the chain, called Steven back. "Steven, Steven, what a habit love is. How do I break it? I don't know who you are, Steven, yet I love you. Or I love something that I think you are—an idea of you based on my own needs. Do you love an idea of me? False ideas, somewhat true, promising. We have become two black holes, draining each other for love. We work so hard for intimacy and there are irreconcilable distances. Not differences, Steven, distances, necessary distances of a blood feud, an enduring blood feud between us. Did I ever know who you truly were? Did I ever love your true self?" He had hung up after the first sentence.

I called John Banks's home in London. "Mr. Alexander Keyes calling for Mr. Banks."

"Papa's not here," his son answered in a prepubic voice.

Mum picked up. "You people have his number. Don't use this one."

"The Cleggan number doesn't ring through." It was mine in Ireland. Keyes often called there. "Mr. Keyes thought he might be in the States."

"He might be," she answered laconically, and rang off. I'd always tried to imagine her and could not.

"John"—I spoke to him anyway—"how am I to get off the island?"

"Dear girl, you're not about to waste your few moments of consciousness in the murk of logic, are you now?"

"Only the animal dealer knew I was coming here. Why would he tell anyone? Why wouldn't he want me to get the gorilla to the buyer?"

I heard the stonecutters' melancholy Happy Hour laughter. I heard their pain rising from the swimming pool.

"If I were you, I'd leave the truck and go home where I belong."

"Oh, John, that poor beast. I can't leave him. Imagine how confused he'll be, how he'll suffer."

"On the contrary. I believe you can leave him. You've left me and you've left your husband. Certainly you can leave him."

"You're more adaptable. Moses is like Diggety. Change terrifies him."

"You've left Diggety."

I no longer wished to speak with John Banks. I wanted to speak to Diggety, to rub his great white chest, to smooth the black velvet of his ears. The white on his chest was the shape of an angel, it was his soul, good and pure.

I called Mr. Froelich's number. I imagined him shuffling to the phone in his slippers, her upstairs listening, listening, waiting. "Yes?"

"Is this Henry Froelich?"

"Why do you ask?"

It was the son, not the father. I could hear the nastiness over the phone. "I need to talk to your father."

"Not here. He's sold your ring and gone to Israel."

"How about your mother?"

"What do you want?"

"I have a medical problem with Moses. His cough is terrible and he's pulling the hair out of his arm and—"

"Where are you calling from?"

"Have your father leave a message for me at the Holiday Inn in Jekyll Island."

"Is that where you are now?"

"Yes."

"And you'll be there tonight, all night?"

"Yes. I'll wait for his message."

"I'll find him."

"The gorilla isn't worth much dead, is he? So you better have your father call me."

He laughed.

"Look, you better find out. He could die."

"Okay, okay. I'll call you. You stay there. I'll get a prescription called in to the pharmacy there. You stay there. I'll call you back in ten minutes."

"Thank you."

I went to my own pain and allowed myself to imagine my Amish wedding ring quilt over my pigskin sofa in J. P. Morgan's cottage on Millionaires' Row. I placed the collection of seventeenth-century French puppets over my Beidermeier bed frame at the Jack Astors'. I yearned to be home with my things, my Diggety, my Steven, my bed. I slipped a fifty under the Tatas' phone, made up the bed with their extra pillows, rinsed out a sink full of beer bottles, looked over their terrace to the pool, to the boardwalk railing over the fragile dunes, and, with the stonecutters and their wives, watched the sun drop into the ocean. The men held camcorders, yelled, "Got it!" as if they would capture the sun, halt time and death. The stonecutters played touch football on the beach. Contact sports were as alien to me as duplicate bridge. My son told me the best part of football was when he made contact with his opponent. I could not imagine that as being wonderful. I'd spent my childhood trying to steer bumper cars out of the paths of the electrified boys trying to hit me. I told my son I would bet money that we were different species. A stranger out of my loins, he looked at me oddly, I at him.

The phone rang. Froelich's son was warmer. "My father said you should stay and wait for the medicine. He begs you to wait for the medicine. My mother wishes you well."

"Tell them to leave it at the desk."

"Dear girl, take a cab to the closest airport and go home. Forget the gorilla. Or go anyplace. Just forget the gorilla."

Dining room B looked like the Chinese emperor's tomb at Sian. As if the stonecutters had just given them a final buffing and set them upright for display on bridge chairs, four hundred stone-faced elders, four to a table, played duplicate bridge in absolute silence. Frozen in silence, playing the same deck again and again. Why did my mother so want to learn to play bridge? I explained to Moses as if I had bought him a Georgia Tech 4XL sweatsuit, as if he were leaning against the door frame of Dining room B doing his own primate study, as if I were Sister Elizabeth, I explained that this was a game, that each of the people had four sets of symbols on cards. "Clubs mean war; spades, death; diamonds, wealth; hearts, love. They don't know they're the dead waiting to be reborn, that they are dealing out their destinies on earth. The game is aptly called bridge. And the stonecutters in the next room, Moses? Waiting to carve the grave markers when the game is over. What card would you add, Moses? Poacher? Zoo? Circus? Oh, of course. Waterfall. Your waterfall. You poor tormented thing, dragging your dream around with you like a dead puppy."

Moses wandered away. I was about to suggest to him that he join me for dinner, I hated dining alone, and then recalled I was Rosalie Tata and that I would probably not be alone long, that I was safer surrounded by crowds and that someone had my picture. Which one? What was I wearing?

In Dining room A of the grand roast beef buffet for the stonecutters and their wives, a black chef sharpened his knife over a side of bloody roast beef, grinned as if he were playing a black chef sharpening his knife over a side of bloody roast beef. And I sat down by a window seat, nibbled on a biscuit, dropped four in my fanny pack for Moses, ordered a ginger ale with a twist of lime as if I were Rosalie Tata, stirred my drink with a straw, looked out at the boardwalk, as if I waited for my husband.

Oh, Steven, of course you won't marry Melanie with her nasty little body, her dog jaw, her cartoon voice. You will marry Celeste, won't you? Celeste, an older ballerina who had been with a prestigious company before her retirement, who is somewhere between artistic and autistic, some days more than others, who stands in positions one and three more often than not, who winds her long and seriously beautiful legs and arms around the columns on my porch. You watch her and wish you too were a column. Diggety watches, thinks of me, keeps smelling her in case, just in case. She isn't I. She is perfectly balanced. She watches the seagulls float onto the lawn on sheets of light and she drifts down the lawn and dances near them, dances, she explains later with a small lisp and a shrug of her ivory shoulders, to Pythagoras. I cannot imagine to what of Pythagoras she dances. Perhaps a mathematical universe of golden triangles and proportions, but she can't balance a checkbook. The seagulls are her footlights and she dances around, between them. On the porch, her cat rolls and writhes to her dancing. It is altogether genuine, magical. I like her in my home. She dances all day from room to room, enchanting, enchanted, until you come from work. You now go to work. You don't know what else to do. Occasionally she spins into the kitchen for a cup of yerba maté tea, which she then forgets and it sits and cools on my good tabletops, but she knows to break open walnuts from our trees and rub the stain of the nut shell into the teacup circles. I don't mind. At dinnertime, having danced all day, she lies wilted, lilylike, on the sofa and waits to be fed, her pale limbs glistening with a delicate perspiration, which you see only as dew and would die to lick but won't. She waits to be fed and watered.

When you explain how things work to her—you are particularly keen on teaching her how the answer machine works—she listens affectionately. When you're home you follow her from room to room and she ignores you affectionately. You pick up her cups and turn on lights. Ah, poor darling, how often you have come upon her in the living room transfixed by a blood red sunset or the first star of evening and it is all you can do not to snap your fingers in front of her face to see if she blinks.

She has a collection of blouses and sweaters and pullovers that constantly slip from one or the other shoulder. Now and then she passes a mirror and reflects on her ivory shoulder and covers it only to have the other exposed. She wears clothes lightly, white and black. You admire her long neck and her grace, but you don't know how to touch her, nor do you know, you realize within weeks of lying together in this bed, where. When she is ready for you she rubs apricot brandy on her tiny round breasts.

You admire the curve and grace of her long fingers on my Belleek teapot. She does also. You bring her clothes from the city, try to keep her attention when you order things from catalogs for her. "See? Do you like this? Winter coats, sneakers, a down robe?" You are afraid she'll wander outside during the winter and return with frost on her legs. You eat sandwiches and canned soup at night. You eat your large meal out with your old friends during the day. She seems to live on Red Delicious apples, New York State cheddar cheese, and Sen-sen. Once you thought you saw her in the window of Papa's Pizza as you drove past, but by the time you'd parked and looked inside, she was gone. Papa hadn't remembered her. You were terrified to hear yourself say,

"You wouldn't." And you wanted to call me and ask what I thought, what you should do.

You are so handsome together. She stunning, you proud and astonished to have such a creature. You watch other people's faces, men and women, to measure their reaction to Celeste, her worth, your worth. You have your hair styled. You look like George Raft. I don't like it. You wear silk poet's shirts and loose pleated slacks. Your new color is celadon. In your daydreams, you pull in front of the Helmsley Palace and open the gull-winged door of your Mercedes 300 SL; she runs from the Palace and slips in beside you. The door folds down and you roll gracefully into traffic. Guests and bellboys watch, look for the cameras, think it's a movie. It is. You and Celeste are often invited to dinner parties. She wears black knits with short skirts that you chose for her and braids her hair in a golden gleaming braid, a gorgeous braid that floats just below her waistline. Every man in the room wants to stroke that braid. She sits still and smiles mysteriously. Sometimes she draws the braid around over her mouth, over her eyes, plays with it, strokes her own face with the tip, chews on it. Now and then a newcomer inadvertently draws her into a conversation about music or apples and she will speak benignly of dancing among dwarf apple trees somewhere in the hills north of Cornell at midnight with little children holding candles until a drunken cow . . . She places a finger over her mouth, smiles, cannot go on. Soon the conversation moves away from her and you drum your fingers on your knee under the table.

I don't condemn you for having chosen Celeste, nor Celeste for living in my home. I understand her. She is me with longer legs and a lobotomy. She has gone many steps farther than I would dare. She is utterly private. But somehow, she has achieved safety and remained a solo act. It is a balance I never struck but, I believe, wished for.

"You've made a mistake, Steven, my sweet, my heart. Skin her. Skin her, split her in half, back to front, roll her out, stretch her above the sofa in the music room, like a flattened map of the world, like two paper cut-out dolls, holding hands, and she can dance with herself eternally, to the music of the spheres, forever, on your wall, front and back above the Chesterfield forever. While she's still almost in full bloom, Steven. Steven?"

"Think hard, dear girl. You may be a bit dysfunctional, all this stress," John Banks told me, kneading my shoulders. *"Your as ifs are a verbal means of escape. You must avoid them. You must stay in a what if mode. You must be alert. Look in everyone's eyes. Know where you are. Make mental maps of escape routes, real ones."*

The boardwalk extended the length of the inn, turned, crossed the dunes, and faced the sea. To the left were tennis courts, to the right, the Dumpsters, the picnic ground, my truck. Here and there through the pines and scrub I caught a gleam of oyster-shell path, the roof of the restroom, the roof of my truck, the Spanish moss chartreuse in the last shaft of sunlight, and, as I dipped my head to the buffet table (they served a short-grained sweet and nutty local rice I loved—the roast beef looked like Moses' arm), I thought I saw, over the restroom roof, I imagined I saw, the ultimate as if: a large and dark liquid King Kong carrying an armful of vegetation, climbing up into a lopsided oak.

Perhaps Steven and John Banks were right. Perhaps I was already dysfunctional, and if I were, I wouldn't know. Time to leave. I made my way up the buffet table to the requisite watermelon basket filled with cantaloupe balls. At my side, someone shoved a six-pack under the tablecloth. As he stood upright, I saw the pink sunburned flesh of an upper arm and I saw the raw skin of Moses' plucked arm and felt a torsion of horror. "Hello Lou Tata" glanced down at my "Hello Rosalie Tata" name tag, then at my blue-black arm, and, as I very smoothly pulled the six-pack from under the tablecloth, dropped the name tag and a twenty in its place, he asked, "You need help?"

"No. I'm fine. Thanks. Thanks a lot." I flashed my crooked dippy smile and left. I was certain the Tatas would work it out.

Next to the front desk was a racked display of Sights to Sea in the South brochures, one for a waterfall in Florida's Busch Gardens. It seemed so improbable, Florida being a flat sheet of oolitic limestone and its only cliffs sinkholes that dropped out of highways and swallowed cars, cows, and houses, but there was a waterfall on the brochure, ludicrously lush and begonia'd, with a handsome pair of gorillas standing beside it. The gorillas were real; the waterfall was man-made. I pocketed the brochure on the small chance that a gorilla looks at pictures.

N I N E

As I'd left it, the truck was closed, silent, the heavy slip lock in place. I carried my six-pack along an oyster-shell path to a small deck under the oak bent from centuries of sea wind. The same wind brushed my hair across my face in silken strokes. The way Moses stroked Dino, John Banks had stroked me with his camel-hair paintbrushes, drew line after line on my body, circling my breasts, the faint and excruciating delicate drift of camel hair. Amazing how the storm of desire overwhelms, and when it's spent, there is nothing to show for it. A tired heart, a few spots of semen. It is entirely gone and a subject of wonder and curiosity but not hunger, no longer that restless hunger, and for that I thank God. "I am alone," I whispered to the sea. "Finally alone."

"Except, dear girl, for the monstrous shadow of beast," the voice of John Banks tolled melancholy with the channel markers.

But the sand was gold with final sunlight, green with algae. Banners of silver shimmered over the sea. Shore birds foraged in the cordgrass on the scarped dune. A bedlam of sandpipers raced along the sudsy edge of tide, pecked at a horseshoe crab struggling to the sea. Pelicans skimmed the surface in wingtip groups.

It was not Moses' beastliness that drew me back to the truck. It was his misery. I could not remove the humanness of that naked arm from my vision, the shudder of his pain from my skin. The existential fear pulsing in each torn hair, hair by hair, was both mine and his. Daisies tearing out their own petals. Where am I? Where am I going? What if she doesn't take me to my waterfall? What if someone is chasing me? What if they put me in a concrete cage again? What if she tries to leave me? What if she forgets my water? What if I run out of food? And rips another handful of hair from his skin. What if Moses kills me? What if Steven has really sent John Banks after me? What will I do if he finds me? Go home? What if I am destroying my self? What if I am ripping out my own heart in exchange for a worthless idea about trusting my universe? What if I'm really wacko? What if they catch me? Who? What if old man Froelich sold my ring and went to Israel? I have insurance on my ring. I can replace it. It doesn't matter. It was too dangerous to wear anyway. But I didn't think Mr. Froelich would have betrayed me. His son would have. What if Mr. Froelich's son made a deal with the man from Animal Control to kill Moses and make it look like an accident so the Froelichs could collect insurance on Moses? What if my very own husband had hired my ex-lover to bring me home, dead or alive? What if? What if?

"Impressive, Linda. You can use logic if you must, can't you?"

"I only used it when I had to, and being so well cared for in my universe, I didn't have to. It never fit well."

"I daresay you're right on. But what about the photograph? Who gave who the photograph?"

"Maybe Mrs. Froelich took it while I was sleeping."

"Maybe. I also have photographs."

"Pig."

The trawlers I'd seen at the wharf came up around the end of the island, riding high through the deep channel to open sea. I watched the boats, caught ragged bits of the Dow Jones and Springsteen from their decks. Someone waved. I toasted his friendship with my beer bottle. I would have liked it to have been the young Greek. Gulls swept off the beach, swarmed the trawlers. I drank beer; the sky drank the wine of night, grew heavy and sweet. Raccoons squeaked near the Dumpsters. High-wire bats planed from their roosts to hunt. Three shark fins cut back and forth in the channel, menacing and mechanical.

And then it was fully night. Too much night with only a shy moon and a distant mercury light over the restroom to light my way. I forced myself to leave the platform, turn around. I was rigid with fear.

"Something in you, Linda, must be driven to go off in the night with an animal-slash-stranger as a witch would."

I tossed my purloined biscuits to the scramble of raccoons in the brush behind the oak, turned to the marginal safety of my truck. As I turned, a branch splintered above me. A scraping, a thud, a crunch on the path, a lifetime. Moses stood upright before me, five deadly feet before me, a bundle of vegetation under one arm, his other arm raised, mouth wide, agape in a grimace of fear. I screamed, jumped backward, threw my beer bottle and his brochure at him, shielded my face. He jumped backward the same distance as I had, our fear of each other being equal, but I had made the error of screaming and throwing. Moses dropped his groceries, dived for me, swept the air away in front of him, and I was swallowed by his being. My heart beat at the shoreline of existence, my blood thrust itself as if to escape. I had no night to shrink into. He swept air and light and life from me, grabbed me by the leg, bit into it, pulled me down on the deck, hit the deck with the side of his fist, which I had no doubt meant, Stay here. Here, in this place.

What haven't women learned about passivity before an angry man? As if Gandhi had discovered something original. Women invented passive resistance when they became women. When the male gets instinctive, you sit still until he allows you to feed him or take him to bed. Acting instinctively yourself, screaming and throwing things, only ignites the ancient fires, which no amount of hairlessness, counseling, philosophy, or vegetarian cuisine can extinguish. So I bent my head in submission and sat absolutely still, limp as if I were already dead. I felt no blood, just the hot swell of tissue on my leg and the supernatural drag of blood cells constricting in my legs when I wake from a nightmare and wrap them around Steven's until his warmth loosens my terror and my blood moves again. If Moses were to have freed me at this moment, I would have, nevertheless, remained paralyzed.

He looked at his non-watch, dropped my leg, looked away, grunted once, squatted on his haunches, laid that great strange hand on my leg, pulled in his lips, sucked them in, bit his lower lip.

. . .

So we sat there in the impenetrable silence of five, ten, how many millions of years of night between us. Glitter-eyed raccoons dared watch us. The wind picked up. Clouds blanketed the stars and it was fully dark. The trawlers fanned out beyond the channel, their lights sweeping the silver sea. Now and then the wind carried a shout, a whine of engine, a crank of gear, as the nets went down. Moses grunted, panted, grunted, sucked in his lips and bit on them, now the upper, now the lower. Steven does the same thing when he's making love, coring a pineapple, struggling with a problem. I remembered Moses rolling the cigarette butt across his lips as if he were I putting on lipstick, in order to understand me. I compressed my own dry lips, sucked them in, bit, and the same feeling of struggle and confusion became mine. I had not known that an expression could produce an emotion. Moses didn't know what to do next, therefore he was frightened, therefore I was in enormous danger, and yet I sat there biting my lip, experimenting and receiving the emotion, fascinated. Stay here. Stay here in this place until I figure this out.

I prayed no one would come and frighten him further. Yes, John Banks, I sat there in the very lap of the irrational, looking for cause and effect. Something in me has always suspected a morally deep universe and I expected morality from the gorilla. He hadn't slashed my flesh like silk, nor squeezed my head to bursting. He'd nipped at me as bitches nip at their puppies. If I had had loose skin under a coat of fur, I wouldn't have had teeth marks. Although if I had not sat in submission, he might have killed me, coat of fur or not. For that's all he'd done, disciplined me. My leg hurt no more than my arm. Moses had thrown me against the hard wood post of the railing and that pressure shot pain up into my shoulders and along my legs and I thought about the first night I let John Banks press me against the iron bars of the cemetery. And I thought I deserved what was happening to me.

What infinitesimal infringement of his territory, what infraction of his dignity, what insult, challenge, could ignite him, send him the wrong message? I had learned the rules with Steven. I didn't know Moses' rules. Reaching down to scratch my leg might draw the red line for me. A sneeze, a snore, could be suicidal. For a while I listened to his breathing and tried to match my rate with his so he would forget me. When he grunted, I grunted, amicably, softly, from the back of my throat. When he coughed, I coughed. His cough was too phlegmy and sharp and, I thought, hurt him. I thought about the reassuring infant language Steven and I used, the grunt and grumble of our own bedtimes. I thought if I could just slide my legs out straight, I'd relieve the pressure of the wood post on my back. I slid one leg in front of me. There was no reaction from Moses. I slid the second leg and his hand squeezed my leg. A small tightening of that squeeze and my leg would split. A jeep parked next to my truck, rolled headlights over us. My heart stopped. But they backed off and drove slowly away. I watched their lights bounce into the next area of the picnic grounds and realized Moses had let me move my head. I turned back to my original hangdog position. It seemed improbable that I would survive.

Night birds called. Boat chains clanked. I could still hear the faint and soothing strains of radio. I heard the beat. The melody was gone, the words erased. Perhaps I was listening to my heart. Near us the raccoons turned the horseshoe crab on its back, dragged it under the deck. I heard them ripping at it, squeak of gristle, crunch of shell, but I heard from another place, as if I were hearing them with part of me and watching myself hear them with the other part of me, like hearing my own voice. Something had pulled back a layer of my brain, a complexity. As if I were on a ship leaving port, my world drifted away from me. The channel markers tolled, echoing John Banks's warning, echoing the painful beat of consciousness, watch out, watch out, echoing what it was the stonecutters were trying to lose as they leaned over the railing, drinking hard and heavy, watching the sun die in the sea, reminding me of something I wanted to forget: the hardness of the earth.

Moses opened his mouth in a yawn, grunted. When I called a command to Diggety, he would stop what he was doing and, before obeying me, look to each side, yawn a large yawn, and obey me. I had always thought the yawn was a nervous displacement of instinct. Perhaps Moses' yawn was a displacement of instinct. I grunted at him and then I spoke very softly in Froelich's singsong voice. "You big cheese, you. You big cheese. I know you're going to kill me."

He released his lips and rewarded me with an avalanche of deep-throated grunts approaching laughter. His eyes looked like my bedroom windows at night when I walked Diggety up the lawn in the dark and my windows, golden and warm, invited me in.

"Moses?" His head jerked up. "How could you be nature red in tooth and claw if you have fingernails just like mine?"

He chuckled, looked at his non-watch, and, as if it were entirely natural, reached across me, pulled a bottle of beer from my six-pack, flipped the cap with his giant thumb, and drank it in one long swallow. I slipped my hand from my side, gave him another, which he took, flipped the cap again and finished half of it, then set it down between us. For the first moment that night I felt I was with a sentient creature.

"Why?" John Banks laughed at me. "Because he drinks beer?"

"No, John Banks, because he is like us in many ways and I am hoping in one way—that of kindness—he will be like us tonight and not kill me."

"We kill."

"You kill. I do not kill."

"Well, dear girl, we'll see what side he takes, won't we? Brute or gentlewoman. But let me remind you he may not improve his personality by drinking beer."

"Hey, you big cheese," I dared. "Old MacDonald had a farm, E-I-E-I-O."

He fiddled with his fingers as if he were trying to pay attention. It seemed possible that I might charm him and save my life. It seemed possible. He liked my voice.

"Just like marriage, right, Moses?" I sang. "Listen, you big cheese, you. What should I do about Steven? What would you do if you couldn't find the can opener?"

He looked at me sharply, belched mightily, looked away.

"I know what you'd do. You'd sit and wait for one to show up, and if it didn't, you'd go out into your juicy blue-green jungle and eat something succulent. An orchid? Morning glories? Take a drink of your waterfall? This could be Africa, couldn't it? A little piece, broken off, floated west? There are morning glories here and thistles. Do you like thistles?"

He rocked to my singsong, laughed in a soft hoot. From the corner of my eye, I saw him glance at me and look away before he was caught.

"You see, Moses, you and I are also playing duplicate bridge. We have the same hands, haven't we? Bridge, Moses. You move across our bridge from instinct toward intellect. I move from my intellect toward instinct and we creep, dash, cross, and recross that tenuous natal bridge between us, for there is one. The wisdom in your eyes is too ancient, too familiar." He had white tufts at his ears, at the corners of his mouth. He was an awesome relative, God-like, the sort one first meets at a funeral, aged, prosperous, strong, who is like and unlike you, a clear impress of the coin, who looks down at you and says, as surprised as you are, "You could have been my daughter." And you respond foolishly, blushing when you hear yourself, "It's never too late," as if you could turn time upside down.

"The wisdom I see in your eyes, Moses, it's just beyond words, something older than consciousness itself but very familiar, a secret we once shared and have forgotten. We are so distant, but we are trying; that is amazing. We are trying to reach each other because we want to survive. Or because I want to survive and you want to go to your waterfall. Steven, you see, no longer tries to reach me. John Banks never did. You wouldn't have liked John Banks. I didn't."

A smart little raccoon crept onto the deck, sniffed at us, came closer. Moses snapped it up, cradled it in his great palm, studied it. With one finger he stroked its tiny head, his own head cocked with curiosity, rubbed the stiff gray scalp of the poor thing, screaming and squirming, and then he squeezed its skull—I heard the crack and went cold—and tossed him off the deck back into the scrub. The scrub fell still. Moses lifted his hindquarters, pulled me up with him, swung his head around, gave me that gaping watermelon mouth, fixed me with eyes that told me something beyond my knowledge, pulled me toward him. As someone buried alive staring out at me from the earth, from under that deep lithic brow, he entered me on a wave of fear, thrill, terror. I threw my hands over my own eyes. His were too human, too filled with meaning I didn't understand. Or no meaning whatsoever, which was more terrifying than any meaning.

"I'm not Dino! I don't know you. I have not harmed you. I'm not Dino. E-I-E-I-O. Here a grunt, there a grunt, everywhere a grunt, grunt."

He sniffed at me, closer and closer, sharp sniffs, and thrust his face forward into my poor corner, sucked my very breath from my lungs, and I wept. My adrenaline having been spent and burned off, I sank into a numbness and wept weakly. "Is this your saint, Grandma, the wild man of the forest, the fur-coated beast who will find lost things? And will he find my courage? For I have lost it. I have lost it."

He pulled my hands from my face, sniffed each of my hands between the fingers, opened them, closed them, turned them over as if he were reading my fortune, replaced my hands against my cheeks. He sniffed up my arms and down my arms. His breath was hot and wet. I had none. My back was pressed hard against the railing. When he had satisfied himself with my fingers and my arms, he began on my foot, carefully removing the sandal and examining between my toes. He sniffed this foot, that foot, dismissed my toes as if they were pebbles. He pushed his face rudely up my legs, against my crotch, sniffed, and, thrusting his great head forward, pulled my hands again from my face. With the hesitation of discovery of an unknown and then with purpose, he licked the lines of tears, my salt, from my cheeks. I felt that raw tongue along my cheekbones, near my ears, down to my jaw. He moved from eye to eye, licking and stinking. Then he leaned backward and sat with his head sunk into his chest as if he had hoped I were something else. Eventually he took my hand in his. His hand was four or five times the size of mine, a hardball in a catcher's mitt. I thought perhaps he'd begin by snapping my fingers off. But he just held my hand. I didn't move a muscle or breathe a breath. I was a small thing before him. And he sat, with all the Morse code of his stomach beating out his messages, sat there, held my hand, bit his lips, upper to lower.

Remember the night, John Banks, when you pressed me for the first time against the wrought-iron fence of the cemetery as we walked away from the pub? It was cold. You reached down to unbutton my coat, pull up my sweater. You were so slow. I felt the great bows of my leg muscles quivering. You had the arrow. You were the predator. The iron sliced into my back. What I felt then, what I always felt with you, even though you may have been faking it, was the newness of myself. The first moment you found my breasts under my blouse, that moment, you held them as if you had never touched a breast before, as if you had found rare tropical fruits, and you held them in wonder. It was always that wonder, that approach, as if I were the New World and you were discovering me, that turned me on. The ending was ordinary; the beginning with you was always the first time. I could not know if you were to devour me or mate me and it felt the way it feels now and I know how perverted I must be because I don't know what the intent of this creature is toward me but somehow there is a sameness, the exaltation of being known, the sharp moment of I am, nailing me in place. I am and I am here. I was about to die in a bloody agony but my head rang with I am. I am and I am here. I had never been so present as at my own death. I was no longer reading the map. I was in the territory.

Moses pushed the cuff of my sweatsuit sleeve up my arm, held my hand to his ear, listened to my watch. He followed the dial with his finger. When he was done he dropped my hand to his lap. I left it there.

TEN

It is I who must contemplate my own funeral. Steven has chosen to bury me on our lakeshore, along an avenue of larch as old as the first settlement. The feathery needles brush softly, drift. The lake sucks dreamily at the shore. Wind-marbled, water and sky are the end papers in my book of life. But Steven has chosen to change the ending. For some reason I cannot fathom, far exceeding the event of my death, Steven has lined the larch avenue as well as the long path from the house to the lake with a good four to five thousand dollars of calla lilies and baby's breath drooping from Victorian wicker stands. There are too many flowers. It has the flavor of wedding and I don't understand it. Of course in a higher sense I am indeed to be joined, wedded to the dream of the lake and the drift of the larch, but Steven doesn't think that way, and he has too many agendas today to bother with the transcendental *conjunctio* of his wife to the universe. When my friend Hannah's daughter was to marry a Sikh cabdriver, turban and all, Hannah took a second mortgage on her home, rented, among other displays, the same wicker stands, filled with the same flowers, and married her daughter to the cabdriver as if he were the Prince of Wales. It was the wedding of the year. The groom's veiled mother sold favors at the wedding. He gave change. Old custom. I understand, Steven. Subsumed, tortured, flattened by my dark and indescribable act, you puff yourself up and present the funeral of the year. But why the wedding atmosphere?

Diggety sits at the bottom of the avenue of lilies, looks up it, waits, wags his tail, waits. He is waiting for me. Surely, he thinks, if all these people are here, she will be here also. There is my husband. His face is flat, unknowable. He is the Jew in church, falsely reverent, immensely painstakingly cautious, correct, terrified, secret. Steven notices two mushrooms growing at the base of a larch. Swiftly he kicks at their imperfection with the soft point of his delicate shoe, crushes them with his sole, scuffs them into the ground with his heel. I'm next. There is something significantly awry at my funeral and I do not understand it. He has chosen well, my husband, planned so impeccably. I wonder if he perhaps had been contemplating my funeral as long as I had contemplated his. He wears his Armani suit, pin-striped, perfect, with a new gleaming pair of soft black slip-on shoes that do not belong outside. He stands there, the ultimate Son of David, his father's fringed white silk shawl over his shoulders, untouchable. Wrapped in his cloud of glory, I in the shroud of shame, his perfection, I take it, illuminates, delineates my imperfection.

There are my friends, estrogen fed, Retin-A'd, glinting with gold in the sun-dappled ceiling of larch. They've had their hair done for today. They wear their good little black numbers so the Angel of Death won't spot them in the crowd of white-robed ones such as myself. Their gold of course is a dead giveaway. They are thrilled and find it difficult to grieve. Erring, as I most always have erred on the side of sensationalism, I have once again illuminated their lives. I give such good gossip. They stand still, hands clasped over their Bally-flat bellies, faces buttered with serenity, grief, and reverence, churning inside. They bend swiftly forward to each other, eyes wide, excited, ask each other questions, titter like squirrels in the trees. "A gorilla?" "What was she wearing? What was she wearing?" "A gorilla?" "Raped and dismembered." They are jealous and triumphant, confused. I'd stuck my baby finger into the plug of the universe. "What was she trying to prove?" "Raped and dismembered." "She asked for it, didn't she?" Ann rubs her gold chain between thumb and forefinger like the silken hem of her baby blanket. "I heard Dian Fossey ordered black bikinis and bras once a year from Bloomies." "I heard they were sitting on the beach, drinking beer." "Raped and dismembered, not necessarily in that order," Dorothy, wise-mouthed Dorothy, cracks. And they contain their giggles with the back of their hands over their mouths when Hannah tells them the joke about the lady who was raped by the gorilla and went into a depression because he never called and never wrote. They repeat the line, giddy, thrilled, terrified. "Never called. Never wrote. Not necessarily in that order." If they could see poor Moses' purple parts, his tiny fruits of the loom of life, no larger than the thimble cones of the larch, they would not speak of rape but of broken necks and crushed skulls. Except for Marian, my friends raise creamy, plucked faces to the front and try to concentrate politely on Steven's reverent tones, all the while wondering if they should leave their husbands and go after him. Not necessarily in that order. Marian raises her eyebrow. It is something she's practiced for years at her bathroom mirror. It has become her quintessential come-on. She is not directing it, however, at my husband. She seems to be directing her raised eyebrow to someone behind the larches. Indeed, there is a news camera rolling. Truly. Discreetly, on the other side of the larches. Local. It isn't like Marian to turn on for the local news.

And there are the children, sleek, guarded, not knowing quite how to behave, hidden, wishing in a good part of their hearts that things could turn backward, that they could once again be the children and I would once again be the mommy and feed them spoon by spoon while I invent stories for them—how ketchup was invented, how to make a frog—instead of this story I invented, the story their father is at the moment at great expense trying to untell. They will divide up the four True Value stores and my jewelry and move up a notch in their yacht or country clubs and try to remember me as if I had been what it was they had wanted me to be. One day they will all read Dian Fossey and decide both of us were really wacko and be done with me.

So far so good, but now I see that Steven has added another element, an element of such disequilibrium, such bravado, it is impossible to plumb the layers of his motivation. It is the reason for Marian's invitational eyebrow. He has added John Banks. John Banks in a British naval uniform stands near the news cameraman on the far side of the larches. Steven, how could you? John Banks stands with his arms crossed. John Banks glinting brighter than my army of gold-flocked friends. John Banks turned out in full gear: medals, stars, stripes, campaign ribbons, gold braid. I had not imagined rank. He wears a patch over one eye. What has happened to your eye, John Banks? Is it just for effect? Because you don't want to look anyone (my husband, my children) straight in the eye? They guess, my friends, Steven's associates, our children, that the Schweppesian specimen is their mother's lover. Who else could he be? I have stunned and silenced my friends. "He has come,"

Steven has explained to my children beforehand, "to honor your mother." They do not meet their father's eyes. "You heard me," Steven hisses at them in his desperation to make amends for all of us. "To honor your mother."

I can imagine the London–New York conversation, the great pauses, the calculated throat clearings. "Of course you'll come. Of course we want you. Linda would have wanted you. I know how much she meant to you, you to her." The entendres, the unsaids. Steven won't take no for an answer, insists on sending a Concorde ticket. Out of absurd manners, John Banks would come. "Respect for the dead," he'd mumble to his wife as she packs for him, "all that rubbish." Cynically, too, he would come. But he would come. He would be curious. And dining out on such an item. "Raise your glasses to my mistress, killed by a gorilla. Great girl," he'd mumble as if he himself had wrestled Tarzana to the jungle floor.

When my mother was dying, a poor and withered black man rolled around the chemo unit in a wheelchair bragging that he had Lou Gehrig's disease: "If it good enough for Lou, it good enough for me." Steven has demonstrated to his complex, moribund satisfaction that any woman who could attract the astonishing figure waiting in the larches, so splendid with power, presence, manners, nobility, can't be all bad. Nor can her husband. Does it give you a sense of power, ownership, Steven, that you owned a woman whom such an other desired? Do the children feel secretly proud that their mother's lover of choice was the Lord of the Admiralty at least, not a decrepit gorilla? So I am to be honored rather than dishonored, desirable rather than perverted, my act of darkness, an act of light. Lord Admiral Nelson over there was far darker an act than my moments with the gorilla.

Steven surveys his scene, rocks on his heels, his hands clasped behind his back. Less than a grieving husband, Steven looks like a department store manager overseeing a new display. Having instructed the saleswomen, run the ads, feathered the merchandise, he now waits to see if the customers buy the package.

"If Linda had an excess . . ." John Banks steps forward at Steven's subtle gesture. My friends are frozen. The faces of my children are atrophied, riveted. "Linda," he addresses me melodramatically. His voice breaks. He turns toward the mourners, clears his throat, speaks in sonorous tones, deeper than I've ever heard in years. It is his pillow voice. My friends shiver. Marian has both eyebrows up. His Englishness stuns them all. Son of a bitch. "I am here because Linda saved my life. Just as I am certain she was trying to save the gorilla's life. If Linda had a fault, it would be an excess of generosity. I am sorry for the pain and sadness Linda has provoked. The terrible loss. She would have wished pain on none of you. Ah, Linda . . ." He faces the grave. "You were so curious, a terrible and wonderful curiosity. You were so good. So very good." He is not talking about my character. He is talking about multiple orgasms. The man is a pig.

Steven stops rocking. Of course there is something deeply sincere about John Banks's words. My erstwhile mourners are left gaping, wondering. The customers have bought the goods but Steven perhaps got more than he bargained for. Steven forces himself forward to shake John Banks's hand. I am so familiar with that hand. John Banks pats Steven's shoulder. They embrace. Man to man. It is odd, that as intimate as I've been with both men, I know them less well than they, at this moment, know each other. There is something disgustingly manly and honorable going on here of which I am not a part. Perhaps what men have in common is not the knowing but an agreement not to know, to go forward and not know. Perhaps that is why men are heroes. These two go forward and will never know because neither ever dared to really know me. The chivalric motto is emblazoned on Steven's J. Press silk ties: "What we don't know won't hurt us."

Ah, Steven, soon I will be leached in the pasture, soon I will drift into the nodes of the larch bark, soon I will become the lake, and I will have completed a greater circle. I will have married earth. But not so for you. You have rewritten my life, denied it so you can live with me at last, live with me as you would have me, not as I was, certainly not as I might have been. I've been packaged. I've been redone and I am now the wonderful wife. I come not to bury Caesar. I come to marry her. I get it. I get it now. You have reaffirmed our wedding vows, brought in a drop-dead best man, and almost, son of father, father of son, given away the bride. Ah, Steven, I feel the gorilla shifting beside me. He moves closer. I feel the horror of that naked arm pressing against my shoulder. We are all so naked. I see you now. You have at last made me what you needed me to be.

ELEVEN

Even at the level of chemical reaction, a system can retreat in its evolution along the same path from which it has come, indicating a primitive holistic memory system. It remembers the initial conditions that made a development possible, the beginnings of each new structure in its development. It is capable of *re-ligio* . . . the linking backward to its origin. Rewind.

It may have been the pulse around me, his breathing in and out, mine, the boom of our blood, the lift and fall of the sumo belly, the leathery chest, the sea beating gently at the beach, the wind, the moss floating on the limbs above me, as if the universe breathed in and out and I rode on its antique breath. I don't know how long I slept. I remember waking up, softly, safely, Moses pressed gently against my shoulder, my hand still resting in his lap, his on my leg, both of us breathing deeply and regularly. He stirred, lifted that great head slowly, looked at me wide-eyed, in wonder. You could be my father. I could be your daughter.

It was a fragile moment, a primeval moment in the Garden, a moment of purity. I suspect it was a moment I'd been seeking all my life. Moses, however, moved to the edge of the deck, turned his back, squatted, crossed his arms over his chest, ignored me as studiously as I've ever been ignored in my life. He coughed his sharp, phlegmy cough. His body shook with coughing. I wanted to reach out and rub his back, rub the stiff silver hairs of his animal manhood, curl up next to him. Then I woke up fully, the innocence of night swept away, and I realized it was an opportunity to escape. If he had truly lost interest in me, I could run to the truck or hide in the restroom.

Ever so slowly, I lifted myself, slid my rear toward the edge of the deck until he barked a single short bark. I froze. But the bark wasn't for me. He repeated it, increased it. It was a bark of alarm. He stood upright, back to the oak, stared at the beach. I imagined his hair bristled. I think it might have. He looked larger.

I had not seen the beach with his eyes. The moon was full on the beach and its skin, liquid, undulated with strange half-lives, thousands of transparent worms, tiny horrid crustaceans, thousands, millions of creatures and half creatures, crawling along their Pleistocene paths. I heard the sound of a forest of autumn leaves swept by strong winds, but it was the creaking armor of an army of ghost crabs swarming toward us in a solid flank. They came forward on brilliant insect locomotion, eyes extended from their sockets on rubbery antennae, swinging as they moved. Some were already on the steps. Moses sprang forward and brought the flats of his hands down on the deck in a thunderous volley, as if he'd bring down the night. He screamed, built to a roaring crescendo. From the oak above us, he tore the splintered limb, swung it around his head. I rolled off the deck onto the shell path, rolled over a railroad tie onto soft sand, rolled silently away from the creatures, over and over again along the beach. Do gorillas swim? Would I be safe in the ocean? Sharks swim. I rolled back toward the deck. I had to make for the restroom or the truck. Upright, gums exposed, teeth gleaming, Moses ripped a leaf from the limb and placed it between his lips, rumbled one last volcanic volley of fury and fear. Unintimidated by his majestic bluff, the crabs marched toward Moses. Poor Moses, having spent his display, leaped from the deck and ran past me into the dark toward his truck.

When I was first married, Steven had brought a dust-filled jar from the garage and asked me to rinse it out in the sink. As the water ran in, the dirt in the jar became spiders, the jar a jar of spiders. I raced to the bathtub, turned the water on full force, tore off my clothes, and climbed in. Steven sat on the toilet, his head in his hands, insisted that it was just dirt, begged me to look into the jar again but I wouldn't look. He ended by asking God what he should do. I never did believe it was just dirt. Hallucination has the same effect as sight. But I felt sorry for him and contained myself thereafter. Moses' reaction was equivalent. He had leaped upward, away, in some diluvial horror, and I wondered as I watched him race away from me toward the truck if we had learned this fear together a long time ago at the edge of a beach, when I was no less an animal than he. I heard the lock slide open, the door flung open, slammed shut, the lock slide shut. From inside. How is he doing it? The creak of springs. His screams faded to the whimpers of a child. The truck rocked back and forth, cries, another coughing spell, sighs, silence.

. . .

I crept toward the restroom bunker. The railroad ties marking the path were loose. I pulled one into the restroom, edged it across the door, between sink pipes and door handle. Pine Sol filled the grouting, the sulfurous dead-horse reek of the toilet bowls. Shaking uncontrollably, I lay down on the concrete floor, my head under a sink, a pack of paper towels for my pillow, my body barricading the metal door. Moonlight shining through the grate of a metal window high in the wall sketched a shimmering square of squares on the floor by my head.

The moon was still in pieces and I had somehow accomplished my own cage. Other than the barricaded door, the only access was through the small windows under the roof. I needed to get back to the truck and find the bag of green alligators. Obviously they would control him. I had no idea how he unlocked the truck. It was possible, if he wanted to, that he could open the door I lay against. A strange and perverse part of me wished to be back on the deck, leaning against that strength, protected. I turned restlessly, vainly trying to adjust my hipbones and breasts to the concrete floor. "Gravity," the dentist had whispered. "Some of us are not meant for gravity. The earth is so hard."

There was something there that night, something geometrical and universally true, a formula about the gorilla and me and Steven. Something Pythagorean. Why, I posed the question, does sitting on the beach drinking beer with a gorilla in the moonlight feel like a date? Because, I offered myself a hypothesis, I'm worried about saying the wrong thing, about giving him the wrong impression. The language was from my teenage years, from slumber parties, talking all night about the great mystery of boys. What are boys really like? I'm worried that he won't like me and that he will like me. I don't know what he is really like. I don't like the way he smells. There is a strange link of words between like as in emotion and like as in an equation of similarity. If I am like him, will he like me?

I was lying on a bale of hay at a fraternity beer blast, in a barn, on a night as humid as this, lying on a bale of moldy hay with Buddy Pfeiffer, who, I heard much later, found a Spanish galleon, became a millionaire, lost his eyebrows in an explosion, had them tattooed back on, not necessarily in that order. We were supposed to be making out, but I made small talk because I didn't want to make out because I couldn't stand the smells, which were of course what had sprung me into this memory: manure in the hay, the boys peeing nearby, the beer in puddles around the keg, the beer on Buddy's breath, and the sweat all around me, his hand on my leg, his knuckles hairy. I didn't like him; he didn't like me. He wasn't like me. Distance is what I felt that night so long ago and it was the same distance I felt sitting there with the gorilla drinking beer at the beach on a hot night and the same distance I have felt all my life and have struggled so unsuccessfully to close. The distance between Buddy/Steven/the man on the train/John Banks and myself, that distance was equal to the distance between me and the gorilla. I drew lines in the moonlight graph on the floor, marked points, one for me, one for Steven, one for the gorilla. The distance between myself and Moses is as profound as the distance between me and Steven. It was an astonishing thought, but I could take it no farther. The moon blinked and the graph disappeared.

"Well, dear girl, whose side was your gorilla on?"

"I'm not sure."

"Quite a temper tantrum."

"You know what I think, John? I think if I'd given him the beer instead of throwing it at him, all of that could have been avoided."

"Perhaps next time you'll try that. You're really stretching it, Linda. I think you may have gone over."

"He was trying to frighten me into giving him the beer. Next time I'll listen to him. Next time I will listen very hard. He was trying to get a beer. You see, he's locked into sequence. His is: I beg, I get. I had broken his pattern. He's not flexible, adaptable, any longer or even very curious, unless he's assessing danger, which, for him, is what I am."

"I'm not certain if your curiosity or your generosity will be your downfall. Now that you've applied them together, you are really in for it. Really."

"All the fairy tales have threes. What's my third fatal flaw?"

"I doubt you'll live long enough to find out."

"If you could tell me I would die by water, I wouldn't fear fire."

Much later I woke to the sounds of Moses grunting with excitement above me. I stood on a sink and looked through the grate of the window. His chain dragging after him, he dashed back and forth under the mercury lamp, collecting Spanish moss, ripping it from the boughs of trees, snapping fronds of saw palmetto, dragging vines. One arm full, as it had been when we met on the path, he climbed up into the oak above the restroom, pulled more ferns and moss from its limbs, stuffed and stepped on them, worked his pile into a nest around himself. And shimmied down in a shower of bark for more. He nested near me, I suspected, purposefully near me. At first he whimpered nervously, coughed. Finally I heard that deep snoring and he slept and I may have also slept for the little that was left of the night. The complaints of gulls following the loaded nets of the night's catch woke me. I heard the fishing boats closer now as they entered the inlet, engines heavy, their sterns deep in the ocean, heading around the island to the Doric wharf at Millionaires' Row.

"Oh, Steven, oh, Steven, why are we so different? Why do we fight? What has happened to trust, to friendship? Did we ever have it? Why do I always feel I love something you're waiting to become? Has it been my timeless role to domesticate you? We worked so hard and we failed. We've got to be a different species."

"It's a figure of speech, dear boy. A figure of speech. Don't worry about it."

As the sun rose, filtered through the smoky celadon fog of morning, I saw Moses on the dunes, lying on his back, feet in the air, one arm reaching out for a trailer of morning glories, the other wadding a bunch of thistles into his mouth. Satisfied, he sat up and stretched his arms out at his sides, just as I do, just as Steven does, yawned, stood on his legs, chewed on a thistle as if he were thinking. Then, facing the barren sand of the highest scarped dune, he beat softly at his chest with cupped hands, beat softly, *pok pok pok,* calling up something, his beat quickening as if something had indeed appeared. I beat my own chest. I felt nothing; saw nothing. Then he thrust his arms akimbo and turned round and round before the dune until he spun, a lumbering whirligig making believe. I saw him there on the dunes, an old and sick gorilla, foolish with his freedom. As I watched him turning, the seeds of place stirred in my head and I could feel my mind closing, sinking into a deep and primitive narrow channel. I felt as if I'd been driving too long, had what Steven called highway hypnotism. My mind kicked off, dropped into a deep place. I will never really know what the mechanisms were. It seemed that the seeds Moses had planted, seeds of place, deeply planted seeds of memory, but more than memory, a presence, his presence, those seeds flowered in my own strange and ancient animal mind and I knew he danced to his waterfall, to his place. When I had questioned John Banks about place, he had said, "One knows." I did not know my place. If Steven is as different from me as Moses is, perhaps Steven came from a different place, was molded in a different environment than I was.

Moses showed me his steaming, thunderous turquoise waterfall again, the brilliant vines and pale orchids and blue ferns and rainbows on fire, and that great sad blue-black face filling the green jungle air, and I smelled the cool sharp smell of the falling water and the dark golden depths of pool that whispered, "Listen. Stand still and listen." I saw him before the waterfall, beating his chest, gleaming blue-black fur and silvered back, joyous and powerful, worshipful. Worshipful. The word jerked me back. The implications that the gorilla worshiped were so enormous and exhausting, I moved from them. Then the two reels took a leap in my mind, spliced, and I was in the movie. Or I saw what Moses saw as if—a condition I was well prepared for—as if I were Moses. I saw as he saw. I suppose hypnotism is the entry into the animal mind. I had put my human mind to sleep and swam in the deep channels of extrasensory ability, like a cat finding its way to its owner's new home, like California ants predicting the earthquake, like the cows I'd seen in Montana forming a circle around their calves before an eclipse, like seeing Moses dance to his waterfall. I saw, he showed me, beyond his waterfall, an escarpment. It is either he or I who walk toward a great ridge and look down into a dried lake bed with mounds of salt and neon alkalines of greens and yellows. Thousands of birds fill pools. Flamingos, endless angled clusters of flamingos, step about in brackish pools, bow politely to each other. Two crocodiles emerge, stiff-legged, and rip at the carcass of a small pig. Miles away, shimmering, I see another ridge, a mirror of the one I stand on. A valley runs between the ridges, forever, diminishing only in perspective. I stare down into the great rift high over the salt beds and the ten thousand birds. And I see the ragged sun and the salt beds and the ridge of ancient rock at my feet and I do not know to whom I listen. Small eruptions of lava and water hiss below me. A young storm boils up from the rift. Soon biblical winds sweep over the escarpment, swallow the sun. I climb back toward the waterfall, rest, drink from my cupped hands, and, when I have the strength, climb into the notch of an ancient tree of twisted branches curling around honey nests, and lie restlessly, breasts and hips seeking softness. The moon and I listen in the notch of the great trees, listen to the drone of bees. It is human talk. The sky cracks open and reveals at the limit of visibility or beyond it, a dark and liquid line of men and women marching across an otherworld horizon. An army of ghosts, the crabs now human, shining selves, luminous, light arcing between their fingers. I stare into the faces, into gorilla eyes, deep, profound, drawing me. My grandmother looks back over her shoulder at me, tries to tell me something but she must move on and I cannot hear her. Lightning slices the sky, looks like pain. A leopard stretches at the edge of the cliff, black velvet paws dangling, watches the storm move in. I tighten my legs and arms around my limb and bury my head in the safe sharp smell of the leaves and bitter bark as thunder shakes the earth.

I closed my eyes from the insistent dream, grasped the handholds of the sweating metal of the plumbing next to my head, but I could not loose myself from the tree buffeted by the storm, sheets of rain ramming its branches. The leopard holds her silken head up to the slashing rain and lightning, whips her tail in fury, challenges the thunder. The thunder growls and the sky snaps shut and the movie is over. And I heard the sound of bullets ripping up the dawn. Someone shooting an alligator? The raccoons? Each other? Backfiring? The gorilla? The sounds were swift and gone. A car left, tires screaming, muffler loose. I slid on my stomach to the cubicle and hid my head against the toilet, listened to the sound of dripping, prayed it wasn't Moses' blood I heard because the sounds outside had been bullets against metal, bullets against my van. Drag of terror in my legs, a bubble and hiss of fear, hot, lava, paralyzing as it filled me. I clutched the sweating metal of the pipes. And I heard one last fishing boat, heard someone with a foreign accent and square nipples shout, "Hey, Miss America, wake up." But I was awake and I had been awake and I had seen all this. And Moses was dead in the van and I heard his blood dripping on the macadam, heard John Banks's voice tolling his terrible word. *"Insurance, dear girl. Insurance. It would seem to me that whoever owns the gorilla carries a good deal of insurance on his life and that he's worth more dead than alive. Someone wishes to collect."*

"And it has to look like an accident. Yes. I know who would do that."

"And you may be in the way."

"Oh, John."

"I know. This is very serious. I do wish you'd just leave."

T W E L V E

When owls eat small creatures, they vomit up the bones and the fur in a ball called a bolus. I was the night's bolus. I heard the metallic pings hit the truck, ricochet from side to side, roll away. I heard the shots rip up the marmalade dawn and spread it and my heart over the ocean. Steven, someone has shot your gorilla. Someone has my picture. My soul flees.

What would I do if Moses were dead? Walk away? What if he were mortally wounded? What if he were only lightly wounded and could conceivably be saved? Who would I turn to? Call Steven. If Moses were dead, someone would want the body. Research? Insurance? They'll come back for the body. I could rent a car and drive home. Go home, go home. I can't. I've gone too far. I've sought the other to find myself and I've gone too far and my *self* is no longer myself. Not only the particle changes; the physicist changes.

I sniffed the Pine Sol on the bathroom floor for its sharpness, dragged myself to a stall, climbed the toilet seat, braced against the gridded window. Pain played on the marimba of my teeth, along my jawbone. I whispered into the funnel of silence left by the gun shots, "Moses." The truck was insulted with holes like the antique pie cupboard in my kitchen. "Moses?"

I stood on the toilet seat, pressed my face against the sharp grid of the window. "I'll grieve for you, Moses. I'll cover you with coffee cups and French fries. I'll paint you with the burial ocher of ketchup. Forgive us, Moses. We're so stupid. So goddamn stupid."

How I needed to go to the truck to hold him, to smooth the pain and surprise from his face, to help him die or help him survive. No, there had been too many bullets. He wouldn't come out from the box stuck with swords like a magician's assistant. I needed to do for him what he'd done for Dino, what he would do, I would like to have thought, for me.

Someone has my picture. They're after me. Someone is after Moses. No one is after either of us. In our town, last summer, a drunk shot all the swans in Swan Pond. It was a prank. Perhaps the same sort of boys who'd whistled "Dixie" at the pier were shooting up Yankees for fun. But I could not forget that someone had my picture. If the shooting and my picture were connected, then whoever shot Moses might be waiting for me in the parking lot, under the deck, just outside the door. Hadn't I heard a car pull out? Was it at the same time? I would wait, I told the knuckles pressed against my eyes. There would be tourists soon, couples and pic-nickers. At my mother's funeral, her mother, in long wraps of black crepe, held an amber bottle of smelling salts to my nose. I took a deep sniff of the Pine Sol and waited. The nightmare fears I'd lived with since adulthood, since wifehood, since motherhood, were manifesting in time, trotting out as if I'd called them up: hairy beasts, men chasing me, men shooting at me, losing my husband, losing myself, losing my home, losing.

"*I get very irritated when I can't find what I'm looking for.*"

"*I know John, I know.*"

The handle of my door turned, the scrape of a key, a knock. "Who is it?" I mumbled a challenge.

There was a long silence, a sigh, a blood red hibiscus under the door. I backed away from it. "Who are you?"

"I'm Paul from Horseheads, New York. I have a degree in electrical engineering from Cornell. I clean park latrines on a barrier island off the coast of Georgia. I am certified sane. Okay? You could stand on a sink and take a look. I left half of my jaw in a rice paddy."

My jaw snapped as I spoke. I couldn't produce the consonants without pain. "What do you use on the floor?"

"Pine Sol."

I climbed down from the toilet, crossed the floor, and climbed onto a sink near the door. Paul from Horseheads' face was collapsed and ravaged but someone who loved him had, this morning, twisted his gray hair into an intricate and familiar French braid. He leaned against a three-wheeled delivery bike, its basket filled with cleaning supplies. He wore rubber thongs and neon orange running shorts. He had no place for weapons. He was tall and thin, narrow-shouldered, not dangerous. Only a woman would have braided his hair so lovingly. Otherwise, I would have thought him gay.

"Go look inside my truck and tell me—"

"They like me to finish the latrines before the tourists come."

I imagined what he would see. I could not answer.

"And then you'll come out?"

Knowing he could be another one of my nightmares, I grunted inconclusively.

His feet crunched on the path as he circled the restroom. I crossed again to my toilet view, tucked my fingers in the grid, watched him. Whatever Paul from Horseheads saw made him whistle. He whistled again, rubbed his hands over his sides, walked around the truck, touching it as if it might explode.

"They got the cab, too, on the driver's side."

I locked my fingers tightly into the grid until the metal cut, balanced myself. My side. They were shooting at me as well. Who? Why? What did I do?

"I'll go get some help."

"Insurance, dear girl, life insurance."

"On who?"

"Obviously, either the gorilla or you or both of you."

"John!"

"Be realistic, Linda. You're the one who has broken the glass. If you cut yourself on the shards, you can't blame it on someone else. You have to pay the price for your actions."

"Steven, he tried to kill me."

"Who, Linda? Who tried to kill you?"

"Whoever has life insurance on Moses."

"Froelich must. He owns him."

"Do you have life insurance on me?"

"Don't be an ass, Linda."

A strange husky sound came from my side of the bunker. Something like a child imitating a train. "Whoo, whoo."

"Whoa!" Paul from Horseheads shouted, jumped backward. "Whoa!" He flattened himself against the truck's door, arms raised above his head, legs spread, like Leonardo da Vinci's geometric man.

"Whoo, whoo," and a crunch of bicycle tires on the shells, the scratch of chain, then onto the macadam, riding the delivery bike, his chain sparking on the pavement, Moses. No hands, clapping his hands, hooting happily, pedaled Paul's bike in circles. Paul fumbled in the pocket of his neon shorts, produced a rusty harmonica, and, with half his jaw, desperately tried to make music. As heavily and slowly as I could, I hummed a few notes of "Old MacDonald."

Paul nodded, connected my notes to each other and more, played fitfully, sucking and blowing. He had little breath from his own fear and only one side of his face worked, but he played his song. I could not understand why he didn't lift a broom to defend himself, open the truck, hide himself. He understood something around the corner, something just around the corner from existence, where he had perhaps gone and lost his face.

Moses made nervous kissing sounds as he passed Paul, sucked his lips in, waved bye-bye, stretched his lipless lips forward, moved his lips, moved his lips, opened them, closed them, made *u* and *o* and *i* and *e* shapes as if he were speaking our language. Where had he learned that? Bye-bye. Moses waved bye-bye, tossed a roll of toilet paper at Paul. Paul caught it with one hand, tossed it back. Moses caught it with one hand, from behind his back, blindly, precisely, and balanced it on his head. Moses chuckled, grinned, his mouth open playfully. One opens the door of fear and out comes play.

"Dear girl . . ." John Banks was in his benevolent Cotswold-altar frame. "Dear girl, your gorilla is in a performance loop now, which indicates he is also in an obedience loop. Get him into the van."

"I have to get off the island, John. I don't know how."

"Start. Take step one, Linda. Just step one."

"You could take my gorilla." Steven's voice had been soft, child-like, as if he weren't really thinking about what he would say, dreamy, his arrow steady in his bow.

"What a marvelous idea, Steven. I'm astonished it hadn't occurred to me. He could ride his little tricycle around the village."

"His collar size is forty-four. He'll need clothes for the plane trip at the very least. And you'll be protected."

I had not been protected. The wires of terror still locked my jaws. With great pain, I could pry them open to speak. My left arm was swollen and blue. My knee pulsed with its bites. I felt almost no sensation in my left hand.

Moses' back was four feet across. His rump dropped over the bicycle seat. Neither his short legs nor the bicycle's framework was visible. He looked like a wheeled creature. I dragged the railroad tie from the door and left the restroom to walk around the building. I approached Moses, clapping loudly as I did. If Moses was performer, I would be audience. I would applaud him into his truck.

He circled and paused before me, beat his cupped hands on his pouch cheeks, *pok pok*, then on his chest to the rhythm of "Old MacDonald," *pok pok pok pok pok.* He thrust his gargantuan face into mine, rocked his head back and forth, dipping it into vague figure eights. I rocked my head in the same Möbius strip. What did it mean? At the Madras Club at luncheon, a barefoot turbaned boy, Dravidian dark, under a cobalt-blue domed ceiling painted with silver stars, stands before me, offering me mulligatawny soup. I am not certain I want it. He rocks his head. What does he mean? He is small and barefoot and excessively polite and unobtrusive and I understand at last, in the pool of embarrassment around me, that he is saying, "The soup will not harm you. I will not harm you." I've seen the head rocking since. Indian millionaires on the airbus to Bombay greeted each other, rocked their heads. Mrs. Froelich rocked her head, moaned, *"Oy vey."* And Paul, with half of his jaw, rocked his head back and forth, inhaled deep chords, exhaled thin weak song as I clapped. It was the potato farmer in Ireland who worked next to my house, greeting me every morning with the same twist of his head as if we could agree about the difficulty of life. It was something I'd seen all over the world, like begging, something human or not human or all of ours, something sympathetic, a sharing of the grief of life. Moses waited, watched my face. I rocked as he had. He rocked in return, barked a husky bark. Moses rocked his head and politely assured me, "I will not harm you. Life is difficult but I will not harm you. I am sympathetic. I am with you."

"Big cheese. Hey you, big cheese. Get in your cage."

Moses looked at me sharply. "Whoo, whoo."

I backed up to the truck and pulled out the bag of green alligators. "Silly Moses, silly silly Moses, get in your cage, you silly piece of cheese. Get in your cage." Brandishing an alligator in each hand like the Sumerian snake goddess at the British Museum, a woman of creative and sacred anger, I approached Moses. Moses pedaled his bicycle away from me and then, on one rear wheel, pedaled a tight circle around me, his body almost parallel to the ground. It was clearly his circus act, clearly the grand finale finish to his death-defying act. I shoved an alligator at the air in front of his face. He jumped from the bicycle, spilling Murphy's Oil Soap, Pine Sol, brushes, toilet paper rolls, turned me around, pushed me toward the truck gently with two hands, bit me on the behind, a nip, a playful nip, pushed me forward again. Somehow I knew he wanted me to run. It was of course not counterintuitive to run.

Paul giggled in crazy hee-haws. He wasn't a man. He wasn't brave. He had betrayed me.

Moses, killer and clown, was playing chase. I was running for my life. His chuckle was no different from a man's, something like a department store Santa's ho-ho-ho. This is it, I thought. This is what happened in the Garden of Eden. A great rough hairy creature and Eve. Running, I was flooded with an immense idea. We're Adam and Eve. If I turn around and offer him an apple, he won't eat me. Forget temptation. If I take him to bed, he won't kill me. That's how it all began—the civilizing of men. It hasn't stopped yet.

Paul from Horseheads sensed something also. "He won't hurt you. He's just chasing you." And had Adam chased Eve around the Garden? Why did she run? On job interviews in Washington, when I was just out of school, I'd been chased around desks. Once a man ran after me in a forest and stopped. Men chasing women. Does it come naturally? Why do we run? Are they really just playing? Paul from Horseheads played a new song. Abadabadaba? Interspecies, that was the Fall. Interspecies. Maybe it wasn't man and woman. It was woman and ape? That was the Fall? Absurd, just when I was about to die I had an inkling of the organizing principle of the sexes, or had I? And they went upon their abadaba honeymoon. Is this the clarity before death—Moses running after me, waving the missing piece of the puzzle at me? "Here, here, you forgot this! Here!" We're a different species. We were formed in different places.

"She was born," my mother said of me, "having forgotten something. I could often see it flicker across her face as if she were about to remember it. We'd see that dreamy look sometimes on her face in the high chair as if she were trying to remember something, listening to something within herself." "Or she's constipated," my father would say.

Moses slowed down. I was dizzy and breathless. I crouched behind the truck. Moses approached, stopped in his tracks, yawned, then lumbered over to hide behind a slender palm tree. Most of him showed on both sides of the palm. He must have thought hiding was funny because he came out from behind the palm tree, closed his eyes, spread his arms, ran around bouncing off trees, bumping into the truck, chuckling, his eyes squeezed closed as if this moment were the funniest moment in the universe. He came dangerously close to us, poked my shoulder lightly with his fingertips, veered off, pirouetted around the parking lot, chuckling until the chuckles were interspersed with deep gasps, then coughs, and he dropped on the macadam and coughed a terrible cough. His chest heaved with deep, phlegmy spasms and we were forgotten. He cowered on his belly, head lowered, arms tucked under, presenting only his broad back to his death.

Cautiously I backed up to the truck and opened its doors as he bent over. "Moses," I sang out to him. "Truck."

He opened his eyes. They were red and wet, almost bloody. Weakened from coughing, he lifted his chain over one arm, moved slowly to the truck. His lethargy might have been a trick because he stopped in front of Paul, stood immense and upright, rocked his head faster and faster, and, monkey that he was also, grinned and grabbed the harmonica from Paul, an alligator from me, hoisted himself into the truck, laid the alligator just outside his cage, and pulled the doors closed behind himself.

"Lock it!" Paul yelled. "Quick!"

I reached to shove the outer lock shut and as I did I felt the electricity of Moses' fingers on mine. He retreated, his arm disappeared into the vent of the roof, head disappeared, the vent screen dropped down. Bolts tightened. I'd forgotten about the vent. Moses was a genius.

I slid against the truck's tire, sat on the ground. Paul slid down next to me.

"I'll need my harmonica back soon," he said, thin and tight, his eyes looking up toward the right of the sky, and I thought he might be mad. We labored to catch our breaths. He held my hand. "Guys with heart wounds sound like Moses—wheezing, gasping. They can't keep things moving in their lungs."

Medic, Vietnam. Of course. "Adam and Even," Paul said. "They took away the *n* from Even because she was odd before God." Crazy. I leaned in the forgiving golden sunlight of that jar of morning, leaned against crazy Paul from Horseheads, alive, leaned into his neck until I felt the carotid vein beating against my lips, kissed his neck gently because he had known somehow to play music.

"Maybe it's contagious. Your jaws, my jaw. It'll ease up. It's from clenching your teeth." Paul drew his fingers lightly over my cheek, reached the back of my neck, pressed in hard with his thumbs, relieved the pain slightly. "They said there was a white woman sleeping on the beach with a black man last night. Some good ole boy just shot you up. You want to report it?"

I shook my head no, shrugged, whimpered tears.

"You think it was an ape and a woman?"

"What?"

"In the Garden of Eden? The way he was playing with you."

I could not stop crying.

"It's okay. It's okay. We'll go to my father-in-law. We'll figure out what to do." He climbed into the truck, patted the seat next to him, but I, in some subcortical tropism, climbed next to the cage, sank to the floor, and rested against a cabbage crate. I knew we were going to Stavros. I knew the woman with the braid and the faint mustache had braided Paul's hair. Moses kneeled on the cage floor, his limbs tucked under his chest and belly, his back exposed. It was the shape of his pain, his weakness.

THIRTEEN

Stavros wasn't home. It was too early for him to open the coffee shop. Paul said he'd drive around for a while. We stopped at a waffle shop, phoned the Holiday Inn. There were no messages or packages at the front desk. We bought a container of Half 'n Half for Moses. A drugstore opened as we drove by. I bought a harmonica, a green plastic plesiosaur with a one-octave keyboard implanted in its midriff. I told the pharmacist that I had a four-hundred-pound relative and I needed to know what kind of over-the-counter cold medicine I could give him and how much. I think he thought I was trying to be funny. He said, "I wouldn't give him any." And called after me as I walked out flushing, "Or give him all of it." Moses willingly traded Paul's rusted harmonica for the new shiny one.

We parked on the pavilion, waited for opening time. Moses handed me newspapers to throw out. I did. When I returned he was knocking something hard and metallic. Tap tap tap. Then he banged his somethings together. I turned the pocket flashlight on his hands. Bullets. Do bullets explode? He sucked on them, banged them against the cage bars, chewed on them.

"Moses, I want those bullets."

He looked at his non-watch.

I held my hand out to him. Moses chewed a bullet. I could hear the bone-bending sound of metal against enamel. "Moses, I want those bullets."

He removed the bullet from his mouth, banged it against his cage bars. I went to the cooler. He was very interested. Mr. Froelich had given us grapes. I offered Moses one through the bars. He reached for it. I put my hand out for the bullet. He gave it to me. I gave him the grape. I offered him another grape. He passed me another bullet. We went one for one. I didn't know how many bullets there were in the cage. I had a limited number of grapes and I thought probably fewer grapes than bullets. "I want all the bullets, Moses. All." I made a circle with my hands.

He rummaged in his hay, gave me two. "Go on. Go get them." I held the whole cluster up to him, out of reach, dangling, swinging it. He pushed all his bullets into a pile.

"All of them."

Grunting with excitement, industrious, he pulled up hay, uncovered more bullets. Dozens more. He pushed them out of the cage at my feet. They rolled away from me. "Good boy. Okay. Good boy." Then he passed me a browned and flattened grape. He was out of bullets. I gave him the bunch of grapes and he ran to the back of the cage to eat them.

"Who are you, anyway, Moses? How much do you really know? Certainly you know the difference between one and all. You're a pretty smart guy, aren't you?" Moses spat grape seeds at me with some projectile force. I had to duck. Then he filled his mouth with water from his pail and spritzed me. When I moved out of target range, he took up his harmonica. Unable to make sounds with it, he banged it on the bars, twisted it like taffy. What he couldn't resolve was controlling his breath, which was why, I supposed, gorillas can't be taught to speak. He scratched his chest, showed me "tickle me, hurry up." I scratched his chest and under his chin. He growled softly, then lay on his belly, on his elbows, crossed his hands under his chin, and scrutinized me, the pink of his gums exposed as his face relaxed. "Had it really been you and I in the Garden, Moses? Chasing each other with snakes? Is that what the Fall was? A woman and an ape? I'd been someplace with you, someplace over the horizon, and part of me is still there. Strange idea, isn't it? Yes, we're different species. But, you know what, Moses, in many ways Steven is as much a stranger to me as you are to me. What after all is species difference? It means we can't reproduce, like donkeys and horses. But maybe sometime when things were looser, when barriers were different, we could, we did. I'll bet chimps and women can breed. Do you think Steven is also a different species? Different than I am? Did we all grow up in different places?" Moses lay on his back, laid the harmonica on his chest, drummed it lightly with his knuckles. Then he rolled over, placed the harmonica on his head, offered up a deep throaty grunt of pleasure and a ground-swelling fart, rolled back to me, placed his great hand over my head so I couldn't see. "He is, Moses. He is so terribly different. I've tried so hard."

Fishermen and early bike renters gathered on the pavilion to wait for Stavros to open. Paul led me to Stavros's easy chair, let it down flat, rolled me onto my stomach, straddled me, massaged my neck and head, pressed circles around my eyes, up to my forehead. We could hear the faint sounds of the plesiosaur keys from the truck in the parking lot across the footbridge, then a furious banging.

My father stopped touching me when I turned eleven. Since then I have never, until now, been touched by a man without a sexual agenda. Paul massaged the occipital muscle at the base of my skull, he explained to me, to release the pain of my jawbone. He hummed above me, abadabadaba, and fell into its rhythm. Under the thin nylon of his neon shorts, Paul's male parts drifted gently over my back. He was almost female, in his touch, his stature, his way, but his parts drifted along the small of my back, keeping rhythm with the press and punch of his massage. I wished I could ignore his manhood.

"I'm Diana." Diana smelled of lemon juice and yellow. "Want me to take over, Paul?"

"She's got enough troubles as it is."

Gay? Are they both gay? Is gay another square on the grid or a coming together? Or the end product of some kind of species hybridization, some massive domestication of man, a drift back toward the original female template? Are the differences between us species really specific, not gender specific? "What we heard was there was a black dude sleeping with a white woman on the beach and some good ole boys decided to shoot the truck up for Jesus."

"The gorilla had her trapped on the beach and then she hid in the ladies' room. Her jaw's pretty frozen."

"Is that how she hurt her arm?"

I wanted to defend Moses, to say he hadn't meant to, that he would have torn it off had he wanted to hurt me. I nodded. Paul's hands were miracles.

"Relax, relax," Paul from Horseheads whispered. "See how tight this is? That's tension. That's really tension." Paul said to Diana, "She was sleeping with him but she wasn't *sleeping* with him."

"That's cool."

I was only something Paul was doing. I could see Diana's knees. I think she was massaging Paul's back in my rhythm. Paul was Diana's and they were both gay.

"Where are you taking the gorilla?" Paul's thumbs were in the small of my back.

"I think someone's chasing me," I mumbled. "He's nearby. He has my picture." My jaw tightened. "I think." Nerves. I yawned it open, heard it crack. "And I think someone's chasing the gorilla."

"Where are you going?"

"Tarpon Springs. But he's very sick. Heart, lungs. I need to keep him alive until we get there."

"You own him?"

"No."

"You steal him?"

"No."

"Who carries the insurance on him?"

"The animal dealer. Following me. I think. Or my husband."

"Far out." He paused above me. "Far out. You're keeping him alive. They're trying to kill him for the money. Why are they trying to kill *you?*"

I shrugged. "I'm not sure they are. I'm not sure the man looking for me is at all interested in the gorilla. I don't know if there's a connection. Moses killed a man. A number of people have a number of reasons to find Moses, none of which I'm sure of, but all of which would do him harm. So I have to get him to Tarpon Springs, where he'll be sold and shipped out of the country."

"He killed a man? So they want to kill him. Wow!"

"Are *you* legal?" Diana asked.

"Maybe. Depends."

"Your old man have life insurance on *you?*" Diana asked. She was tough.

I shrugged.

"Who else would chase you?"

I didn't want to tell them about John Banks.

"So you want to get away from someone, or a couple of some-ones, waiting for you over the bridge. So we get you off the island without crossing the bridge. Hey, Diana, what about your uncle's barge? If we can get her down to the St. Lucie, she could cross over on your uncle's barge. Whoever's following her won't figure that one out." He bent down to me. "Diana's uncle takes empty barges from the Atlantic to New Orleans across Okeechobee. He could get you to the west coast, below Tarpon Springs. Diana, see if your dad—"

"I have money," I told Paul.

Paul bent down next to my head. "You oughta be more careful who you tell that to. What's your name?"

"Linda."

"Listen, Linda, I've got a stethoscope in my truck. Let's go listen to your friend's insides before Stavros gets here."

Moses pressed one hand into the ground, swiveled over it like a gymnast, leaned against the bars. I fed him a tunafish sandwich, which he autopsied before eating.

"Snort at him. It's like asking permission."

Paul snorted. I held the stethoscope against Moses' chest, Paul listened.

"What?"

He offered me the instrument.

It was too close to life, too fragile. Moses was to have been strength and comfort to me, not loss and death, something eternal. I did not want to hear his mortality. Even so, I placed the stetho-scope over my ears and against his heart. He looked away. His heart boomed like a freight train lumbering up a rough hill. The roar of his blood filled my head, echoed in a terrible beat. I think I can. I think I can. It didn't seem as if he could much longer. Paul and I looked at each other. He tilted his head, shrugged a shoulder.

"He's lived a long time like this probably, so maybe he can last. I don't know. I guess he could drop on you any minute."

"Why am I doing this, then?"

"It's the right thing to do. It's good and true and beautiful."

I had not really felt until that moment that there was anything good, true, or beautiful in what I was doing other than buying myself some time. Paul had added another element that had somewhere already existed, had begun to bloom when I watched the beauty of Moses dancing in the shimmer of sunrise, when I thought he was dead in the truck. I wanted to help him. I knew how very deeply I wanted to help him, oddly, at the moment when I found that I could not.

"Would you do what I'm doing?"

"If I were free."

I looked at him quizzically, but he would go no farther. It was all right. I was carrying enough problems of my own and had just added another. Moses spat grape seeds at us. Paul spat them back at him. They laughed. Moses tried to get Paul to tickle him. "Awesome," Paul whispered. "Awesome." Moses spritzed Paul. Paul spritzed Moses. Both giggled wildly. Where would gay fit on my grid? Moses grabbed Paul's arm, pulled it gently toward his bars, held Paul's wrist up to look at his watch, cocked his head to listen, followed the movement of the dial with his finger, then released Paul and looked at his own wrist, cocked his head to listen to his own non-watch.

"This son of a bitch can make believe. If he can make believe, he's as crazy as we are."

"He tells me his dreams. He wants to go to a waterfall." Why was it safe to tell that to Paul? Why was Paul safe?

"In my past life I had a girlfriend who did bit parts in a movie and there was a lion in it and he'd sit in front of her every time he saw her and show her his place. She knew he was asking her to take him home. Hey, you old sucker. A waterfall? Busch Gardens. Yeah. That's okay. That's okay. You don't need that chain on him anymore, do you? I'll get a pair of pliers."

We heard Stavros yelling. Paul spat one last grape seed at Moses, laughed, "Gotcha!" and jumped out of the truck. "I'll talk to Stavros. Give me ten minutes."

Hadn't my eldest son walked to school every day holding a football in each hand so that his elbows were forced out away from his body? Hadn't he walked apelike until at last he could walk that way without the footballs and look tough? Hadn't his dream of manhood been the hirsute and rough, the violent and inarticulate? Does a man dream of being gentle, of giving comfort? I had given him gentle toys and household tasks. But he was a man and he became what he needed to become. I could not imagine what gene had programmed such desires, what throwback. Where did such hormones come from? What lay in those ancient wires? How could we have lived the same millions and millions of years and become so different? My second son had more of me in him, hated contact sports, walked gracefully, built a harpsichord from antique woods. My husband worried for years that he might be gay. He wasn't. He was just more like me. My first son, however, was, at last, all male and all male, it seemed, somehow, now, was very ape, brutish, possibly chimplike, generically ape. Not gorilla. Gorilla as in Moses was too dignified, too aloof, too contained, too silent, too gentle, too wise. "It wasn't you and I mixing it up in the Garden, Moses. But there's a long and riddled story here and I can almost touch it. I know it someplace in the marrow of my own bones, Moses, and you know it also. It's why zoo visitors stand mesmerized before your compound. They know. We all know. We don't know what, but we know. We've always known we are also what we are not."

"You see, John, my questions made everyone, as well as Steven, very uncomfortable. I felt . . . I felt as if we were all in the hold of a ship and I was the only one at the porthole but no one would look out of it nor did they wish to hear what I saw. I told them again and again that if they looked out they would no longer be frightened but they were too frightened to look out. They finally closed the porthole so they wouldn't have to listen to me. Because they are not aware of the broken part that is lost, that I yearn for. Or they are afraid to be aware of it."

"Dear girl, do you hear yourself? You aren't thinking very well. You're thinking in circles."

"She's very upset, John. And she should be. Someone's shooting at her. She's being chased. She hasn't had a good night's sleep or a decent meal."

"Steven, I was in gorilla time last night. It's a puddle, its circle expanding, encompassing more and more until it encompasses the whole and the center is everywhere."

"She's never been exactly linear, John."

"Oh, Steven, I knew there was something else and I've kept asking. There is more. I've caught a glimpse of something deep, something powerful, something beyond myself which is, even so, myself."

"What do you think my wife means, John?"

"What do you mean, dear girl?"

"That I am also what I am not."

"I see," they both said. Neither saw, nor would they ever see. John Banks listened well, but he listened as if he were tracking prey. It had

taken me years to realize his interest in my talk was not sympathetic. Steven's was, although John Banks understood me better. I could fool Steven. I could not fool John Banks.

"Another thing you should know, John. We never liked the same movies. Linda memorized African Queen. She always wanted to civilize Humphrey Bogart. And I wanted to be James Bond. I knew James Bond backward and forward."

"Tell John about the football weekends, Steven. Let's talk about aggressive fantasies. 'Don't interrupt me, Linda. Wait until the commercial.' For entire weekends, Steven sat in a miasma of aggression. I didn't exist."

"Aha!" John Banks said. I could hear his fingers tapping on his desk. "Men like action, Steven. Women like meaningful movies about character, relationships. Perfectly normal, hormonal."

"So who's right, John?" Steven had become more John Banks's sycophant than I had been.

"No one's right, Steven," I answered. "We're different species. It's not hormonal."

"Look, Linda, sweetheart, whatever happened last night—and you have every reason to be paranoid—is upsetting, whether it happened or not. So why don't you check into the Holiday Inn for a couple of days, use the Jacuzzi, eat rich food, sleep. I'll come down and get you."

"No."

"No?"

"Not yet."

"Why?"

"I'm doing this to find out who I am, Steven. But I can't until I find out as well who you are."

"She means what you are, Steven. She may be serious about this species business."

"John, are you trying to make Steven think I'm crazy?"

I laid the back of my hand on the bars. Moses sat upright,

touched my hand cautiously with his fingertips, then very lightly drew the back of his knuckles over mine. I might have been in the Sistine Chapel. He might have been God.

When I returned to the pavilion, Stavros was snapping one suspender against his belly and yelling into the pay phone about my shooting. Diana offered me a cup of coffee, looked into my eyes significantly, which startled me. Stavros grinned, listened to Paul, grinned, nodded, and, in a flurry of quarters, dimes, nuggets of English in a field of Greek, called his brother with the barge, called another brother in Tarpon Springs. "Three thousand! American. Port Arthur. Mayaca. Caloosahatchee. Fort Myers. Tarpon Springs."

He leaned away from the phone. "He wants to know what a gorilla's worth."

I shrugged. He didn't need to know. He was too excited, too sharp-nosed, for me. It would take three days, maybe two. They would drive my truck to Stuart and load it onto the barge. The gorilla and I would fly out of Jekyll Island. We'd meet the barge at Indiantown on the St. Lucie. From there we'd cross Lake Okeechobee. I listened in a soft trance, agreed to everything: places, times, cars, boats, planes. I would cross the lake on the barge, away from the canals, off the highways, so no one would see the truck. Stavros would pick me up where the Caloosahatchee meets the Okeechobee Waterway. The Indian words were musical. The Tarpon Springs run would be the most dangerous but Stavros knew the back roads and would protect me. Stavros nodded yes yes yes to me.

"In advance."

I looked at Paul.

"In case it doesn't work." Paul was embarrassed by Stavros.

"Three thousand," Stavros announced.

"Okay."

IIis face fell. I'd agreed too quickly. He should have asked for more. He called his brother again, yelled on the phone in my behalf. I recognized the as if. "My brother says four thousand." He yelled into the phone. "Okay. Okay." And hung up as if he were angry. There was no brother. There was no choice.

"Hey, you," Stavros addressed gentle Paul. "Off your ass and find Everett. We got a job for him." Paul flushed with embarrassment.

I took my checkbook from my fanny pack. "Let's go, then. Let's go as soon as possible. Half now, half at Tarpon Springs."

"All now. In case."

"Three thousand now. If you want four thousand, two now, two when we get there."

Stavros grinned at my shrewdness. I spoke his language. "Sure. Half now, half later." He was too excited. Why? We weren't after all talking about enough money to buy a new fishing boat or to change his destiny. He snapped his suspenders as he walked from the pavilion over the bridge, hit the back of my truck as he passed it.

His grin hung in the air after he left. There was something too greedy, too hungry, about Stavros.

F O U R T E E N

Everett Everett's airport was a sandy spit above the beach, a World War II hangar, a Cessna 310, an outhouse painted in camouflage brown and khaki, polkadotted with bullet holes, as if riddling surfaces were a local habit and not something I should take personally. An orange wind sock swelled and throbbed in the light trades like the throat of a frog in love. Everett Everett, somewhat lacking in chin, wore a Chem Tech Feed hat, a stiff-starched white shirt, and state trooper sunglasses. A lovely low-rider belly, much like Moses', cantilevered bravely over short, skinny legs. The blazing buckle on his leather belt read "Lake Okeechobee Speckled Perch Contest Second Place." He squeezed a black rubber ball in his right hand, shifted it quickly to his left hand, shook my hand hard, returned the ball to his right, squeezed, apologized, "Trigger finger." He was a young forty, already sloppy and thin-haired on Fat Boy BBQ beans and Bob Evans's sausage gravy and biscuits. His voice was high, his eyes lively, his lips, of all things, rosebud. Everett Everett's mainmost job, he told me, like his daddy and his granddaddy, was game warden. "Family all outlaws, regular gang, before statehood. Hung out in the Florida swamps, hung out with the Seminoles, poached, stole right along with them. Made us all game wardens and Baptists. Must be up to four hundred God-fearing cousins at the reunion every year."

His shirt pocket was stuffed with red-topped syringes. He was not afraid of animals, had rounded up the chimps after Hurricane Andrew. "Mean little sons of bitches, them chimps," he told me. "Eat their own kids if they can." His ears flamed when he looked at Moses in his cage. He patted the syringes in his shirt pocket. Moses snapped his chin at him, grunted two sharp warning barks. Everett Everett leaned forward. "Quick as a snake," he said, and darted Moses' naked arm. And said again, "Quick as a snake. You use one of these syringes on 'gators, one on the chimps I rounded up. So two should do just fine for your monkey. Thirty minutes we can load him." He invited me outside with a jerk of his chin. "Stavros sprung for sandwiches and cold beer. And this." He gave me a plastic bag of Mars Bars with a Christmas tag on it. From Paul.

"I have to nap."

"Here?"

I shrugged.

Everett Everett turned the brim of his cap backward and left, I knew, to polish his plane, tinker with the engine, clean the cockpit windshield. Moses grunted a warning again. I stroked his arm. He would not look at me. I sat beside him next to the cage, rested my head against the bars. Moses listened to something inside himself. His eyes shifted as he listened. He leaned his great back against the bars, near my shoulder, dropped his head on his chest, dozed off. Then he remembered my presence and was alert and alarmed, grumbled.

"Just me, you big cheese, just me." I snorted up the back of my palate to him.

He snorted, checked the gorilla time on his wrist, examined the stuff of his nose, satisfied, lifted my pocket flashlight, smelled it, turned it over carefully, respectfully because it was mine and strange, laid it down where he had found it. He was the most gentle creature in the universe.

Moses wrapped his sausage fingers around the bars and I folded my hand and rubbed across the rough warm leather of his fingers. He begged me for something, reached toward the Mars Bars. I gave him one. He unwrapped it carefully, passed the wrapper out to me, ate the bar slowly.

"My mother's mind was so liquid she couldn't play bridge. Think of the nuances. She was brilliant but she died wishing she could play bridge. She had a sea mind. Maybe I have also. All those stupid stone-faced people at the hotel could play bridge, Moses. My mother couldn't, not because she was stupid but because her mind was so liquid she couldn't think in straight lines. 'Think straight, Linda,' Steven says. 'Think straight. Let's get this straightened out.' You and I don't think straight, Moses. That's why we get in so much trouble around here."

He looked away, moved to the back of his cage, sat in his tub, extended his lower lip, twisted it sideways like a man shaving. He'd stripped his arm enough. Now he plucked hairs from his upper lip. He pulled his lip out as far as he could to search for hairs. When he could find no more to pluck, he sat still, dwelling in his dreamtime, eyes shifting as if he were seeing other places in his head, places he'd been, smells, tastes, frequencies, distances, sounds, starlight, moonlight, magnetic pull, pheromones, electric currents, his own song lines. I think gorillas live in circles, think in clusters. I lay back and closed my eyes, shivered with exhaustion. "Oh, Moses. Where did I go wrong with Steven? Are we truly phylogenetic enemies? Were we always enemies? I know why you're so different. We have different histories. We're different species. But why is Steven so different? Do Steven and I have different histories, different childhoods in the infancy of our kind?"

Moses fumbled in my hair for the antique comb, lifted it out carefully, brought it into the cage with him, tasted the mother-of-pearl ridge, the tortoise-shell teeth, bent his head, held the comb on his head, bent his head toward me, offered me the comb through the bars. He sought my attention with his soft adenoidal snort. I knew what he wanted. It was a simple charade. I pressed against the cage and ran the teeth over the top of his head, down the back of his shoulders. He shuddered. "Where did you learn the beauty of silence, Moses? Where did I learn to talk?" Those dark ancient eager eyes brushed over me. I felt the hot flash of the creation we once shared. "Did we love each other once?"

"Anything's possible." Paul leaned against the door of the truck, whispered.

I flushed with embarrassment.

"I've got medicine."

"Why are you whispering?"

"Stole it." Paul gave me a prescription vial with Stavros's name on the directions. "It goes under the tongue."

Moses came to the front of the cage. "Stick out the tongue, old buddy." Paul stuck his tongue out; Moses took Paul's arm, listened to his watch, stuck out his tongue. "C'mere, Linda. You have to do this."

I stuck out my tongue. Moses stuck out his tongue. "Closer, Linda. Get in there."

I moved closer. Our tongues touched. I reached up and slipped the tablets under Moses' enormous tongue, into that trap of mouth. Moses wiped his arm across his mouth, as if my taste were polluting. Paul laughed.

"Wait until I tell my husband." I rinsed my mouth away from Moses' sight so I wouldn't offend him.

"Get some antibiotics when you get to Tarpon Springs. And watch out. Okay? You'll be okay, huh?"

"Are you trying to tell me something, Paul?"

He looked away. A muscle jumped in his cheek. "Just watch out. Stavros isn't what he seems to be."

"Who is?"

I could not imagine the control Stavros had over him, but the relationship between them must have been other than the true and the good and the beautiful of which he'd spoken so longingly, so enviously.

Moses swept piles of straw toward me, sat up, stuffed the straw under his legs, behind his back, made an oval shallow night nest in his tub, took one final glance at me to make certain I was in place. Moses rolled forward, took one foot in both hands, rolled over, and slept on his side. My arms weren't long enough to mimic him but I curled up facing him. His breath fanned my hair. If Moses thinks in circles, they no longer expand or never did expand. Mine still expand. He stored all the information he needed for his world, except we stole him and took him to our world.

Something was poking gently at my arm, grazing along it, poking. I brushed it away, turned over. It moved over my back. I opened an eye, rolled my head slightly to watch him. He had stretched out on his belly, rested on one elbow, his little legs drawn up under him. He held a long straw and poked at me, sniffed the end of the straw, poked in a new place. He was exploring me, point by point, an acupuncturist, busy, fastidiously poking and sniffing, grunting, examining. Hair, cheek, neck, ear, shoulder, breast, rib cage, hip, thigh, poke and sniff. I lifted my arm for him. Underarm. Nose. I sneezed. He leaped backward, waited, stretched out on his belly. Mouth. I opened my mouth and let him rub saliva on his straw. He stuck his tongue out, tasted the straw. The inside of his gums were bright pink. Then he sat intently pant-grunting at me. It was the longest he'd ever spent looking into my eyes. And I knew what he wanted to know. So I pulled a straw from his cage, pushed it down under my sweats, slipped it across myself, and passed it to him. He sniffed it hard and long and when he had mapped what he needed to know about me, he sighed, took one final glance at me, again rolled onto his back, held one foot with both hands, slept deeply, his old-world cluster, perhaps, forced into expanding enough to contain my new scents. "Maybe, Moses, maybe your circles are expanding again. Maybe this time around they'll include me." At the Masai Mara, from under a dining tent, I had offered a baboon a breakfast roll. The guide caught my wrist, stopped me. "Don't feed him, madam. You will change his habits."

"Linda, why did you lift the—"

"Because I wanted to let some light and air—"

"Why the hell can't you let me finish a goddamn sentence for once in your life?"

"Because I knew what you were going to say." I said this to Steven's back as he walked away from me, slammed door after door between us. "Oh, Steven, how fragile you are, how easily diminished. Dear Steven, communication isn't about finishing sentences. Communication is about passing information. I lifted the curtain because you use that protein shampoo and it molds up on the shower curtain where you splash so I lifted the curtain and opened the window so there would be light and air on the mold. I know what you're about to say. It isn't intuitive. It's just that I can enter your loop at almost any point, given a word or two. You don't need to finish a sentence. Just because you think in straight lines and I think in expanding puddles does not mean I don't respect you. I think in puddles and I get your information faster than I would if I were to think linearly. My thinking process is liquid, like my mother's. Yours is linear, a single narrow one-way path cut across savannahs, over mountains, hacked through jungle, toward such suicidal stupidities as unified field theory and manifest destiny. I think as if I came from moving water, not hard earth. I'm making my own maps. They are not quite accurate to yours. I am, after all, Sister Elizabeth."

"And I'm Howdy Doodie and I'm going out to buy a new shower curtain liner. And *this* one, leave alone."

"*Steven, my friend, let me tell you something about women. Your wife was always looking for patterns. Relating the unrelated. In her own good and kind way she was trying to make whole the universe, to heal.*"

"*Yes, I was, John. I really was. You see, Steven, you* were *the unrelated. I was trying to relate to you, to teach you to love, to show you how to love children, friends, me. It was a struggle. It didn't come naturally. I meant no harm, ever. You understand that, don't you, Steven? That I meant no harm?*"

"*Dear girl, allow me to speak both for Steven and myself. None of us meant you harm. Believe me.*"

"*What are you two doing? Bonding, for God's sake?*"

"Departing!" Everett Everett stood above me.

Moses rose to his legs and arms, wavered. We managed somehow to roll him out, prop him up against Everett Everett, who was, amazingly, strong enough to support Moses' great unbalanced weight. He lifted Moses' arm, dropped it over his own shoulder, maneuvered him toward the plane. Moses' eyes rolled up in his head. We led him toward the open cockpit door of the plane. All was well until the wind sock flapped. Moses tensed, screamed, shook us loose, lumbered away from us, scrambled up a tree. Wind socks didn't belong in Moses' circles.

Everett Everett turned his cap around, winding up to think. "That there's a buttload of monkey. Sure hope he comes down before he falls down." He shook his head. He turned his cap around again, looked at his watch. "We got six or seven minutes. Come look here." He spread a map over the fuselage. "See here. We fly at nine thousand feet, a hundred sixty knots, takes one point fifty-two hours. We fly down the coast to Stuart, then turn here into the St. Lucie. Granddaddy Everett was engineer on the St. Lucie when they dug it, straight as a string. I drop you here at Indiantown. You pick up the barge here where the St. Lucie crosses Highway 710. He takes you around the south end of the lake to Moorehaven. Here Stavros meets you and takes you up through the sugar fields to Tarpon Springs. That away."

"Can't I pick up the barge here, Mr. Everett, at the head of the river in Stuart?"

He swiveled his cap again. I tried not to smile. "I thought about that. Stuart, everybody's sober and Baptist. Indiantown, everybody's drunk and Catholic. Used to be a Christian town. Born and raised in Indiantown. Now it's a honky-tonk picker town. Drugs, beer, shootings. All citrus season they got a graveyard carnival, lights, noise, pickers drunk as skunks. So you can fly in darklike over the lights and into this field right behind my old high school. You land dark. You take off dark. You'll be okay there. That barge should be in just about sunrise. Five-thirty, six."

"Sunrise? Wait a *minute.* What am I supposed to do all *night?*"

He turned the brim of his cap backward. "Just hole up. We'll shoot your friend up good. Shouldn't be no problem."

I tried to keep the fury from my voice. "Isn't it possible for you to leave *here* later so we can meet the barge when it arrives?"

He opened the map again, drew his finger from Cuba to Jacksonville. "You can't fly over the ocean past midnight. Major southeast front coming in. Isobars are real close coming in."

"So fly inland." I did not know what an isobar was. I knew I didn't want to spend the night by the river with a gorilla or, for that matter, without a gorilla.

"Over Okeechobee? No, ma'am. That's a mean lake. You stay off its back. The weather builds up over Okeechobee, you wanna watch out. Hell, nobody ever crosses the center of the lake, boat or plane. They wouldn't find you out there if anything happened. So we gotta head out while the weather permits."

"Goddamnit! What am I going to do with him all night?"

He blinked. Women don't swear. He folded up the map. "Hey, lady, this isn't my idea. Far as I'm concerned, I'm doing it for the money only. And I'm not asking no questions. But an animal like that is better off dead. That naked arm, pulling out his hairs. Ole guy, he's suffering. Just like them chimps, lost, running. He's better off dead."

My resolve shattered like a teacup. I blew my nose and turned away. He was talking about Moses and about myself.

"Okay?" Everett Everett asked my back. "I don't mean you no harm. Stavros says you ain't safe here."

"Sure." I retrieved the peanut-butter cups, the harmonica, the alligators, the nitroglycerin pills.

I stood under the tree and held the harmonica out to Moses. He ignored me, swiveled on his rump, turned to look out at the sea. Everett Everett stood under the tree. "Forgive me, Mr. Everett. I'm very nervous."

"Don't you worry none." Moses swiveled so that he sat directly over Everett Everett's head. "That sure is a buttload of monkey. Sure hope he comes down before he falls down." It did not surprise me that Everett Everett would repeat himself. Everett Everett sent "come, kitty kitty" kissing sounds up to Moses. "Females sometimes respond," Everett Everett explained.

In his Jack Benny gesture, Moses drew his hand over his cheek downward to his mouth, held his chin, cupped it, cupped his elbow with his free hand.

"He's considering coming down."

Moses lifted his chin, turned away.

"Well, one thing, we know he ain't a female." Everett Everett made believe he'd broken his leg, hopped about, fell down, cried out ouches and ows. "Can't fool him no way."

Moses urinated precisely from his limb. Everett Everett, laughing, hotfooted out of range of the splashing waters, hit his knee, laughed. "Wowhee, that's good aim there, fella." Moses folded his arms and looked down at his navel. "Well, you got about three li'l ole minutes before you drop outta there like a piece of ripe fruit."

"It may be the wind sock. Can you dismantle the wind sock, Mr. Everett?"

He lowered the wind sock. Moses watched carefully. "You can tell if a critter's ready to kill or play. This guy is playing. You ever see a kill? I seen a panther at Barley Barber Swamp get a coon. Had his teeth in the coon's neck, just about to kill him, and the look on his face was gentle like a baby's. Innocent. Coon's screaming. Panther looks like his mama's rocking him. That's a real killer. This guy's just horsing around."

Moses looked at his non-watch, slid down the tree, flashed by me, grabbed the harmonica. I threw the alligator at the back of his head to stop him. Without looking, he scooped it effortlessly from its trajectory, headed for Everett Everett, who stumbled into the outhouse. Moses didn't stop to open the door. It splintered around him but he had spent his wakefulness, it seemed, and he collapsed against the inside wall of the outhouse, sliding down it to Everett Everett's cowboy boots. Everett Everett sat on the john laughing, hitting his knee. Then he stepped over Moses, holding that lovely belly of his. "Guess he needs more darts than a 'gator."

Moses rose, barked weakly, rolled over and over toward Everett Everett's back, staggered upright. I laughed so hard, I could barely manage to shout, "Oh, God, Mr. Everett, look out!"

"Whoops. Whoops."

Moses beat Everett Everett on the head with the rubber alligator. Everett Everett laughed as he ran, their tummies leading the way. We all three laughed. Everett Everett's tummy would be solid. If I were to lay my head on it, certainly I would hear Bob Evans's little pork sausages beating out "Dixie" on the drums of Bob Evans's old-fashioned sourdough biscuits.

I tossed Everett Everett an alligator. He caught it as precisely as Moses had. "Get him to chase you into the plane," I yelled.

"Goddamn, I love a gal with a sense a humor."

He hopped into the plane. Moses, eyes screwed upward in laughter, his mouth opened in a play-face, chuckling, hopped into the plane after him. But then Everett Everett swung about, waved his alligator at Moses. Moses stopped dead at the cockpit, backed up. Everett Everett turned on him, waved the alligator in his face. Moses slumped to the floor because the tranquilizer was at last in business. He held his alligator in his great hand, lay back on the floor between the seats, and slept. Everett Everett shook his head. "Well, I'll be. Critters always surprise you. He treats that 'gator just like a gun. He knows it's a weapon. Just depends who's holding on to it. Made it into a game. You ole monkey, you played a joke, didn't you?"

*"I don't know, John Banks. Here we've split your rational universe asunder
and what do we find? Play. It's all quite Buddhist, isn't it? The universe
at play."*

*"Dear girl, dear stupid girl, this is not play. None of this is play.
That's where you're making the mistake. Leaving your husband, leaving
me—those are serious issues, dangerous issues, not playful ones. You're not
going to get away with this, Linda. There's going to be a price."*

"What are you talking about, John?"

"I'm talking about you and me."

"That's over."

*"I'm not going to tell this to your husband, Linda, but I want you to
know that somehow, some way, you'll be punished for what you've done.
That's the way it works."*

"Buttload of monkey. But look there at that li'l ole pecker. Size of
a green bean." We both looked down at a little bald spot and a
tiny peg that was Moses' sex. "Tee-ninier." Everett Everett removed his cap, scratched his head, wondering how such a small
thing could work.

"Dear me," John Banks exclaimed. *"Not a terribly impressive coupling
device, would you say, Steven? I would have thought it would be a great
deal larger. Wouldn't you have, Steven?"*

*"The Jolly Green Giant and his tiny little peas. He must have a great
personality, Linda."*

"Cute, Steven, cute."

Everett Everett strapped Moses to each of the four seats with the
seat belts and bungee cords, turned his cap forward, started up the
engine. As we lifted over the night sea, I realized Everett Everett
could also be a dangerous man. And Stavros. And Steven. But most
of all John Banks. Most of all.

FIFTEEN

So much for Saint-Exupéry, so much for *West with the Night* and the nightscapes that nourish the soul. We flew off the island east into the night. Moses stank in great sour green clouds of fermenting cabbages and apples. I could hear his stomach over the engine noise. We flew low and tight along the barrier islands. Trawlers bobbed in a black rough ocean, winked out.

From under his headphones Everett Everett yelled to me about Daddy Everett when he was warden, alligators, willow trees on floating islands on Lake Okeechobee planted by Granddaddy Everett when he was warden, air boats, quilting bees, and why didn't I come on up front and sit by him where the air was a lot better. Everett Everett's mama hid all the pencils in the house. She made him wear long curls until he was five. The Indians at school all smelled of smoke. He couldn't talk to his mama when she was piecing. She had a quilt over her bed said "Old Quilters Never Die. They Just Go to Pieces." Everett Everett slapped his knee, chuckled, asked me why I didn't come on up front and sit by him where the air was a lot better. I thought about Moses' gestures, Steven's use of his hands as he talks, about Everett Everett's mother's fingers piecing quilts in candlelight. I wondered if women's fine motor skills are part and package of refined thinking skills. And why not? How lonely Mrs. Everett Everett must have felt in her surround of grunt-faced men, what comfort piecing gave her.

"My daddy's Everett Everett. His daddy's Everett Everett. My brother's Everett Everett, and he's got two sons Everett Everett, and one of them has a kid and didn't name him Everett Everett. First time." He shook his head at the family tragedy.

"What did he name him?"

"Don't know. Sure wish we could open a window."

In Moses' defense I explained to Everett Everett the outside possibility that gorillas control the gas in their intestines to communicate in just the way we control the air in our lungs to speak to each other.

He yelled, "Jacksonville."

"And at this very moment over Jacksonville, Moses may not be farting as much as he is philosophizing."

"Makes sense to me. Just a difference between headwind and tailwind. I got a preacher with the same problem."

I laughed. I watched his shoulders shake with laughter until two titanic blocks of air collided around us, caught us in the sudden vise. We bolted, jolted, bucked, and shuddered. Moses stirred, snapped a bungee. Everett Everett tilted the plane toward the sea to find a safer passage. "Descending." Everett Everett stopped talking, stopped laughing, started singing sad and blue, and I was alone, a winged dragon, naked in the night.

"Is this, then," I asked Moses, "the day of my metamorphosis?" Lightning cracked the sky like a thug's rock at a store window. The greater the expanse of night, the smaller my heart. Fear drummed in my head, in my chest, drowned the engine roar. At any moment Moses could wake up, backhand the thin skin between me and the night. The night pressing up against the window felt as lonely as Dino's death.

There was no landscape, no point of light, no tribal fire, no barrier, no limit below, above. The window was black and reflective as a dog's eye. How I longed for the logic of landscape, a road, a bridge, perimeter, parameter, my home, but as I searched I saw, rising up like a dim shape in a faded negative, clouds of dust, volcanic dust swirling around a hut of mud and hides tied over a thick frame. Humped cattle walk slowly under a horizon of smoking volcanoes. Moses is roped to a stake. Behind him two men, laughing, take turns whipping him. "Vero Beach," Everett Everett called back to me.

I've lain with Diggety, his whole warm strong silken back pressed against mine, and I've listened to his breathing until his breath was mine and I felt the engine of his body and his legs pounding, twitching in his sleep, the breath heavy, small yips and barks, as he dreamt running, and I, with my hands on his hips, slipped into his dog dreamtime. I can remember the first time, waking up startled, moments after I'd drifted off to sleep, because I was dreaming of a place I'd never been but that was exactingly, eidetically clear to me. It was a small European street with wooden phone poles set very closely together, a stone fountain in the center of the street, a large and angry shaggy ram at the fountain. A sluggish, narrow band of dirty water ran under an aqueduct. It was a very old stone bridge with arched supports. And I think it was Holland. At least I recall waking and thinking I was seeing Holland and wondering if Holland had aqueducts. I entered Diggety's dreamtime again and again. There were no other places. I only saw that street, the ram, the fountain, and the aqueduct when Diggety slept with me, when he ran in his sleep, dreaming, yipping, his muscles pounding under his silken fur. I wasn't there with Diggety. I was seeing what he dreamt. It did not surprise me that I could see Moses' dreams, the smoking valleys, the salt beds, the cliffs, Danakil, mortal dreams and immortal dreams. I believed that waterfall. I had reason to believe it. Although Diggety had been bred and born near our home, I found on his pedigree that his grandfather on his sire's side was a champion in Holland. Maybe I'd known it and forgotten it; maybe I hadn't. If Diggety could dream his father's dream and I could dream his, why couldn't I dream Moses' dream?

I saw the volcanoes of Danakil. I saw the Danakil dust. I saw Moses being whipped. I thought about Moses holding his alligator in his hand, his harmonica in the other. How I wanted to spread myself over Moses, hide in his bedrock comfort. I reached under my shirt and held my breasts. They were warm, friendly, responsive. When I am deeply frightened or my hands are cold or I am lonely, I often slip my hands over my warm breasts and if my thumbs warm the nipples, it is all mine, the waves of pleasure in my blood, and if my hands were to touch my belly lightly and reach within myself and think of a lover, still, I am all mine. Anyone, someone who needs healing, but no one I know or care to know. Not you, John Banks, not you, Steven, not you, Everett Everett. Possibly my self. Possibly someone like myself. If death is lonely, truth is lonelier still, orgasm loneliest.

"Melbourne." Everett removed his earphones and yelled back to me. "I'll bet you got a nice husband and kids back home."

"Yes, I do." I dropped my hands to my lap and folded them neatly.

"Then you must be the baby."

"How's that, Mr. Everett?"

"I'm the baby and I figure you're the baby. People run away who need more attention. They usually the baby."

"You are wrong in my case. I was the only child."

"Well, I've never been the smartest guy. Good, but not smart. You want a blanket? Behind you in the baggage compartment. Behind the seat. Anybody ever tell you you're one hell of a woman?"

"Can't hear you."

He managed not to repeat himself, sang instead, a soft whining dah-dah-dah the very soul of you, something about gaining complete control of you, and I thought maybe just maybe he was singing to his plane.

"Be careful, Linda. He's coming on to you."

"Don't be ridiculous, Steven."

"Ten minutes ago, Linda, he was the class clown. Now he's singing sad songs to you. Be careful, dear wife. Unless . . ." Steven laughed. "John? Unless she wants a cracker in her soup."

They both laughed.

"Yet again, dear child, yet again the Universal Joint meets the Great Divide. And to what end? This neotenous second-place winner of the Lake Okeechobee Speckled Perch Competition? You expect him to fill the emptiness? Why, you'd be better off with the gorilla."

"Listen to him whining, Linda. It's not a song. It's a fucking mating call."

"You never liked me when I was sad, Steven."

"Sad men attract women. I'm learning that. Sad women do not attract men."

"Where are you learning that, Steven? My sheets aren't even cold yet."

"Not precisely a mating call, Steven, dear boy. You are listening to the original treachery of man. It's a faked infant cry—sad, hungry, in pain. And a kiss is not just a kiss. A kiss is the suckling sound of a hungry infant. Prehominid man was trying to trick prehominid woman to turn her hormones on." John Banks has remembered everything he's ever learned. Could he be a shrink?

"You see, dear girl, this is so subliminal, it's subcortical. This is an infant cry, a prehominid deception, the first lie. Send a kiss to say you're hungry, then roll them over and mount them. Certainly gives new meaning to the phrase turning a trick, *doesn't it?"* Both men cackled. *"The future tense of lie is lay."* They roared at themselves. Pigs. Grown male *is an oyxmoron.*

"Right you are, John. You see, Linda, your Moses didn't fall for Everett Everett's suckling kisses, the baby talk, the broken wing. He pissed on him. Why? Because Moses is all male. Remember, in the movie theater, after the children were grown and married, you heard someone call "Mom" from the rear of the theater and you jumped up and yelled, during the movie, "What?" You knew your kids were out of town. You're just wired for female, Linda. You wanted me to be a grown-up and take care of you. But you also wanted a baby who could turn on your hormones. It's not easy to do both. I think the problem in our marriage is when to be the baby and when to be the boss. Wouldn't you say, John, that's the basis of the imbalance?"

"I don't believe this, Steven. Has John become our marriage counselor?"

"Think what happened when you met John Banks, Linda. A man hurting, a man in trouble, a man hungry."

"Steven! You discuss me with John Banks?"

"Only insofar as it might help him to find you. Otherwise, no."

"Steven, I'm shocked."

"So was I, Linda."

I mimicked John Banks's tones. "Assuming, dear boys, assuming sex comes naturally, why did the male have to make believe he was a hungry baby in order to attract a female? I thought everyone went into estrus and had a great old time. Come one, come all. Why did I have to tempt you with an apple? I was appeasing you, not tempting you."

"John, old buddy, do you feel anyone tickling you?"

"Dear boy, the noon wife is getting dangerous. She's using logic."

"Look, John Banks. You and Steven are both babies and tyrants. You had to tease me out of the water because I was a different species. I stayed in the water because I wanted nothing to do with either of you."

"What water?"

"Maybe I think in puddles because I came from water. Maybe that's why my mother's mind was liquid."

"Jesus X. Christ, Linda. Your mind isn't liquid. It's a sieve."

"And when I came out you chased me around the Garden and ever since then I've been offering you food and taking you to bed so you wouldn't eat me or beat me."

"Now, now, dear girl."

"Are you aware that men are the only species on earth, except for parasites, who do not feed themselves? If I hadn't been domesticated in the household of man and determined useful, which God knows I am, I would have been just one step lower on the food chain. I perhaps am. 'Don't chase boys,' my mother taught me. 'Boys are supposed to chase you.' "

"Odd, Linda, I've always thought and felt I was being domesticated in the household of woman. Odd."

"Talk to her, John. Talk to her."

"Steven, I daresay your wife is in touch with her inner bitch, not reality."

I knelt on my seat and opened the compartment behind me. I felt as if I had no skin. I was holding the blanket in my hand when the plane hit a pocket and threw me off the seat onto Moses. He grunted. I held my breath. Everett Everett struggled with crosswinds. I held myself above Moses gingerly, lifted myself very slowly. One arm to pull myself up to my seat, one leg off his body. He grunted, threw his loose arm gently over my back. Everett Everett did not see me or hear me. It was all right to sink down, to lay my cheek against Moses' cheek, to close the space between his body and my own. Massive bedrock, massive intrusion, gneiss and schist, igneous flame, quaking and quickening of muscle and nerve. "You are earth, Moses. Sweet, solid earth. I am water." His breath lifted my hair. I was safe. His eyelashes blinked, grazed my cheeks, a butterfly kiss. I matched my breathing to his, in and out, as slowly as I could. I sank farther into his being, into his strength, into his peace, until finally, instead of the frail and bouncing plane, I rode him through the night.

"Linda, get off him. Get off him this minute. Goddamnit."

"Dear girl, you'll be fine. You don't have to do that. Really, old girl. Get off him."

"I don't have to listen to you. I'm a mermaid. You are only chimps."

"Them chimps I caught?"

"Yes?" I closed my eyes, rocked with the plane. I lifted my shirt and pulled the gorilla's mouth to my heart. He covered my breast with his great long lips. "What is the difference, then, John Banks, between sensual and sexual? This is not sexual." I felt no urgency, just a warm relief as if I'd wet my bed.

We meet at the edge of the ocean. I will not leave the water. I am small and sleek, graceful and hairless, bright, upright. I sing. He is large and awkward. He grunts and is covered with hair. He mimics my sounds. He offers me leaves and sticks. I sit on the sand. His eyes are gentle. His belly rumbles with pleasure. We taste each other's tongues. We roll over and over in the sand, tickling each other. He is laughter. I am song. But where is Steven? Steven is jumping up and down, screaming at me from the edge of the beach. I turn to him, and away. I follow the gorilla. He is covered with hair and walks beside me like Diggety. Chewing sticks, I follow him, singing. At last we climb into green and rest by the waterfall. Lianas, orchids, the skein of falling water, wrap around me. I float on them in the pool of water. He won't go into the pool. He can't swim. He can't sing. He can't control his breath. He can't play the harmonica.

"I went to see them chimps I caught in the zoo? They tore up a pigeon, live. Tore it right up. Temperamental little bastards."

He took me to his waterfall, silver splashing over us, wove me in the cradle of lianas and honeysuckle vines and orchids, rocked me in the blue-green of his gorilla time.

"Now them gorillas next to them chimps, they had little bunny rabbits living in the rocks in their compound? Never bothered them. Gorillas just sit around, touch each other now and then, just calm and peaceful like they praying. Chimps run around picking lice, picking fights, chattering, grinning, all nervous like, telling each other they won't rip them up, won't steal the food, won't kill their babies. Lies. All that grinning, all the chitter-chatter. Remind me of some people I know. Yup. Little bastards, remind me of some people I know. Plane's steady now. You need a hand? You all right?"

I think amoebic dysentery. I think giardia. I think a buttload of monkey. Stavros said to me before I left, "If anyone stops me and asks about you, I'll tell him I bought the truck and you took off to Cuba with a big black guy." Men hurt women who do weird things. I was doing something very weird.

So I climbed into my seat, tucked the blanket under my chin, around my knees. I took deep breaths, held his touch, his scent, his power around me, penetrated his peace. Everett Everett wiped the interior of the windshield with his sleeve. "Don't trust them chimps a bit. The males bugger each other. Mean little sons of bitches, them chimps. Now your guy, he's okay. Sense a humor."

"He killed a man, Mr. Everett. That's why we're running."

Everett Everett was quiet for a while. Then he said, "Must of had cause. He's not a killer." Then he said, "Come up front a bit."

"That's okay."

"I gotta show you where we are."

A moment by the river with Everett Everett, with his trigger finger and his rosebud lips, would be short and swift and dumb. Aah, dumb. Terribly, abysmally dumb. I hate dumb. But he would stay with me, fill the emptiness of my night with that lovely creature belly, his happy nervous little thing, I'm certain, poking away, nothing serious.

"Linda, which one? Which one? Which one are you talking about?"

"Aah, Steven, I don't know."

He wasn't stupid. He was uncultured. He was strong, considerate, had a good sense of humor. He was gentle and kind. If I were to lead him on, I could get him to stay by the riverside with me through the night. He would be easy. Just until the barge came. He would keep alligators and snakes from my legs.

"Not the gorilla, Linda, for God's sake. He'll kill you."

"I'd rather die by my accident than your intention."

"You don't think your wife's referring to us, do you, Steven?"

I was referring to John Banks, not Steven, but I dared not make the possibility any more real by speaking it.

"Orlando!" Everett Everett changed songs and whined about what he would do if I were far away and he was blue dah dah dah dah. It was true. I could feel the frenzy of a baby's cry bypass my heart and drop right into the hotpot of my hormones. Female animals respond to infant cries from any species. "Look," I heard, "I'm really only a baby. I need care. I won't do you no harm."

"We're a different species, Everett Everett. You *will* do me harm. With cries and lies and wild shiner ties you'll pull me up like a perch." I covered my ears with Steven's ski jacket and tied the sleeves under my chin. I heard the rasp of old Froelich's voice: "The gorilla, he's a gorilla. Your husband you should be afraid of."

So if I really came from the water . . . maybe I'd been an asexual egg layer when I was in the sea. Maybe I had a small, sleek, singing husband whom I left behind. Certainly it wasn't Moses who lured me from the waters with infant cries. Never. Moses has too much dignity. He wouldn't lie. It was Steven as chimp, and Everett Everett as chimp or something like a chimp then, devious, clever, political, hungry, volatile, temperamental.

I sat down on the seat next to Everett Everett. "How are your isobars doing?"

"Closer." He put his hand on my knee, patted it, left it. "Little bit now. That's Stuart. We're turning off the coast and down the St. Lucie. Soon I'll turn my lights off, onc't I see the carnival lights. Now look out there. The moon is on your left. Okay? The river is in the same direction as the moon. Over there head of us up there. See the two lights blinking about three o'clock? Those the Florida Power and Light towers on the south end of the lake. The river's south and east of those towers. It leads into the lake. So keep the towers behind you to the right, the moon in front of you, and head down to the river. Look. River runs east-west, Highway 710 runs south-north. Where they cross is where you wanna be."

"Highway 710," I repeated. "What's that at twelve o'clock?"

He dipped the plane toward a smoky circle of lights. "That's it. That's the carnival. That's Indiantown. See those two blue lights? That's my ole high school, the parking lot. Lost my virginity in that parking lot. They got lights in it now. All Guatemalans, now. Guatemalans and muck. Used to be a white town. Now it's all pickers. Buncha monkeys. Lettuce, beans, melons. Citrus season now. Then they go on up to Alabama, Georgia, work apples in New York, then back to the jungle."

I lifted his hand from my knee, patted it, placed it on his knee.

"I'm sorry. I'm just a hot, crazy guy."

"That's okay. I'm not."

He circled the carnival, descended into its circle. I expected to see Dino flagging us in. "Hold on, now." He shut his lights, then his engine. "Hold on." In literature, there can be no coincidence. In life, we expect it. I looked down on a dirty little carnival, stuck on the edge of agribusiness land without the cleansing benefit of Coney Island's sea breezes. We glided silently into a pinkish hazy smudge, over the bit of town, a few cars moving on the highway, fields of school buses, downward over the last smear of streetlights, the two swarming blue circles of mercury lamps in the school yard where Everett Everett lost his southern virginity. Moses stirred, whined.

"Maybe you can find your virginity down there, Everett."

"Huh? Oh yeah." And he laughed because he had no idea what I meant, figured it out. "Funny thing about virginity. You meet someone like you, you get it back again."

We hit a washboard, bounced in the wake of a thousand plows. "Goddamn, they *always* planted this east-west. Goddamn."

Everett turned his landing lights on. We still could not see. The propeller threw sticks and pulp against the windshield. Black plastic sheets flapped before us, behind us, followed us as we lifted them up from mounded fields.

"God-danged Film Gard. It's all in my wheels and my prop. God damn. Supposed to keep out *weeds,* not airplanes."

"Jesus, Everett."

"Tomatoes. Just tomatoes. Wowhee, someone's gonna hate me in the morning. Wowhee. Hang in there, honey." He was talking to the plane. The plane bucked and stopped, a rubbery sound in its props, in its wheels. I looked out through the plaster of tomato pulp, broken stakes, green. Everett Everett jumped out, wiped the windshield. Moses rose, a seat attached to his leg, tilted, rolled out of the door. The seat bumped after him. I followed. Moses sat on a mound like a man on a long subway ride, arms dangling between his spread legs. He lifted his head and sniffed around him, then, having found something, he stuck his alligator upright between his toes on one foot and his harmonica upright between his toes on the other, ate tomato greens with both hands. We had cut a wide swath of the field, destroyed thousands of plants, torn up miles of the black plastic protecting the mounds.

"Coulda been worse. Coulda been cows."

I unwound strips of Film Gard from the wheels and the prop. They were knotted in tightly. Everett Everett scraped the cockpit windows. We heard shouts. Lights came on, distantly. "Jesus, I better get my ole Dixie ass out of here before it gets shot off." Everett Everett turned me around away from him. "Now look, that there's the river down there. You can smell it."

I smelled nothing. I hoped he wasn't going to kiss me. I hoped I wasn't going to cling to him. He whispered, "Honey, what did you-all do back there with that there gorilla?"

"Nothing. I was too scared to move."

"That's what I thought. That's what I thought," he reassured himself. "Now. Lights back a you, over your shoulder, moon at your left? Smell? There'll be a breeze from up it near dawn. Now listen, honey, the buses pick them pygmies up around five-thirty, six, so get down out of sight about then. Stavros says his brother should be here by dawn. You just keep your eyes on those two blinking lights, keep them behind you on your right. I'll dart him again and I've got more darts for you. Just keep the towers at your back and you'll be facing the St. Lucie. High trees, smell of water, Highway—"

"Seven ten intersects north and south."

"Right." He took his hands from my shoulders. I turned around, stepped backward. "That brother of Stavros? He don't come, I'll know about it. I'll come find you. Daddy Everett would cut off my head and stuff me with wild shiners if I didn't take care of a woman. So you listen. Now this is important. Jesus, I hate to leave you out here. Now look, you get in trouble, you find the railroad tracks and walk them up to the towers, just head for the towers. Okay? They parallel the highway. You get to the power plant, they got a tourist site nobody goes to. It's where I lost my virginity the second time. Barley Barber Swamp, old cypress slough. You go in there and I'll find you. There's shelter and toilets and running water and a boardwalk. You just follow those tracks, the towers in front of you, the moon behind you. You know about snakes and such? Just watch where you walk. Stay on the board-walk up there." He walked toward the plane, swung into it.

"I can't see them in the dark, Everett," I whispered.

"Who?"

My voice was so small. "Snakes and alligators."

"They don't come out in the *dark*. They're out in the sun, them and the 'gators. Anything happens, I'll come in. You remember there." He leaned out of the plane's door. "Everett Everett. I'm your safe harbor. You need anything, anything, any time, I'm your safe harbor."

"Thank you."

"I mean it. All them pickers looking for drugs. You white, they figure you got drugs. Listen, I told you I'm the baby. I never done no wrong, neither. I'll come back. You get going. Get on."

"I know."

"So get going. Get outta here."

I didn't know if he was talking to me or himself. He started his engine, roared up the field in a north-south direction, lifted great strips of plastic but did not entangle his plane. I released the bungee cord and detached Moses from his plane seat. Moses sniffed around him again, jerked his chin at me to tell me to come with him, took my hand, led me down the length of the ruts. Now and then we had to wait while he stuck his alligator and harmonica back in place between his toes. We walked down a dusty road. The moon was not to my left, the blinking lights not at my back. Moses was taking me to the carnival, toward the calliope music, toward the bursts of words: death-defying, thrill of a lifetime, three tries for a buck.

S I X T E E N

Uneasily, under a wheel of fiery stars, between threatening ditches, we made our odd-fellow way toward the streak of north-south headlights on the highway. Something had shifted. Moses now chose to stay close to me rather than keep me with him. He burst forward in furtive sprints, then slowed to vague circles, sniffing the night air often. The air had that close sulfurous smell preceding a storm. I hoped Everett Everett could outfly it, that Moses and I could find shelter from it. The shouts we'd heard from the field drifted closer. Moonlight shellacked the eastern portions of the telephone poles. An incandescent haze drew us toward the center of the town, past fields, small houses, and hundreds of old muffin-roofed school buses in every space possible, their windows shattered, sides dented, stenciled roughly: Fla. Citrus Co-op, Dole, Tropicana, Ruby Red, something in Japanese, Ltd. Hills of packing crates, buckets, baskets, marked the road. A wealth of oranges and grapefruit filled the ditches at the corners where overloaded trucks had taken the turns too fast.

Moses warned me in a series of low-pitched hoots, ended in a growl as two boy-size men came stumbling toward us, holding between them a big fat mama in a bright red spangled dress, walking alongside her as if they'd stolen a cow. They sang sad Spanish songs, fell into the ruts and ditches, lifted each other out. One hid behind a phone pole and peed in the moonlight while the mama waited patiently, stupidly, on the road, and the other stroked her star-spangled behind. The men were tiny, their fingers lemur-long, twice the length of their palms, their legs bandy, too short for their upper bodies, their faces the triangular flat-eyed unblinking faces of ancient Maya, with monkey tails tucked into stiff new little-boy dungarees.

Moses grunted a warning bark as they came near, stood on his fours, elbows out, shoulders high, hair bristling, staring them down. Stunned by the apparition of woman and gorilla, unable to focus, they stopped and stared up at us. The sequined mama broke into tears, wiped her nose with her sleeve. Finally, one announced: *"Está un singing telegram."* He poked his friend with his elbow. "Sing 'Felicidad,' Singing Telegram." And I realized they thought Moses was wearing a gorilla suit. "Singing telegram," they explained to the mama, who nodded blearily. Moses barked, bent his arm in a gesture that only Dino might have shown him, hit the inside of his elbow with one hand, thrust a fist up in their faces. They howled with laughter, rolled on the ground. Moses stood erect, beat his chest with *pok*s that echoed down the road, screamed. They threw their arms above their heads and ran down the road into the dark, screaming also, *"¡Dios! ¡Dios!"* The mama ran after them, her immense behind rolling out fiery stars, another heaven herself. Everett Everett had chosen the right town. We were a hallucination among hallucinations.

By the time we reached the four-cornered intersection that was Indiantown, Moses panted too hard, slumped against doorways. I suspected another tranquilizer would slow the work of his heavily burdened heart. Two patrol cars waited for action in the school yard, interior lights on, each scrub-faced officer reading the newspaper. I backed behind a Latino bodega, into a yard. Moses held his nose up in the air. His half-dollar nostrils opened wide. He sniffed sharply as if he'd been here before, needed to locate something, someone. Have you mapped this place in your lifetime? I don't know your history, Moses. Is a piece of it here?

The rain gathered itself in heavy drops, then in pounding sheets. Lightning split the sky. Cabbage palm metronomes swayed to the beat of the storm, Moses screamed up into its boil, provoked the thunder, slapped at the rain's sting on his head as if he were killing flies. I tried to jimmy the doors of a one-story brick school, a Carnegie library, boarded up, housing authority, liquor store, Assembly of God church. Nothing gave way. We huddled under the metal awning of Fashin Center without the *o*. Moses peeled an orange with his teeth and sucked it. In the wash of rain, the window of the Fashin Center became a glorious fish tank of fuchsias, reds, turquoises, spangled and sequined dresses for little girls and big mamas, blatantly sexy, cheap and shiny, hooked on string and hung on wire hangers like tropical fish. My poor face among the dresses was pale and sickly like the white belly of Steven's Horror House mermaid, faded as if I had been in the water too long.

The police cars pulled away. The carnival lights turned off one by one. The little long-fingered people held newspapers over their heads, scurried from the carnival grounds, yelled, *"Ai, ai,"* as the rain slashed Indiantown. Moses grabbed my hand and pulled me across the highway with such force, I thought my arm would loosen from its socket. He'd locked in to something, another sort of socket, one of memory and meaning. I ran with him as fast as I could. We rounded the back of Funland, USA, from truck to truck, stopped under a lit door before a gatepost grotesque: a peeling, faded painting of a bloodthirsty gorilla. Moses touched the face lightly with his knuckles, crushed the truck door open with his shoulder, snapped his chin at me, took my hand. I followed him in.

Lights clicked off around us. Doors closed. Voices in the dark dropped, vanished. He'd taken me to yet another dark ride, another Horror House. I groped along the narrow track, hands on the filthy walls, hit a pile of greasy packing quilts, a crate of engine oil, tools, yet another pale mermaid with white Rubbermaid breasts the size of the star-spangled mama's. Why are mermaids always white? I followed the track until I came to the train, the grip cars with their leather seats and crossbars. Moses, exploring also, offered me a series of abrupt low-pitched grunts, soft and reassuring. I made the same sound to him, carried an armload of packing quilts to the little train, climbed into the last car. Moses climbed into the car attached to mine. My sweatsuit was soaked. I took it off, wrung it out, draped it over the back of the car, hung my sandals upside down to drain. With great rubbery slaps of cheeks and lips and a rattle of teeth, Moses shook himself dry. I shivered under the greasy quilts, grateful for them. I threw a quilt over him. I could hear the singing of the hole in his heart, the song of his death, the labored rise and fall of his chest. At Tarpon Springs, someone would know how to medicate him.

"I could take you home with me, Moses. You'd be so comfortable. I have a wonderful house. It's a cage, but it's also a house. My house has twenty-seven rooms. I have china. I have dinner plates and tea sets made of money. I have carpets deeper than your fur. You could roll on them. You couldn't sleep in my bed because my husband and Diggety are there. Sweet Diggety is a third of your size and has human eyes like yours. He's in love with me and I with him. He's my dog and I'm his woman and he's suffering now that I've left him and he's waiting for me, sitting under my fur coats in the front hall closet, waiting, brokenhearted as if I'd died. When my husband and I sleep in our bed there's an arc of hostility, an angry flickering circuitry. Diggety lies between us to break the circuit, lies with his ears up, his paws pressed together before him, sphinxlike, and listens to us. No tickles, no pats. He pushes my hand off with his nose. He is entirely purposeful. We are to go to sleep, to be quiet, to lie still, and not fight. When we are finally quiet, I feel the weight change on the bed. Like a mother tiptoeing from her infant's bedroom, Diggety steps cautiously, lightly, over our limbs, slips on his belly off the bed, and pads into the bathroom. I hear him settle his body on the cool tiles, sigh, stretch out. Later, later, I feel him lay his great head on the side of my bed, near my head, as if he were checking my breath. I touch his head lightly from my sleep and he goes back to the bathroom, takes a deep sigh, and settles down on the tiles. Like you, Moses, like you. I could make believe you are Diggety and I am home. Oh, Moses, Moses, are you as lonely as I am?"

Moses rolled over. Beads of his rainwater fell on me as he shook. They were his words caressing me.

"You'd like Diggety, Moses. He has a big head like yours and long black shiny fur and a leather nose and pads. When he was a puppy, Moses, he looked just like you. He's sweet and gentle and powerful like you. He was born with a splash of white on his chest. It's the shape of an angel, the shape of his soul. I stroke it. He licks my face when I do. We kiss, we cuddle. I lay my cheek against his. He bats his eyelashes across my cheek like a butterfly. He takes my hand in his mouth and leads me away from danger, from fallen trees and thin ice, from Steven's loud words. He takes my hand in his mouth, gently, leads me upstairs to my bed, says, "Stay here with me where you are safe. Don't leave me."

"Diggety," I called out into the night because I knew he'd hear me. "Diggety. I want you with me. I love you, my Diggety. I cannot bear to be without you. I'll come back for you. You are my child, my lover, you are my sea heart. Come, Diggety, come." I bit my knuckles to hold back my tears. "You're my Diggety for now, Moses, you big cheese. Or I'm your Diggety. It doesn't matter. We're together and I won't leave you until I know you are safe. I hear your heart crying. You'll be safe soon. I won't leave you, Moses, until you are safe."

Moses sighed. The sigh was caught in a cough. I wondered if his heart was so weak and so stressed that his lungs were filling with liquid. When the children were infants I would open my mouth to get them to open their mouths and then I would stick in a spoon. I opened my mouth. "Moses, watch me."

He rose on an elbow. I stuck out my tongue. He stuck out his tongue. I licked my lips. He licked his lips. I, yes, I touched the end of his tongue with mine. He licked my tongue, the inside of my mouth, my lips, and I snapped the pill bottle open, keeping my tongue busy on his, around his. I bit down lightly, held his tongue in place, laid the tiny pills gently under it. I thought about amoebic dysentery, about giardia, about God knows what would get me in the liver, but he continued to move his tongue over my lips until I withdrew. Then he lay back, tented the quilt over his head, his legs tent poles supporting it, turning it in circles with his feet until the quilt flattened and he slept. It was one of the more brilliant and most stupid things I'd done, French-kissing a gorilla. I listened to Moses' breathing, listened to the heavy hollow drum of rain on the metal roof of the truck, slashing rain and thunder. The earth, on rewind, turns dry. The bushes come loose in my hands. A brown ostrich races away, eggbeating sand. I thought of the policewoman's magnificent seed-queen behind, spewing fertility on a barren land. Is this the trip she made? Here a gully of wet soil and a pool, bullrushes. I eat leaves. It can't be me. I held my head with my hands because it seemed it would burst like a Ruby Red grapefruit in the gutter, and I felt the chill of sleep take me but I could not give in to it because I had to think what I would do if the barge did not arrive. I could do nothing. And finally, deeply fatigued, ashamed, and frightened, I gave in to those racking sobs of childhood, of terrible, unbearable loss.

"What's today, Steven?"

"Tuesday."

"It's liver cookie day. Diggety expects his liver cookies on Tuesday."

"He doesn't know it's Tuesday or Bulgaria. What are you talking about?"

"On Tuesdays Diggety sits by the refrigerator and waits for his cookies."

"Is that what you're crying about? Diggety's liver cookies?"

"There, there, Linda, Steven. Linda isn't crying over the dog. She's crying over loss. She is crying with remorse because she's left you, Steven."

"I'm crying over Diggety. He doesn't understand how I could leave him."

"Come home, Linda. No one understands."

"Marry Celeste, Steven. She'll make liver cookies and frost them in cream cheese and draw have-a-nice-day faces on them and Diggety will love her. Don't marry Melanie. She won't be nice to Diggety."

"Jesus, John, what should I say to her?"

"We'll talk about this, old boy. We'll talk. Don't worry."

Moses didn't like my weeping. He snorted, vaulted from his car to my car, held the rail sides and the seat back with his feet/hands, lowered himself slowly closer and closer until his sumo belly grazed me, then lifted up suddenly, held his sad, furrowed bucket face. His eyes welled up with liquid. If he had ever been a sea creature, he would have salty tears. "Doesn't cry," Mrs. Froelich said, "but his eyes fill with tears if you yell at him." He had no tears, just sadness, a direct and unwavering wet gaze of pain as he looked down on me, examined me curiously, sympathetically. I was a sad little frightened shining sea creature who wept when things were too close or too bright.

I did not breathe, for my chest might touch his. Again he lowered himself in infinitely small degrees, his sad and noble head not inches from my own, his majestic body a blanket of comfort, covering me lightly as if I were eggshell, and I was, and still very delicately, cautiously settled his body over mine so that it touched, a union of sorts, rested a moment, long enough to lick the tears from my face, and then, as if burned by whatever flame leaped between us, some original sin of husbandry, perhaps the original sin itself, he catapulted from the grip car and raced in a maelstrom of banging and rattling and hooting, terrified by what he'd done, horrified, mortified, having tasted me, polluted, raced up the track toward the light and the back entrance. The contact was as terrifying to him and to myself as it was intimate. I touched my cheeks where he had cleansed me. "Moses," I whispered into the dark. "Moses?"

"Linda! Are you crazy? Are you out of your mind?"

"His blood is the same as mine, Steven, but his heart is at the center of the universe and he touched me with it."

He answered from someplace above me, not far, snorting. Desperate to be near him, I pushed the car along the track toward his sounds. I must have tripped a lever, for Moses fell into the car behind me, fell, but too lightly, bounced. "Oh, God, Moses." I touched a gorilla who was dead or stuffed, cold and dead. It was not

Moses. With a squeak and grind, the straw-stuffed gorilla ascended back to the rafters, stored until the next time the train passed over the segment of track. Moses was in the rafters also, torso flat out on a large crossbeam, legs and arms over the side, and beyond him, just above him, against the wall, the stuffed gorilla. Someone, I supposed, he had known once, something, a memory, a smell, that had drawn him to Funland, USA. He probably knew many carnivals, many dark rides, many cages. Poor gentle creature, his career had been frightening people. The garish painting on the outside of the truck might, after all, have been an advertisement for Moses.

"Dear girl, how I've warned you. You take one step over the line into the irrational, suddenly there's no return. And the catch is, you don't know which step it is . . . and you're gone."

"Is it you I'm really talking with, John Banks, or is it my idea of you? Are you and Steven playing left brain, right brain for me? Have I been so inculcated that you both think in my head, that my thoughts are filtered through you?"

I may have slept. I sensed Steven beside me and reached out for him. He was hard and hollow. We had not shared childhood. We had not shared the childhood of our creation. We had not shared ancient places. We did not know each other and would never.

"Talk to me, Steven. Just talk to me."

"I'm reading."

"The hospital called. Sarah did something to her leg at school and is on her way to the emergency room. I think we should drive up."

"Don't be silly, Linda. Wait until they tell us how bad the break is," and then he rolled over and slept while I prayed through grinding teeth over my daughter's flesh and her bones and remembered all the Band-Aids and vitamins and was furious with Steven because he could sleep while the flesh of my flesh lay broken. I shook him.

"What?"

"How can you sleep?"

"It may be nothing. Wait until they call," and dropped away again. And I hated him for how alone I felt and part of me wished Sarah's accident to be a really bad one so I could demonstrate to Steven how unfeeling he was.

"There's no point driving four hundred miles if she just sprained an ankle. Use your head."

"Our maps are so different, Steven. We think so differently. You're so damn good at yes/no, so binary. You don't use your heart."

He folded his pillow over his ears so my anger wouldn't disturb him.

"Oh, Steven, direct from Funland, U.S.A., I forgive you, Steven. All these years we have mistakenly tried to be alike and were so betrayed when we sensed the differences. Emotion is in a separate place in your head, Steven. You keep it in place. It doesn't spill over into logic. You're right but I'm not wrong. We see the world so differently. Then, Steven, I felt betrayed. Now, I still feel betrayed but I understand. I don't use my head the way you use your head."

I was, for example, entirely unable that night in the catacombs of Funland to imagine, struggle as I might, what possible course of action was left open to me should the barge not arrive. "Remember, honey, the light's east, the river's south, the red blinkers are west, slightly north, the road to town's parallel to the river, the highway's crosswise north-south to the river."

"Don't tell me directions, Everett Everett. Tell me things—billboards and traffic lights, things."

"Dear girl, Steven has asked that I go over this species business with

you, clarify some of the issues. The differences between you and Steven, and you and me, for all that, are hormonal. They are not species differences, but gender differences."

"Nope. Moses and I are as profoundly different as Steven and I. The difference between Moses and me is a species difference acquired through separation of one ancestor species into different places, niches, as they say, to create different species. And I think that holds true for Steven and myself. We were cooked in different ovens. We're different species from different places."

"How would you explain the differences between female gorillas and male gorillas, Linda? That is not a species difference. That is hormonal."

"They aren't natural enemies. They don't fight so I guess they think alike. Steven and I fight."

"Well, of course. You both are vastly more intelligent and sensitive than gorillas."

"Then we should have learned by now to be good friends, like female and male gorillas, like Diggety and me. Men and women were raised, formed, molded, forged by different environments, different places. Steven and I come from different places."

"Well, let's go on to this business of men thinking in straight lines, linearly, because they hacked their way in paths across the world. And the business of women thinking in puddles because they come from the sea. All of this has been explained very simply. Hand movements shaped the brain, probably preceded language, shaped language. Men threw spears and rocks with one hand while women made round pots and round baskets with two hands and stayed at home in the circle of their campfires while men struck out. The way we see it, the linear logical pattern of men's behavior is an advance over a primitive, round, clustered, circle pattern of thinking that you and, forgive me, the gorilla share, from which men have, thank God, evolved. If hunting made the man, basket-weaving made the woman."

"Nice, John. Very nice. Just because it's logical doesn't mean it's true. It

may be that you have limited, binary, compartmentalized minds because you trigger-fingered spear-chuckers could only figure out how to use one hand at a time. And my brain is expanded because I used both hands. But if I'm correct, it may be that I swam with both hands and that's what created my superior mind . . . carving it, distributing information evenly, everywhere. It isn't just hormones. The whole blueprint, the wiring, is totally different. It's not hormones."

"She's out to sea again, isn't she, John?"

"She's out to lunch, Steven. Out to lunch."

"I didn't realize you were listening, my Steven."

"Don't denigrate the linear, Linda." John Banks laughed. "The shortest distance between a man and a woman is a straight line."

Steven laughed. "John, old boy, did you hear about the blind man who walked into the fish market and said, 'Good morning, ladies?' Maybe they did come from the sea, maybe Linda's right." I laughed with them and remembered my grandmother and stopped laughing.

"Dear girl, I believe what you are seeing is that we've really surpassed you on the old scale."

How could I explain to John Banks the shimmer of the moonlight grid on the bathroom floor? That the gorilla licked the tears from my face? "Did you say surpass or suppress?"

"Dear girl, we are, as a group, single-minded."

"Narrow-minded, Mr. Banks."

"It's men who are the true geniuses," Steven added.

"And, my dear husband, it's men who are the true murderers and sex deviants."

"Dear one, our minds are more efficient, analytical. Focused."

"No way, John. They're simpler, separate. Your centers don't connect from area to area. You're compartmentalized. That's what makes you dangerous. Your information is locked into place. Ours is diffused. We have more connectors from one side of the brain to the other. You don't compute the subtleties of the heart, the sights, the sounds of the world."

"Dear girl . . ." John sighed. "If we took time to do all that, nothing would get done. Roads wouldn't be built. Cities wouldn't rise in the air. We wouldn't go to the moon."

"Ah, John Banks, so what? I once asked you how one knows what the right place is. You answered, 'One knows.' I've never known. Never known."

"I believe this is a question for you, Steven." John Banks and Steven had rehearsed.

"Yes. Yes, it is. Linda, darling, the right place is home, is here, with me, safe. You are in a dangerous place. No matter what the limitations of home are, no matter what the dangers to your soul, the danger to your life is enormous and you belong here. Think of your self, sweetheart."

"So I'm the can opener, after all. Listen, guys, I thought I was reaching for my self and instead I've touched Being. I'm not going to give that up. I have to work this out."

"Well, I daresay, your little wife is adding courage to curiosity. She's in for it."

"She'll never come home. Never."

"¿A dónde está Tropicana? ¿A dónde está Dole?"

"Ruby Red. Ruby Red. Over here. ¡Aquí! ¡Aquí!"

The long-fingered pickers were going to the trees, their heads wrapped in rags, their arms covered. I heard the horns and rumble of buses, smelled the stink of exhaust, heard carnival voices approaching, near us. Moses grunted, stirred, sprang down next to me almost as I opened my eyes. He shot up the track toward the door and the tawny dawn. I had to get into my sweats and sandals. I ran after him through the carnival grounds and caught up to him as he faltered before a shelf of dozens of stuffed animals, almost as large as himself, all rosebud-lipped, baby-faced, plush—an immense neoteny of gargantuan puppies, pussies, Mickey Mice waiting for life, the first touch of daylight glinting on their glass eyes.

He thrust himself upright, let out a roar, beat his chest. When he saw me, he touched a rear foot with his hand, growled, burst into an attack run, screamed viciously, stopped a foot short of me, slapped the ground between us.

He had lain on me and licked the tears from my face. "Forget it, you big cheese. Forget it. We have to find the river." I put my hand out and touched his, then slipped my hand into his, a hardball in a catcher's mitt. He looked away, yawned, and I knew the attack was over. I had approached him too quickly, had become one of the odd animals. I jerked my chin toward the exit, led him back to the alley behind the carnival, down into the yards toward the St. Lucie.

He ran with me through backyards of shacks. Dirty sheets were nailed over broken windows and torn screen doors. I heard a baby cry. Forgotten cars, overturned boats, old engines, cement mixers, broken buses with fresh cardboard windows, palm trees. Chained dogs stirred, growled, cowered. Chickens, chicken wire, rust and ruin, a hill of liquor bottles, a pile of turtle shells, a home-drawn street sign: Toughluck Lane. Moses pulled a bunch of bananas from a tree, tucked them under his arm. "*¿A dónde está Tropicana? ¡Yo, yo, Tropicana!*" From the step of the Deliveries Only door of the Kountry Kitchen, Moses plucked a carton of Half 'n Half. We ran through a hammock of oak, a twist of primrose willow, a border of cane, barriers of packing crates, an alligator on a rope, tin sheds, burning rubber, bus diesel. Moses grunted with pleasure, a soft purring grunt, a reassuring stay-together-we're-all-right grunt. Moses was having a grand time.

"Did you . . . did he . . . Linda, have you screwed the gorilla?"
  "Steven!"
  "Well?"

"I think John Banks is hunting me and I think he's going to hurt me, to punish me because I left him."

"Don't be ridiculous."

The St. Lucie was empty, amber at my feet. The steamy broth of morning hung in the canopy of trees. An alligator floated near me, only its teacup eyes above water. A soft-shelled turtle the size of a bicycle tire flipped sideways off the bank. I could hear the putt-putt of a small boat but could not see it. Faint peach light tinged the eastern end of the river where I strained my eyes looking for the barge. I would not let myself think what if. I sat on the sloped pebbly concrete of a launch where nothing from brush or water could surprise me. I heard the crush of Moses' feet behind me, watched his dark reflection in the water, holding his Half 'n Half bottle in one hand, his bananas in the other, leaning over me, opening his mouth, enveloping my head. I watched without fear as I disappeared in the amber water, until he'd swallowed my head for as brief a moment as he had lain on top of me. It was another intimacy, another test. This time he was not afraid of what he'd done. This time he patted my head and sat down beside me, grunted with pleasure, drank his Half 'n Half, stripped his bananas carefully with his lips, ate slowly, threw banana skins into the canal. An eagle oiled his feathers on a dead tree. Two wood storks hopped from treetop to treetop. Moses pulled tree snails from the sides of old oaks, sucked out the muscle, ate clusters of eggs. He foraged in the grasses, returned with a green stalk torn from a palmetto, soft dark fruits of a custard apple tree. He spread his treats out around him, looked up at me, did not offer me any, lay back, his legs crossed up in the air. He was an African emperor in black silk wrinkled gloves, eating grapes. With thumb and forefinger, Moses chose one delicacy after the other, dropped each into his vast mouth. The alligator lifted from the water and dragged its long prehensile self up onto the far bank.

Moses rolled over onto his belly, rested on his elbows, foraged among his treats with his lips. Birds rose in threes and fours from the trees above us—great herons and lesser herons, blue and white, huge wood storks, wing spans darkening the sky, the creak and shiver of their feathers like ship timbers in a rough sea, thin-throated tin-lizzie honks, a nation of lifted wing, clamor, flap, all pipe and trumpet, horn and honk, an Audubon abundance, a wilderness not three minutes from the delivery door of the Kountry Kitchen, from the pay phone at the front door of the Kountry Kitchen, from Steven's morning voice.

"I called to find out how Diggety is doing."

"He's limping."

"Are you giving him C's?"

"You didn't leave a note."

"Give him four thousand, two in the morning, two at night."

"Where are you?"

"It doesn't matter where."

"All right, Linda, have it your way. I can only do so much."

"Don't forget Diggety."

"Sure, Linda. Sure. Listen, he hasn't hurt you, has he?"

"Who?"

"The gorilla."

"No."

"Have you done anything with him?"

"Like what?"

A compact car pulled up behind me. An old waitress holding a ring of keys walked toward the front door of the Kountry Kitchen. Moses sprinted at her in an attack run, slapped the concrete in front of her, screamed.

"Singing telegram," I shouted over to her.

"Not bad," she allowed. "Not bad." She watched Moses' antics politely, patted the oversize polka-dot bow on her ponytail, and turned to the box of doughnuts at the front door, apologized. "Gotta shake the dew off the old kidneys. Coffee'll be up in five minutes."

We returned to the St. Lucie. The sun sent its first bronze blush up the river, tipped the horizon, rose up in a red and gold coronation, a triumph of silica bead, dew drop, glint of rain, speck of mica in the sand, trembling, all of them, in the new creation. Moses scratched himself laconically with a palmetto frond, scratched his belly, under his arms, his crotch, poked me for a few good measures. The buses rumbled off to the orchards. The little long-fingered people were returning to the trees. Two old black men in a fishing boat puttered up the St. Lucie, touched the brims of straw hats as they passed us.

"I think in puddles because I came from water."

"Dear girl, you are as earth-born and -bound as the rest of us. Don't be silly."

"I know I came from water."

"Explain that one, Linda. John is having trouble understanding you."

"I can't, Steven. I'm sorry, John. It's just something I suspect."

Perhaps the cow in Tasmania wasn't drowning. Perhaps she was trying to get back into the sea so her newborn child wouldn't be eaten. Perhaps I too had been on the food chain, a small, pale, and gracile ape, who lived near the marshes, the swamps, along riverbanks, with tender-fleshed infants whom the chimps stole and ate unless she escaped to the water. "Mean little bastards," Everett Everett said. "Eat their own kids if they can." I watched the parfait tinge of pink flame up into a turquoise-shot sky and then I saw the barges slipping up the river, slipping along before the sun as if the sun itself were pushing them toward me. Okay, I said to no one. Okay.

S E V E N T E E N

Lady of Shreveport was the sort of harbor tug made heroic in children's stories, once red, now gray, snub-nosed, its sides scraped, its windows streaked with salt and dirt. A winch-and-cable system attached one of the two barges to the tug. The second barge was attached to the side of the first. My truck, unconvincingly camouflaged in fishnet, was tied down on the outside barge. Moses stuck his alligator between his toes on one foot, harmonica between his toes on the other foot, the bottle of cream in a hand, leaped from the lip of the concrete onto the barge, into the truck, laid his do-not-disturb alligator in front of his cage, climbed into his tub. I heard him panting heavily. I stepped onto the barge.

"Hey!" the pilot yelled at me. I turned. He hit his chest with his fist. "Andre."

"Okay, Andre." He was not Stavros's brother; he was not Greek. But it was my truck on his barge, I assured myself, and my things in my truck, with the welcome addition of a package of J. C. Penney undershirts, two pairs of nylon neon orange shorts, a pack of Fisherman's Friend, and a bale of fresh hay. "Good Paul. Good Paul."

Andre walked stiff-legged in the same strut that I'd learned too well from Moses meant trouble. He wore a knit cap, wading boots, an army-issue khaki sweater, shrunken and tight, gun straps on the shoulders, moth holes on the chest, and the unmistakable threat of an erection in his pants. The sweater's ribbing rose high above his belly button, his pants well below, and right down the exposed rubber white belly flesh, a thick curly mean streak, too pubic, menacing. He was Cajun, I would guess, and smelled of fish, wet wool, garlic, sweat, bourbon. I did not offer him my name. He scowled, started his engine.

I changed into Paul's clothes, sat cross-legged on the deck in the sparkling grace of light after a rainstorm, and combed my hair dry with my fingers. Our wake sucked and rushed between rotted launches and pilings. Blue herons flapped ahead of us, hopscotched on rubbery legs up the marly banks. I heard the deep call of pig frogs, saw the cool perfection of a red-shouldered hawk snatch a gar from the water before us. Fish flashed, mocked the graceless effort of the alligator on land. Turkey vultures warmed their wings along the banks, lifted and rose in the thermals. An egret examined me in a lazy dip. From a water orchid center, dozens of gar, like light, exploded in a silver circle. We moved slowly up the river toward the lake. The day climbed behind us on shoals of light.

Two round-bellied, pink-faced men in a lustrous sportfishing boat, shark-shaped, swivel-seated, frosted the water in languid V's as they zipped around us. One leaned over the side, shouted between his hands, "You the gal with the gorilla? Everett . . ." The words were lost in the engine noise. Everett. I waved at him. He circled again, slowed. "Kin," he explained by way of introduction. "You okay?"

"Fine," I yelled. "Both fine." And dared to blow a kiss for Everett Everett, who'd sent an Everett or two.

He swung around and yelled to Andre, "They got manatees at Mayaca." Andre scowled. The Everetts circled us again, lifted their shark nose, and roared down river. Kin. Everett Everett watched over me. I was not yet safe. But I was not unsafe.

Moses sat in his cage, breathing croupy bubbles, rubbing a piece of burlap rag between his fingers, his big bucket face furrowed with concern. I held a cup of apple juice through the bars. He drank dutifully as I held the cup, listened as I told him about manatees and mermaids and sex-starved sailors making love to them in the shallows, that male manatees had six-foot members. He sipped and looked over the rim, locked his eyes into mine in a weary gaze of pain and beauty, a question.

"We're okay, Moses. You'll be with other gorillas, not the skins of old friends. By tonight, I promise."

With the soft gargle of an old man lying down in bed, Moses cleared his throat, took his tub to the back of the cage, lay down, put his tub over his head, turned over so that a shaft of light fell on the silver of his back. The light etched the horizontal stripes of the whip, the old wounded flesh of his dream, of the dust at Danakil, the humped cattle, the stake, the laughing men. I saw his dream.

"Oh, Moses, what have we done to you? Come here. Come."

He brought his tub to me, sat in it, leaned against the cage, his back to me, let me trace the history of the wounds across his shoulders. He shuddered under my fingers. "Your dreams are mine, Moses. You big cheese, you wizard beast, your dreams are mine." I kneaded his spine with my knuckles, stroked his neck, each stroke smoothing the horror of his exile, his torture, his confusion in our terrible world.

"The dust of Danakil, the rift cliffs, the shimmery salt beds, the cauldrons of natron and smoke, the obsidian man fishing at the lake, and the waterfall, always the waterfall. Are you taking me on a trip, Moses? Your history and gorilla history, wanderings, round and round, from the sea to the desert to your jungle?" I rubbed his chest so he could sleep. "The walk's almost over, sweetheart. You rest. You sleep."

"What did I tell you, John? She's fucking the gorilla."

"Have you . . . Linda, have you? Jesus. Have you?"

"Have I what, Steven?"

"Have you slept with him?"

"Next to him."

"Do you want to?"

"I touched his tongue with mine and got him to taste my mouth so I could put nitroglycerin pills under his tongue and I couldn't—"

"That's disgusting."

"I'm confronting the dark and unspeakable, Steven. Disgusting is not an issue. Also I'm trying to keep him alive so Froelich doesn't stick you with a huge lawsuit for damages."

"If it's a choice between letting him have a heart attack, Linda, and French kissing a filthy beast, as far as I'm concerned . . ."

Moses wrapped his fingers around the bars and I drew my knuckles slowly across his. He passed a handful of hay to me. I shoved it back to him. Moses tossed the straw on his head, on his neck. Then he passed me his burlap rag. I passed his rag back to him and he rolled on his back and tossed it up in the air with his feet, much the same as he'd done with the packing quilt. I thought he might have bounced a ball on his feet as his circus trick. He lay on his belly, knelt on his elbows, eyes crossed with intention, carefully pushed straws aside, one at a time, back and forth, until he found something else for me and passed it to me: a tiny piece of Mars Bar wrapper. I took it, offered it back to him. He shook it off with his hand. I didn't know what else to do. He pig-grunted, screeched, looked hard at me, put out his hand. Oh. I offered him a grape. He wouldn't touch it. How can we judge their intelligence when we don't know what they know? I gave him half of a Mars Bar. He unwrapped it fastidiously, tore off a corner, returned the rest of the wrapper, ate the candy. When he was finished he searched around in the straw for another coin to trade. His trading face was sincere, honest, eager, earnest, a straightforward clear gaze into my eyes. For the remaining half of the candy bar, he offered me the second piece of wrapper. We were not trading. We were doing symbols.

We sailed under a concrete bridge into the bowl of water that was Port Mayaca. A few fishermen waited in glossy boats, peaked hats turned backward against the wind from the lake. A couple in white pants and blue-striped shirts stood on the deck of a three-tiered yacht out of West Palm Beach, searched the water with binoculars, focused on me. A part of me I hated wished I could dazzle them with my ring so I didn't look like the cheap girlfriend of the tugboat pilot. I was, after all, who they were. A life of passion and luxury comes unknit so fast, one wonders if it were ever whole.

The locks were formidable, an army engineer's dream of punishing the lake for killing thousands of early settlers in the hurricane of 1926. To the right, far up—level, I suspected, with the lake—was a government-issue clapboard harbormaster's house, a small white forties house with a swing, a dog, a barbecue. A very old live oak, once a landmark on a sultry overhung oxbow, now shaded the harbormaster's lawn. The banks across from it were buttressed with modern walls of rip-rap boulders. Above the rip-rap, manicured stretches of grass rose to the lip of the bowl. There, on an unpaved road, three black men leaned against the hood of a rusted Bonneville with long bamboo fishing poles stuck out its rear windows. Shading their eyes with their hands, they drank from paper bags, watched the white folks who watched for the manatees, the water separating all of us.

At the top of the locks, in front of the house, two small children in plaid pajamas tossed lettuce and white bread into the water until their mother called them back inside. The couple on the yacht put their binoculars away, moved their boat aside for Andre's unwieldy crafts. The manatees had left. The locks would open.

Andre gestured to a mooring dolphin empty except for a pelican. "I takes first this boat and this barge and comes back for you."

"No. Me first."

He scratched his head. "Better here. People. No wind, no trouble. Sit. Wait. Twenny minute."

"No."

"I leaves you here. I takes first barge through. I come back twenny minute, maybe thirty."

Andre was confused by me, scratched his head, didn't know how to talk to me, tried harder, orchestrated his words with his hands, large patting motions, telling one of us to calm down and behave. "The current she is worse on other side, waves. Here is calm, nice. You sit and be nice. Sit." One thing my host didn't want was trouble. Andre pulled off his sweater and pants to what might have been khaki trunks, what might have been underwear. The pubic strip went right up to his chin. He pulled on a scuba mask and fins, rolled over the side, tossed cables onto the barge,

climbed aboard, pinched my rear end, for want, I thought, of
words. I looked at him blankly. He nodded and turned away,
reassured perhaps that I was a woman and he was a man and
everything was okay, his pinch a question, an animal repartee. Pig.
Throwback pig. Andre tied my barge up to a mooring dolphin,
dropped his flippers and mask near me, put his sweater and pants
on, hopped over the winch to his tug, and chugged away with his
one barge before him, moved slowly away from me, between the
mooring dolphins, an audience of pelicans, the sportfishermen, the
arrogant three-tiered yacht from Palm Beach. I disliked him leaving me stranded more than I disliked him.

A red light stopped flashing. A long buzzing signal announced
the clearing. The huge black and yellow striped curves of steel
opened slowly. Andre steered his barge into the lock, cut his
engine, jumped over the winch to push-pole the barge off the sides,
straightening it in the holding area. When the gates closed,
another signal split the air. A red light flashed, a signal blurted.
The snub nose of Andre's tug passed through the lock, lifted. The
yacht went through. The fishermen went through. The Bonneville pulled away. The pelican never moved from his mooring
dolphin.

I waited on the edge of my barge, my feet dangling in the
water. A choppy breeze carried the acrid smell of burnt sugar,
rocked the barge, brushed my forehead. Moisture from the swamps
and the saw-grass rivers of the Everglades beyond us rose toward
immense shelves of cotton bale clouds high above the lake, great
brilliant white rolls of power piling up for the afternoon's storm.
Moses sat in his tub, dozing, his head on his chest. Now and then
he belched to me and I belched back. I could not help thinking
about the whip wounds, about the fork of the crutch Dino had held
at his neck, about God knows what cruelty we'd inflicted on him.
Moses came out of his cage to be with me but would come only as

far as the truck. He sat in its shade, watched me with his furrowed, worried face. He feared the water but dreamed of a waterfall. "Do you fear water the way we would fear God? Are you in awe of water?" I took his hand, tugged. "Come on, you big cheese. Come sit with me." He barked a warning bark, backed up, took his place by the truck. "Did you really leave the savannah and go to the jungle, Moses? Is that the dream you've shown me? Were you afraid to go into the sea? I think I left the land and went into the sea. When I lie in the hammock, Moses, between two monkey firs in my backyard, Diggety moves under me, back and forth, passes under me, lifts me, nudges me, rolls his back along my sides, pushes me sideways. It is as if we were in the sea together. I close my eyes and make believe we're swimming. Do you know, Moses, that Diggety is terrified of his own puppies but if a baby comes to the house he does nothing but lick its feet and hands, will not leave its side? Why does he prefer human babies to dog babies? Do you think, perhaps, he was our nursemaid in the bullrushes? Our guide in the sea?"

Clouds piled higher. The sun crept up the sky like a lion, tawny, brutal. More than twenty minutes. More than thirty minutes. Sun-splintered light in the bowl glinted, flashed, fractured the horizon until there was no horizon and everything that was up was down, the clouds in the water, the water in the sky. From the corner of my eye I saw a dappled movement. The blank spot in the water the size of my Suburban became a manatee, following her, the size of Steven's Porsche, her calf, swimming alongside the barge, barrel rolling, rubbing the barge, looking up at me each with one small eye, a puppy Cabbage Patch doll face, someone from the Macy's Thanksgiving parade, dirigibles floating in water, their wizened arms hanging downward, their little faces approaching tentatively, sun-dappled, the signature of propellers along the mother's back in a geometry of pain. With the lightest flip of her tail, the mother was off to a murky stretch of water hyacinth and returned with a stalk in her mouth. The baby pushed a piece of bread toward her mouth with her flippers. Her mouth was a vacuum cleaner, without fangs, without jaws, without fear. Without fear. They had nothing to fear but the cruelty of men. The mother's tail had been shredded by a propeller.

Steven sighed. "I've never been cruel to you."

"Steven, our brains are so different, our perceptions so different, you wouldn't know what cruel is. It could be a smirk when I park the car too far from the curb, a finger tapping on a tabletop while you wait for me to make a decision about the menu."

"Manatees rub up against propellers, cuddle boats, suck the engines. It's not all men's fault."

"I know. I know. Don't I rub up against the propeller? Don't I suck the engine? You've seen my scars."

They nibbled my feet. They chirped and squealed and enticed me with somersaults, half gainers, belly rolls, arching, stretching. If the sky could be in the water and the water in the sky, certainly I could pull off my clothes, put on the mask and fins, roll into the sun-fractured water a million years ago, five million years ago, down, green, filtered, streaked. How was it that I, so terrified of the earth's night, could drop so easily into the water's deep? I was no longer what I was, but what I had been was a sea creature, my body, my genes, my hormones, my brain, my perceptions, had to have been molded by the gentle sea.

"Listen, John Banks, the gorilla thinks in wholes, tight dense deep clusters that do not expand, land-locked circles. He was never in the sea. I think in puddles because there, in front of me, is what I was."

"She's convinced of this water business, John."

"Certainly, dear boy. And apes don't swim. But how it impacts on your marriage is the real consideration."

I could make out the scarred back of the mother hanging near us while her calf nibbled at me, rolled on its belly, glided upside down. I scratched its belly. Watching cautiously, faced away from me, the mother snapped her tail, steered herself around toward me with her flippers, then approached, weightless, wonderful, pressed against me. She swam in front of me, looked back at me, swam around me, inspected me, touched my knees with a flipper. I felt the delicate bones of fingers inside.

I rolled on my belly, let my arms float in the water. They nibbled at me, ate bread, sucked up my skin, around my face, exploring me, rubbed against me, floated off, sank down, rose up like balloons. With her strange and wizened flipper/arms the mother stroked me. If Steven had done this, I would never have left his bed. John Banks was incapable of such tenderness.

"What were you before you were this? Cows? Dogs? Mermaids? Those were graceful arms. Did you weave and sing? Are you the mermaids? Was I? You stayed in the sea, didn't you? Why didn't you go back to earth? Why did I? The earth is so hard." I folded my hand over her flipper hand, hand such as it was, such as mine would have been if I had stayed in the water.

I looked at my hand, at my fingers, at the skin between finger and thumb. The sun shone through my hand, and for a stunning instant, I saw the webbing between my thumb and forefinger, pink and translucent, a quarter moon of vestigial skin, and it burst in my head, lit up my primitive tracks. One sees God, one sees the Mother of God, one sees one's self. I knew something. I didn't know the details, but I knew something big. A part of the sea in the pinch of my thumb, my remnant, my history, my truth, my sea-sign, the piece of my puzzle, my place.

"Let's get this straight, dear girl. If you have webbing because you were in the sea, it follows a priori that the gorilla doesn't have webbing because he was in the jungle, so why don't you just look at his hands?"

The manatees surfaced to breathe, sprayed me with water, dived into the dark. The mother surfaced with an algae green board in her mouth, released it, let it bob between us. The mother swam up to me, held my face between her two flippers. "I was with you once," I said. I held her head between my two hands, and for one brief watery moment we saw each other, and then she released me, sank downward, sank sank into her green void, and was gone. The green board bobbed where they had been.

"Steven, remember the cow in Tasmania? I don't think she was drowning. I think she wanted to take her baby back into the water before it became someone's pastrami. I think she remembered that the sea was a safe place. Horses became hippos and cows became whales and dogs became seals. Why do I hear Diggety barking?"

"He misses you. You've broken his heart."

"Tell him I am stalking the core of myself in the hope of becoming more human. Tell him my legs straightened out, grew strong as I swam, began to grow together, but I didn't stay long enough for them to become a tail."

I knelt near Moses at his place against the truck. "Moses, Moses. When I was in the sea, you were walking up the rift to your waterfall, weren't you?" I held Moses' gray-soled feet. "I returned to the earth, sleek and streamlined, long-legged and supple in my form, a swimmer, my nose shielded with bone, my fat in my buttocks for floating, my breasts full for floating and feeding, my backbone straight." I touched the half-dollar nostrils that could never close underwater. "You could never swim, Moses, never. I stood upright. The water taught me to walk, Moses. The water taught me to sing. I held my breath and sang. My body naked, my hair long, some senses precise, some almost gone. I wept tears to take the salt from my body. Did I learn to sweat salt? I went into the sea four-legged. I came out two-legged. I was horizontal in the water. I was horizontal and vertical in the shallows and, finally, vertical on the land. I walked upright in the marshes, then on the beaches. Do you see, Moses? The way your peace was formed in your head, the way you have the peace and abundance of the jungle in the marrow of your bone, that way, I carry the gentleness and abundance of the sea with me. It's like growing up very, very rich." I looked at the fold between his thumb and forefinger. There was no webbing, none at all.

"Diggety, listen. The way you stand in the water on your rear legs, and offer me your paws, and we dance in the shallows? Enough of that, Diggety darling, and you'll walk upright. And if you ever learn to control your breath, you'll be able to speak. Okay, Diggety?"

E I G H T E E N

"Let us say, dear girl, that on this pathetic bit of evidence we've eliminated the gorilla and proven, perhaps, that he was not ever a swimmer. But let us also not forget that I am also human. I am also upright. I am also naked. Did I not swim in the sea as well?"

"No, not as an ape, much earlier. We all began in the sea. I returned to it. I don't know why you are so like me, but I do know that you are so different because you didn't return to the sea. We both left the sea millions and millions of years ago. We came out together. We probably lived peacefully in an abundant world. But when the earth turned hard and barren, hot and parched, I went back in. We were ancestor apes, generic. You remained on earth. I was molded by the sea currents, you by the rough

rock and hot crust of a dry and barren earth. A hard place. My brain is an
utterly different physical machine."

"Let's get this straight, Linda."

"See? Let's get it straight. You're always getting things straight, aren't
you? That's how your brain works."

"Words, Linda."

"Words are tools, John. They have feedback. They can change your
brain and other people's brains. They are the ultimate tools. Women are
much better with them than with your screwdrivers and forklifts. We're
trying to domesticate you with words. That's why you don't listen."

"All right, all right. Let's get back to . . . uh, our line of thinking. We
all came from the sea, did we not?"

"Yes, but I went back in without you." I rolled over on my belly and
drifted into gorilla time. I could feel the marrow of peace in my own bones.
"This is the piece of puzzle I've sought. It's the water I've dreamt. The moon at
my window told me, but I couldn't hear. Oh, Steven, my sea self was the
missing link."

Moses growled softly, rubbed his great smooth hands up and down
my body, smoothing it, rolled me over, smoothed me here and
there. His hands were priests' hands, hands that had never worked,
never killed, never struggled. I hoped I wouldn't have an orgasm
because it would be an impossible secret to keep. "I came out
almost human. The manatee never returned to land. Moses never
went into the sea. But I was a dusky, hairy little ape and I went in
and I learned to sing and swim and came out sea pale like my face
in the tropical fish tank, faded, white."

"Notice her nipples, Steven. She insists this is not sexual but sensual. I say
her nipples are hardening. Linda!" There was alarm in John Banks's
voice. I'd never heard alarm before. "I think you better roll away from him.
What if he smells something?"

"Remember once, John, on a beach, at night, you tickled me under my armpits and I came and you laughed at me?"

"It's the sun, Steven, old fellow. She's had too much sun."

"You know why I love to have my back rubbed, Moses? Because that's where the action used to be, back in my old estrus days."

Moses spread the lips of my mouth, picked things from my teeth, pulled at my tongue, sniffed, touched.

"Linda?" Steven approached me as tentatively as the manatee had, as if I were truly another species. "Are you saying you went back into the water without us?"

"Steven, dear boy, don't try to follow her thinking. Stay in control here. Remember, she said she thinks in puddles and we think in straight lines, earth lines. She is about to conclude that we weren't in the water with her at all, that we aren't her natural husbands. And that is dangerous. She's really off the wall, Steven. We should get her home and give her time to rest. I mean, your wife thinks she is the missing link."

"I don't think she'll come home, John."

"Chin up, old boy. She'll come to her senses. Of course she will."

"Do you think she's in love with him?"

"The gorilla?" John Banks laughed. "No more than she's in love with your dog. I daresay, old sport, you're both going to need a little rest."

"Look, Steven, look at the sun through my pinch. It looks like the shell of my mother's cameo, doesn't it? So delicate, so mortal and immortal at the same time."

"She's very fatigued, disoriented. I also think she's taking this business of being a different species than we are far too seriously. I'm of the opinion, old boy, that we have to change our tactics or we might lose her altogether."

"What I think may make no sense to you. But it's my own map, my own territory. I don't expect you to share it in any way. I am Sister Elizabeth."

"*I have a brother-in-law with webbed toes, John. Men are webbed also.*"

"*True, Steven, and we have, among other things, nipples. Explain that, Miss Link.*"

"*Those are* my *nipples you're wearing, guys. And my webbing. I'm the template. You're the rough copy.*"

"*Listen, Linda, sweetheart, the time is now; the problem is here. I want you to come home. I want to help you.*"

I held my hand up to the sun, looked through the web as if I could see the other side of myself, and tried to remember. "*Something happened, Steven. Something that is still with me, that separates us from each other, that keeps me from our home. I've always wondered why you never liked me to touch you, why you felt I talked too much, why you could load the station wagon so well when we took a trip, why you would get lost in the woods even if you had a map, why I could lead you out. My brain is entirely different, my perceptions, my rules, my ways, my world. We have lived together in separate universes, parallel. All this time. The can opener.*" *I felt a weight of stone in my chest, a terrible sadness, the lonely presence of truth, the can opener, the soap.*

"*Why, dear girl, aren't these just gender differences?*"

"*Because it goes deeper than egg laying, too much deeper. It's in the blueprint of brain. It doesn't come from the addition or subtraction of hormones. The brain drives us and we're going in different directions in different machines. Redefine gender. Redefine species. You men keep organizing the universe. It doesn't always fit your plan.*"

"*I daresay you are wrong. I know there are anatomical brain differences, but I say it's gender.*"

"*So what, John. I say it's species. I say it's history. I say it's place. I say place shapes nature and my nature is different from yours. Too different. I don't care what you call the differences. They are, whatever you call them, irreconcilable.*"

I sat with Moses at the side of the truck, put my hand in his, told him about spring, about the fireflies on my lawn, a million of them sprinkled over the wet grass like the stars above them, one for each star. I told him about the smell of rain-bruised peony petals, about the Oriental poppies that opened when the peonies did, about the thin purple perfection of the Japanese iris. "When the black raspberries are ripe, Diggety and I pick them. Diggety will wait for me to go into the woods and pick raspberries. He'll wait forever. I don't know where I'll be. You'll be lying in a zoo someplace with baby gorillas climbing all over you and a female watching you as she piles straw on her head, flowers in the straw. Diggety will be waiting for me to go into the woods and eat raspberries with him."

The gates ground closed behind us. The water rose in the lock. The mother chirped at the side of the barge. I knelt near her, put out my remarkable hand, and held her remarkable flipper close to the barge to protect her as we went through the locks. Her baby glided upside down beneath her, watching, safe, as the forward gates opened and we passed out of the locks into a higher Okeechobee level. On the right side of the bank, an old place, not buttressed, I saw what might have been a dappled back swimming before us and then I saw both of them clearly as they swam into a marsh to feed. Bullrushes swayed, opened, closed over them.

I spread the fresh bale of hay alongside the cage, spread it smooth as if I were making my own bed at home, spread it soft. Moses watched me when I wasn't looking at him. I could catch the swift turn of head. I played "Old MacDonald" on his plesiosaur for him. He would not come over, would not move his lips, would not play. I opened his cage door, something I'd never done. He scrambled to the back of his cage, watched me without making eye contact. I had never been in his cage. I reached for his tub. I heard a terrifying *whoosh*, the sound of the brushes descending, surrounding me in a car wash, enveloping, exploding. He lunged at me. He was swollen to twice his size, his hair fully extended, standing up on end. I screamed and tossed the tub at him. Moses caught it, sat in it, crossed his arms on his chest, looked away from me. The nimbus of hair flattened down, his crest dropped, his face opened, folded into his play face. He chuckled. A gorilla's joke. Diggety's joke is to run up behind me, shove himself between my legs, and lift me. I know Diggety runs off laughing. Moses had fooled me. I suppose I had paled, for he stood, shook his head rapidly from side to side, told me he had meant no harm.

I settled myself on the straw with Mrs. Froelich's blanket and Paul's Fisherman's Friend on my tongue, curled down, waited for Moses. I thought of all the nights I had waited in bed for Steven, quiet, making believe I slept, the light on, waiting, waiting all those nights for someone who never was what I waited for. For whom had I been waiting? Not quite Steven. Perhaps someone I'd known in the sea, someone I'd shared my childhood with.

"Do you understand the breakthrough I've made, Steven? Do you understand I've entered some sort of natural consciousness? That the world has come alive for me? I've tasted the fruit, Steven. It's sweet and compelling. In some small way, I've returned to the Garden. I'm no longer yearning at the gates. Don't you get it? Why are you talking about being in love or being crazy? Why are you talking about me as if I were the enemy? Why are you hunting me?"

Moses came from his cage slowly, sniffed me, belched softly, snorted through his adenoids. I acknowledged him with a snort of my own, permitting him to enter my space. He dropped his tub in the straw, lay on his back, his knees pulled up to his belly, his hands lightly drumming his chest. I put my head on his chest. He pulled up a hank of my hair delicately, let it float down, examined it in the light, played with it very gently.

"The sea is different, Moses. There we had no territory to

defend. Things floated away. That's why you're different. You were never in the sea. You're into territory, not things."

Moses' hands said, "Hurry up, tickle me." I scratched his belly, under his arms. He chuckled.

"You ain't got no pinch, my friend." I lifted his fingers. "This little Moses went to the jungle and this little Steven stayed home in the savannah, the orangutans took to the trees, and this little lady went way way way out into the sea."

He scratched his stomach, belched, turned, looked over his back at me, invited me to groom him. "You were right about place, John. Everything has its place. Your place and my place were vastly different. Place shapes. Moses stayed in his blue-black jungle pocket, under his waterfall, ate all he wanted, fought with no one. Peace is in his bones, in his genes, in his blueprint. I went into the sea, grew round, gentle, and smart on seaweed. You stayed on the savannah and scratched out a living. And I use the words *scratched out* advisedly." I stroked the dusky skin of Moses' naked arm. I tickled his wounded back. Now and then he moved to direct me to a new spot, grunted when I reached it. In the rock and lull of the barge, in the movement of the water, I dozed, dreamed, drifted, my hands tucked deep into his royal silver fur. "You see, Moses, I really could have been a little ape, hoop-legged like you are, with my sex under my tailbone, like your ladies, and my nose concave like yours, and covered with hair like you. And in the water, when my legs straightened out, my sex moved from under my tail to under my belly. I lost my hair. I came out ready to speak, ready to walk, not ready to be mounted. I was no longer an ancestor ape, chimp, or whatever we had been. You had become a gorilla. Steven and John had become chimps. I was almost human. You know what, Moses?" I sat up with the idea. "That's why men had to grow such long penises. They had to stretch when we changed: stretch penises." I laughed. Moses chuckled, sucked on the soles of my feet, between my toes. I could barely sit still. "And that's why a male manatee has a member six feet long. He had to accommodate to his lady's new sea shape, poor thing."

"You enjoyed it. I felt you."

"I was trying to accommodate you, John. I hated it."

"But what does she mean, John? What does this really mean for you and me?"

"Nothing, Steven. It's all poppycock. I'd say it's time to grab her and take her home. She needs help. It's of course in our favor that she thinks she's a sea creature. She may leave the gorilla behind."

"If she thinks she's a sea creature, she may leave all of us behind. Oh, God, John, she'll wander around the house like the Little Mermaid until I throw her back into the sea."

"Long skirts, my friend, and lots of Prozac."

Steven laughed, but not easily. "I guess I better close off her accounts."

"Not yet. We don't want her to do anything desperate."

"We've got to move."

"Agreed." John Banks rested his hand on Steven's forearm.

"Steven, Steven, don't listen to him. You know me better than John Banks does. He isn't helping you here. You're a better man, a kinder man. He's a dangerous man, brutal. Don't use him, Steven. He'll ruin everything. He's not on your side, Steven. I'll work this out without fireworks and plans of action. Try not to think in straight lines, Steven. Try not to grab. Try, Steven, try. Get rid of John Banks. Get rid of his mentality. He's a killer. Come to my side."

"What choices have I got, Linda?"

"Trust, patience."

"You've blown those years ago."

I heard Diggety barking. "Steven, tell Diggety to keep practicing in the water." I heard the wind chimes on the back porch.

Diggety has webbed feet. Diggety swims overhand. Diggety saves me instinctively in the water. How long did it take for Diggety to change his learned process of saving a human life into an instinct? Diggety has been with me that long. Longer than Steven? A long, long time. Maybe Diggety was in the water with me. Maybe that's what's between us. Thousands and thousands of lives of friendship.

"You see, dear girl, it's a matter of sacrifice. To whom and what are you willing to sacrifice. You are sacrificing some particularly vital parts of your life for some poorly interpreted dreams about waterfalls which may or may not exist, some fanciful idea about saving the gorilla, at the expense of your marriage, your husband, your husband's financial security, and, if I may, at the expense of your sanity. For what? A gorilla who is about to die any moment? For what, Linda? A handful of dreams? This is pure self-indulgence. If you want to take action based on the romantic interpretation of your dreams, that's your business. The business at hand, however, the immediate, if I may add, pressing, dire business at hand, is getting the gorilla to Tarpon Springs before he dies so Steven doesn't have the pants sued off him. Steven's rental contract makes him responsible for the gorilla. So don't even consider a dramatic interlude at Busch Gardens under the waterfall. You must get him to Tarpon Springs safely and then rethink your life. Then, dear girl, if you really are leaving your husband . . ."

"No, John. I don't like you. Steven trusts you."

"Don't play with me, Linda."

"You're a frightening man, John Banks. I want nothing to do with you."

Moses moved back into his cage. I rolled over to watch him. He rifled through the straw, found something, held it between his lips, returned to me, snorted, lay on his back, put the square piece of paper on his chest. He drummed on the paper. I dared not pick it up, but I elbowed closer and closer until I could make it out in the dim light of the truck. His treasure was a scrap of glossy paper, slimed and chewed, crushed and stained. It was a torn part of the Busch Gardens brochure and in particular it was the portion of the brochure on which a gorilla stood beneath a waterfall. Moses was not trading for a Mars Bar. He was trading dreams. His great hand over my head as if it were a basketball, he rubbed my hair between his fingers.

"Maybe Stavros would take us there. Maybe." I snorted at him.

He snorted at me. I lay back, wondered how I could take him to his waterfall, what it would cost me, what it would cost Steven. I slept and heard, someplace back in my sleep, my own snoring. Steven had accused me of snoring as many times as I'd denied it. I heard my snores and then I felt a heat above me and a pressure and it was the pressure of Moses' strange thin lips on my lips, trying to keep me quiet, muffling my snores. I pushed him away before I thought I oughtn't, but he wasn't upset. He simply, gently, placed his hand over my mouth. I poked him in the ribs until he pulled his hand away. I woke up once, popped another Fisherman's Friend, asked him if I smelled as bad to him as he smelled to me, gave him a Fisherman's Friend, but he was deeply asleep on his back, belching, farting, grumbling, and, under it all, I could hear the wind through the hole in his heart. Liquid, I poured through the squares of logic.

"Steven, Moses went upland. He's shown me: from the Ethiopian plain, to the highlands, down the Rift Valley, along the salt beds and the burning natron, to a lake with flamingos, to a cliff, deep into the jungle, to a waterfall. He ate leaves and fruit. I've seen his trip; I've seen mine. I can only imagine yours from what I know of you. It wasn't nice. You ate flesh and drank blood. I'm going to take Moses to Busch Gardens. He's going to die and I want him to get to the waterfall before he dies. I know how angry you'll be. But I must do this."

"*The gorilla comes first. Is that right, Linda?*"

"*Oh, Steven.*"

"*That's right, isn't it, Linda? He comes first. You don't care about me. That's what you're saying, isn't it?*"

"*If you could think in puddles, you wouldn't have to force me into binary decision making. I don't like yes or no questions. I'll never touch a computer again. It's bad for my soul. All of you come first. I'm exhausted.*"

Moses rolled me over and took nibble bites of my behind, very delicately. Bite, bite, bite. I giggled. "*It is only a suspicion that the gorilla* thinks *in clusters, John Banks, but I am dead certain he nibbles in clusters.*"

"*You were always naughty, dear girl, but this is going too far. I've warned you, haven't I?*"

Later, I heard footsteps and looked up to see Andre, the bright sun behind him, a bottle of wine and two glasses in his hands, come a-courting, but his face was frozen as he looked down at us. I heard him whisper, "*Mon Dieu.*" He tripped on something as he left. It was very hot, noon, I imagined. Halfway. The engines started up.

N I N E T E E N

"Steven?"

"I'm right here, Linda. Are you okay?"

"Now that I know the nature of the beast, seen the nature of men, and know the nature of woman, I've considered the nature of man and I believe I know what happened, Steven. You were a chimp. Or something like a chimp, something brutish."

"Come off it, Linda."

"You were a chimp. By the time I came out of the sea you were a full-blooded killer and now you're a half-blooded killer because you took us as wives. Half chimp and half human. You're a hybrid. And that's why you're dangerous and unpredictable, because you're divided at the core and I never know if you're going to be like me or like that other brutish part."

"Linda, I realize you—"

"Human means woman, not man. You're an addition to woman. I'm the template. You added the bad stuff."

"I never minded equal rights. But this is carrying it too far. Much too far. What about daughters?"

"My daughter rarely partakes of your brute. My daughter's brain is like mine."

"Is that so, Linda? How is it she doesn't speak to you?"

"Because I didn't tell her the truth about men and marriage. Because I couldn't tell her until you died."

"It's a bad dream, Linda. You're having a bad dream."

"Cain and Abel. And you killed my firstborn and took me, that bloody day on the beach. You didn't know whether to eat me or mate me, but you overwhelmed me. Kill the men and the children, rape the women. As Mr. Froelich would say, 'So what else is new?' "

It was past one. Moses, restless in the sultry heat, snored, gasped, sputtered, rolled back and forth, scratched his stomach, his crotch, threw an arm above his head, batted flies from his nose. The truck was steamy with his heat and smells. I walked out on the deck to eat a sandwich.

"Why must we replay this, Linda?"

"We replayed it every day in a million ways for millions of years and I'm tired. I'm tired of being the same. I'm tired of being equal. I'm different. I'm very, very different and I'm tired of fighting. I came out of the water singing, but my first words were, 'Don't, please don't.' "

"John, listen to her." Steven's voice was plaintive.

"Your little wife certainly has a new interpretation of the Big Bang theory." John Banks laughed. Steven didn't.

"And we had your children, Steven. They were too big and it hurt and they had, many of them, fur and fangs. You were half and half. Steven, you're less than the rest. Everett Everett is half human/half chimp. Andre

is almost completely brute. But you, John Banks, disguised, undercover, are
the pure specimen, the most dangerous. Perhaps the ultimate manipulation
has been domesticating the brute in men. 'The gorilla, he is what he is. It's
your husband you should be afraid of.' "

"Because," I told Mr. Froelich, who knows a lot about animals even
though he keeps Mrs. Froelich prisoner, "because Steven is the hybrid."

"Oy, girlie, are you going to get in trouble."

"Half and half. Get this down, Steven. We can use it. She's getting this
from the bloody cream her gorilla's drinking."

"Like her chartreuse dolphins, right, John?"

The sky was bottle blue, the sun blistering. Brown funnels of
burning sugar from the cane fields spread over the lake. I couldn't
see a shoreline. The two red eyes of the power plant lights were
lower than they ought to have been, behind us rather than to the
left. Everett Everett had said no one crosses the lake. Nevertheless,
as if we were perched on an immense ball, the water curved
downward all around, curved away from the horizon, disappeared
into a brassy acid radiance.

"Yo, Andre, Andre," I called. "Where are we going?"

"Okee Tante. Stavros, he is late."

That told me nothing. "Why are we crossing the lake?"

"To get to Okee Tante." He grinned, shrugged, ignored me.
There was nothing to do except go back into the truck and give
myself to the sweat and heat of the straw and Moses. Andre offered
no explanation. It would mean nothing to ask and probably be
dangerous to confront. Stavros, with his red suspenders and his
Byzantine mind, of course, was involved.

Midafternoon, when I next looked out from the truck, remnant
streamers drifted from the grape-ice underbellies of storm clouds.
We were entering a somber territory of sawgrass, cattails, bullrushes. Far away, the clouds sagged, loosed long straight rain lines.

Near us, in the swamps, frogs called in the rain. Andre unloaded the empty barge at a launch site, entered a canal, pulled up at a trailer park called, indeed, Okee Tante, docked at a launch next to Lightsey's Seafood Restaurant. Lightsey's windows were draped in fishnet and glass balls, the parking lot palms still hung with Christmas lights.

I laid an alligator at the cage door and followed Andre into the restaurant. It was dark and cool and well after lunch hour. Except for a dozen or so Seminoles at a long table and a single man in a Cubaverra jacket at the back of the room, the place was empty. We sat down next to three manacled lobsters in a glass tank. They looked at me with Mrs. Froelich's hyperthyroid eyes. The Seminoles joked about the alligator they were eating, drank from sweating pitchers of iced tea. The men wore traditional ribboned shirts, Serengeti sunglasses, big gold watches; the women, stretch pants and Disneyland T-shirts. All had big chests, strong arms, heavy gentle faces, small hips. The Cubaverra jacket sitting at a table in the back of the restaurant looked out a window to the parking lot, drove cigarettes into the ashtray, one after the other, tapped the top of a long narrow white florist's box on the table. He was Mexican, I imagined, pear-shaped, with narrow shoulders, a thick waist, fat hips, designer hair. His waist was too thick. Money-belt thick? It was his anniversary and he was waiting for his wife. It wasn't his anniversary and he was waiting for Stavros. The box held long-stemmed roses. The box held a shotgun. Linda, I told myself, only hindsight can draw the distinction between paranoia and intelligence. You better move. He stood. A white truck pulled up. He waved. Another truck came in too fast, tires squealing. It was time to move. I told Andre I had to go to the ladies' room. He grabbed my wrist roughly and pulled me back into the booth. "Sit." Hindsight came too soon.

The Indians turned, watched. A man at the head of the table half stood. Andre released my wrist, growled, "Order first."

"Fried clams and a beer." I didn't think I would ever eat seafood again. I was ashamed before the lobsters. I could no longer assume animals didn't know, didn't feel.

Andre grunted. I walked slowly around the Seminoles' table toward the side of the restaurant to the ladies' room. As I passed the man who had stood, I said very softly, "Don't let him follow me."

The restroom was on the porch. I climbed over the protective railing, over the side of the porch, slipped into the canal, swam around the back of the tug, kept Diggety's Being with me, stroking evenly through the canal, held him with me so nothing with jaws wanted me, climbed aboard the barge, kicked out the bricks in front of my tires, ripped off a tarp from the windshield, blitzed the truck up the launch ramp into the trailer park. The barge bounced and slammed the water behind me. Andre ran from the restaurant. John Banks was in the second car, blocking Stavros, who shouted and waved his arms. "Linda! Linda! Stop." In my mirror I saw the Mexican with the flower box, but he was too late, for I drove out of the trailer park and headed toward the town, toward Highway 710, toward the red eyes of the power plant, where I would find Everett Everett's swamp. I knew they were after me. All of them, in some sort of Girl with the Golden Goose parade. I wondered how much, after all, poor Moses was worth.

When had it happened that I would sacrifice my self for this creature? Perhaps millions of years ago, perhaps this week. When I felt the peace in the marrow of his bones? When I recognized him as me and me as him, more and less? It had happened as if there had never been a choice. It had happened when I saw his majesty denigrated to a circus act, the rotten meatloaf, the belly dance. It had happened when I saw his naked arm, saw the ancient pain in his eyes, the weariness, saw the whip stripes from Danakil, heard the hole in his heart, saw the waterfall.

Two or three miles out of town, the belly of the sky split open. Rain slashed at the saw grass, at the groves, at me. There was something celebratory about its power, its madness, its own abandon. I was Moses' leopard at the edge of the cliff. I growled at the thunder and slashed my tail at the lightning. I swung wild curves around the orange trucks, swung into blinding rain, in and out of the passing lane, swung in a rhythm when I was ready to pass. Nothing could stop me. I couldn't see the red lights. I could see them. I passed the landscaped entrance to the power company, took a left into a U-Pick-Em Grove down the road, drove deep into the grassy avenues of burdened orange trees as far as I could. Stavros would pass me; John Banks would pass me. I suspected the man in the Cubaverra jacket would be with Stavros. I grabbed a tarp and an armful of net. Moses refused to get out of the truck. I pulled up my T-shirt and showed him a breast. Breasts don't turn gorillas on; rear ends do.

I believe, for Moses, my breast was a sign of authority. Whatever it was, it worked. He took his tub and ran with me through the orange trees. Rain beat at us, swept us forward to the highway. There, I saw Stavros turning his truck around at the entrance to the power company, saw a second shape with him, watched them head back toward Okeechobee. At the first break in traffic we ran across the highway, ducked into a stand of palms. Very soon John Banks pulled in, turned around, drove back toward Okeechobee. Moses and I slipped along the border palms until we found a gate and a sign that read Barley Barber Swamp.

Not because he wanted to get in but because he liked to squeeze locks, Moses squeezed the lock open and we started down a straight shell road, flanked on one side by railroad tracks, on the

other by a perfect waterway for alligators. Dead turtles were caught
on the railroad tracks. The rain drummed on their shells. There
was no place to hide. I could only hope the rain would continue to
clutch us in its fist and drive us forward.

We had not gone far when Moses lay on his side on the road,
catching his breath, heaving. I heard a rattle in his chest I hadn't
heard before. I gave Moses some nitroglycerin. I rubbed his back,
the great bony shield of muscle, the soft leather of his chest.
I stroked the long fur of his shoulder. "My beautiful wizard beast.
You really are the wild man of the forest, aren't you? My grandmother's saint who's come to help me find what I've lost." I
rubbed under his chin, lifted and smoothed the velvet nap of
his fur. He sighed a long deep quivering sigh, caught his breath,
stopped panting, raised himself slowly, made that soft cough
sound, almost as if it were my name, called me to come with
him.

How long it took us to walk the road to the parking lot of the
swamp, I don't know. It was forever for Moses. We moved on a few
paces at a time until we could take shelter under a thatched open hut
with benches. "A chickee—" the wooden sign read, "—typical
Seminole dwelling. Notice the woven roof." We noticed also the
water fountain, a candy machine filled with Mr. Nature's Unsalted
Trail Mix, Mr. Nature's Unsalted Oriental Nut Mix, and an assort-
ment of Mrs. Nature's Dried Fruit. Nailed to a support column, an
educational environmental less-than-reassuring poster displayed
large to small silhouettes of wildlife in the swamp: bear, alligator,
deer, bobcat, raccoon, indigo, rattler, oh my God, green tree snake,
cottonmouth moccasin, a vast collection of spiders, and an unneces-
sary warning to stay on the boardwalk that circled the swamp for a
mile and arrived back at the chickee. I pressed the pedal of the water
fountain with my foot. Moses took a sip. He stepped on the pedal
again and again, pushed the water back into the fountainhead with

his finger, drank it, stood on it, hung upside down, washed his feet, let it run on his face, down his arms. When he was bored with the fountain, he banged on the glass of the candy machine. All I had in my pockets were his tranquilizers and a pocket flashlight, no quarters. Moses backhanded the candy machine, lifted it, slammed it again and again on the concrete floor until it sprang something from its interior, then pulled the machine apart like a loaf of French bread. When he lost interest in the food, he pulled his tub over his head, rolled onto his side, laid his alligator next to him, and went to sleep. His chest heaved with the effort he'd just made.

How I wanted my own alligator. I climbed on top of a picnic table, covered myself with the tarp, heard the rain stop, heard the drip-drip of the swamp and its buzz and hum of sounds, zippers, rockers squeaking, screen doors swinging, all the sounds of the silhouettes swelling to life. I heard the ancient footsteps of Indians, the soft paddle of canoes, murmuring, and I woke up with a feeling of presence at the back of my neck, raised hackles, a light pressure, a cold presence that I couldn't identify until I stood and a small brown snake dropped from the back of my shirt to the bench of the picnic table, sat up on its tail, looked at me, slithered past me, onto the boardwalk, into the swamp. I screamed. Moses raised an edge of his tub to watch me. I tore off my clothes and screamed. I stamped my feet, clenched my fists, my body rigid as an Irish girl dancing a jig. Moses went to the water fountain, stepped on the pedal, filled his mouth, came at me with his mouth filled, stood over me. I could not stop screaming. He stood looking at me with his mouth full, then sat down in front of me on his powerful haunches, lifted me onto his lap. I opened my mouth to scream. He let the water fall from his mouth into mine. It might have been mimicry. I after all had given him water to make him feel better. Or was he stuffing my mouth to keep me from screaming just as he had covered my mouth to keep me from snoring? Or was he giving me a drink of water because he loved me? He screwed his face into funny shapes, sucked in his cheeks, pulled his lower lip up over his nose.

"It wasn't the snake, Moses. It was everything and the snake. We have to go in there, Moses. Nightwatchmen. We can't sit out here. Many snakes. Many many snakes, leeches, jiggers, ants, mosquitoes, spiders. Maybe Everett Everett will come." Moses, hearing me speak, decided I was finished screaming, ignored me to complete the gutting of the candy machine.

I wrapped the tarp, the nets, my clothes, into a ball, started down the boardwalk. It was covered with old leaves. Moses raced clumsily around me, in front of me, back and forth, euphoric, on three legs, his hands filled with his Mr. and Mrs. Nature baggies, stuck between his toes, in his mouth, a pile under one arm. I moved far more cautiously. Shafts of sunlight filtered through the canopy of giant cypresses. Drip, slosh, movement, secret movement, trees looped with snakes and moss, green tree snakes, wisps of fog, pockets of black, green, and blue, bruises of light, stretches of rippling black swamp water.

There was only one cypress we could climb. It stood in the center of the swamp, at the boardwalk, its flanks girdled by a strangler fig, its limbs horizontal. "Indicating," the sign read, "that it was the mother cypress of the grove and is at least eight hundred years old." Her sons and daughters towered and spread about us, their arms lifted to the final rays of the sun. But below, where I was, night already drifted among the shadows, slid down the vines. I slung layers and layers of fishnet around the cypress's leader and limbs until I had a strong hammock for Moses. Birds rooked in trees above us, boisterous. Hundreds? Branches bent under great birds. I saw wood storks with their polished cream neck feathers. Like a theater crowd settling in

their seats, hordes of grackles fussed, grumbled, fell silent as
Moses came near.

Moses stood in a curve of the boardwalk, under a bit of open
sky, looked intensely at something in the trees. I called him. He
stayed where he was, his back to me, stared at the space above
him in the trees. I stood next to him, saw the setting sun, a fiery
ball, slipping down into the power company reservoir, the calico
sky turning red, igniting water and air. Moses spread his arms
and turned in circles under the sun, to the sun. I spread my arms
and turned in circles with him, light, naked, mad, joy bubbling
up in my chest.

When only small traces of the sun filtered through the trees,
Moses picked up his bags of food, I my own bundle. The grackles
started up again. Moses climbed the mother cypress, pulled Spanish moss into his nest, threw it over his head, over his body, tucked
it under his behind. I climbed to the limb above him, pulled the
tarp over myself, pressed myself into the arms of the old dead tree,
into the cancer of vine and fig around her smooth silken surface,
pressed my forehead against her, against the silhouettes swelling
around me, against the night which had come too quickly. Moses
slept and dreamed. I saw his waterfall, saw a female watching him,
saw her lay straw and flowers on her head, dance around him in
circles, saw little male gorillas climb on him, stroke him, sit at his
feet and absorb his silvery power, saw him scratch himself, beat on
his chest with pleasure. It was a good dream.

*Mr. Froelich leans on his elbows on the fence. He wears Wailing Wall
robes. "Girlie, the gorilla, he is what he is. Be afraid of your husband."*

"Your son is trying to kill the gorilla."

"What else is new?"

I wrapped an arm around a limb, held it like a pillow to my cheek, breathed in the moist sap of the swamp, cool in my lungs, of moonflowers blooming, of the deep secret salty immortal sap of the majestic creature below me. I watched the swift braid of water as a solitary creature slipped through it beneath us. I pressed against the mother cypress and let my sap flow into her dry wood. I tingled with something. I think it was my Being.

John Banks is tapping a desktop, using all his fingers so he sounds like a running animal. He is very impatient. "Linda, as usual, there are some holes in your logic. For one, if we were on the savannah and you were in the sea, how did we reproduce?"

"We didn't. I had a husband in the sea. You were on land. When the grass started to dry, you unseamed the little foragers for the grass in their intestines, ate the grass, ate the intestines, ate them. It wasn't man who became a hunter. By hunting you became a man. If there had been enough vegetation, you would have been something different. But those were hard times. You grew volatile, cruel, destructive, killer, aggressive, dominant, devious, deviant. God knows it isn't something I carry. I didn't hunt. By not hunting, I became woman. Too little muscle and bone, too much heart. Too little fang and fur. And yes, John, too much curiosity, too much trust, innocent. You were right. By the time I emerged, you'd drunk the blood. You were a full-blooded killer. Real men don't eat quiche because they can't kill it."

"Talk to her, John. You've got to talk to her."

"Dear girl, did your little husband stay in the sea and become a porpoise or a seal?"

"You killed him on the beach, John. Cannibal, Cain, Abel. You killed your brother on the beach. You were big. You had dense muscles, fangs, fur. You ran fast, caught me. That was the original sin, the mixing of blood between us. I was almost human. You were not. That was the Fall."

Both John Banks and Steven fell silent with the possibility, found arguments.

"May I remind you of mules and horses, Linda?"

"Chimp and human, John, human being woman," I repeated, fascinated. "Men are hybrids. That's why you're so dangerous, because you're unpredictable, because you have a double nature."

"Linda." Steven's voice was so thin and tired. "There are certain interspecies barriers."

"I daresay, old boy, what is true now might not have been true then. Hell, she might have been an egg layer. And there are experiments we've heard about with women and chimps. Back then, things may have been different. Look at the duck-billed platypus—a mammal who lays eggs. There may have been fewer barriers. Or different barriers. Humans and chimps did branch off much later than the gorilla. And their DNA structures are almost identical. However, what I would like you to clarify, dear girl, since there are thousands of far more qualified scholars than yourself, if I may, examining all of these ideas, how is it they've found none of this?"

"My bones are underwater. My tools are pebbles and shells and song. Find them."

"So, let me get this straight. It was a female something and a male something else. A large chimp-something. Something like Austrolopithecus africanus, *who was small and gracile, and* robustus, *who was large and rough."*

"Why are you patronizing her, John?"

"So she thinks we're taking her seriously."

"She's not right, is she?"

"Of course not, Steven. Don't be a fool."

"What does it matter if I'm right or wrong, Steven? I'm making my own map. I've found my own territory. You can make your own maps. This is my story, not yours. That little female sea creature was the template, is still the template for the human. The brutes added a few things: murder,

aggression, different perceptions of the world, different thinking processes,
an anatomically different brain, a preference for things, not people. You
can't blame it all on testosterone. It's in your wiring, ancient tracks laid
down in hard times. Testosterone only ignites the wiring. This goes deeper
than hormones, deeper than gender. This is in the anatomy, in the blue-
print. You are both myself and another thing, Steven, a lethal anomaly.
Chimp and me. Hybrid. You are an unnatural species, divided. You carry
my sea genes, your earth genes. There is an animosity of hormones between
us that dates back to the Miocene."

"What's your take on an animosity of hormones, John?"

"Nice phrase. Felt it."

"I too. The age-old battle of the sexes, I suspect."

"But does she mean between men and women? Or something divisive in
our selves? Our own battle?"

"Probably both. Interesting. I'd never thought of that, but we are of two
natures, we men, aren't we? Bit more of the brute in us, and some husband
also. An uneasy mix, I daresay. And they, the women, are of one.
Interesting."

"Well, it hardly means we're unnatural."

"Of course not."

Moses prodded my bottom with his feet. Small feet. I tickled
them. They couldn't grab. Clean-skinned, childlike. Moses sat
upright in his nest, scratched his head, dribbling trail mix from
one hand to the other, rubbed it on his belly, tossed it over his head,
bounced raisins from one palm to the other.

"It was a terrible moment there on the beach and then the odd mixed
children born with full coats of hair and fangs and the fleeing across the
desert to green, implanted as we were with your brutality, which might be,
now that I think of it, the origin of the distinction between good and evil.
That may very well be the framework—the divided self of man. If evil is

aggression, if evil is dominance, if evil is murder, if evil is torture, if evil is rape, if evil is sexual deviance, if evil—"

"Are you getting any of this down, Steven? It would be useful."

"To prove me incompetent in court? I am incompetent. I could never really change you or your sons. You are still, after all, at this very moment, hunting me. God knows none of that's in my line and Moses certainly doesn't have evil in his soul, which means that the original line of primates did not carry it because he's older than both of us."

"Will you listen to her. My, my, Steven."

"She's very serious, John. Let her be."

"You know what the real proof of all this is, for me? Neither of you likes to be touched. Neither of you. You are so antiquely afraid of the universe, you don't like to be touched. You have to control it."

"Oh, Linda."

John Banks cleared his throat. "Well, under certain circumstances, I don't mind a good touch."

I knew the circumstances. They were rare and specific. That and the way they could load a station wagon. And the can opener. And the soap.

Night moths floated by, thin as Kleenex, huge, lit on the fiery-tongued orchids of the tree trunks. I saw a pair of emerald eyes steady in the water. Splash, grunt, flash, thrash. I shuddered.

"Linda, sweetheart, listen to me. Let's say you and I may have been separate millions of years ago and you have some memories that I don't, but we've also spent millions of years together. We're not that different. Certainly you and the gorilla have less in common than you and I."

"Oh, Steven, darling Steven, Moses lived in peace for millions of years. You didn't. He grazed all those years as I did. He found his niche and he stayed in it. He's wired for peace and gentleness. You have your killer soul and my human soul, a war in your heart. Sometimes there is more of one, less of the other, but you remain a divided self. There is dark matter in your heart. Remember the stripe up Andre's body? That's what the self-hatred* *and the hunger is all about: the self-hatred of a divided self, earth self and sea self, brute self, gentle self, within you. It's your battle and it's a terrible one. You could never understand that I wasn't the enemy. That you yourselves are, that you can't help yourselves."*

"She's not coming home."

"Don't be silly, dear boy. Of course she is."

"You're not, are you, Linda?"

A truck pulled in. I heard a real screen door. I hadn't noticed a building. I would have to tranquilize Moses soon. There would be others. A man yelled to someone else. "Well, Ah'll be. Goddamned bear got the candy machine again. Musta been a couple of 'em." A truck drove away. There would be others. I had no choice but to sit up and listen in the world of velvet moss and leather fern and jiggers. Moses reached out once and patted me on the thigh. The Florida Seaboard Railroad train hooted. Moses hooted back, beat his chest weakly. A green snake with golden eyes glided up the strangler fig near me, became the tree itself, hooked around me, looped down away from me and up again at my feet, slid to the end of the limb, dropped down to the fence railing. I heard its progress in the dry leaves on the boardwalk. Everett Everett, you said they didn't come out at night. I heard the shriek of a whippoorwill, hoot of owl, pipe of quail, a wonder of sound, the thunder of an alligator grunt, pig frogs, drums of pulse, scraping, ratchet, and rasp, the throb of the Jew's harp night, the thin scream of a nation of mosquitoes. Moses would hear intruders for me. Moses would roar and send death away. Four young owls, fluting, chirping, swooped from vines, sailed over the swamp water. One sat on the fence railing, looked at me, flew a little higher on the cypress limb, turned his head to look down at me, judged me, dropped from the limb to catch a dragonfly on the surface of the water. Owls mean change, owls mean death, owls mean relocation.

T W E N T Y

I listened for the murderous footsteps on the bridge of the board-walk. If Moses roared, he would alert half of central Florida, certainly all my hunters. I gave him a peanut-butter cup, looked at my watch. I desperately wanted him with me, but he would expose us. Moses touched my shoulder. His hand fell away, heavily. I was left to listen for myself. I heard other progressions in the leaves: clicks, coughs, whispers. The soft movement of a j-stroke from a canoe, my imag-ination. The Indian ghosts had come to trade. Something buzzed, swarmed angrily inside the tree. I tucked the tarp under my chin, over my head. I heard footsteps on the boardwalk, a soft padded crunch on cornflakes, footsteps in two directions. The night moths lit on air plants and orchids and waited. I waited. The frogs were still. The birds listened. I forced myself to think. Stavros, his head ripe with the cheese of profit, looks for me. He's sold the gorilla to someone. There will be a plane, a truck, others. Everett Everett will fly in to save me as he promised. Yes, but not to save me, to win me, to savor the adventure, a white Christian knight, and he'll screw it up because he's a romantic. Also he lied about the snakes. He would be no match for John Banks. Steven is home in the control center. John Banks is nearby.

A grackle sang a descending scale. It was one of a thousand night notes, but I heard it and it might have been E-I-E-I-O. It might have been Paul. Paul who was not a hunter. Paul who was not brave, who was not free. I heard two forms approaching from the left, saw two pocket flashlights and the iridescent wavy line I'd seen in the Pennsylvania woods, but there was another density in the night behind me. Two sets. Moses stirred. I held my breath. The grackle sang again and I knew Paul was near. I did not know if that was good or bad. I scratched Moses' chest. He shuddered but made no sound.

When my daughter started dating, she asked endlessly why she couldn't find a boy like Daddy.

And I would answer lightly, "You won't. Daddy's the result of years of training. Find one who's willing to let you train him. Like we trained the dogs. No punishment, positive reinforcement. It takes years for a boy to become a human." I was using the term *human* loosely. Then.

"But they do, don't they, become human?"

I am no longer using it loosely. "Of course," I had said, lying. "It depends on how well you train them. And of course, they often revert. They can't help reverting."

"I know. I've heard Daddy about the soap slivers."

"Well, that's what makes the world go around." Shamed for my weaknesses, I betrayed my daughter. She was so young. I had been so young. How could we tell these things to each other? Only later when my friends and I shook our heads and sighed, "Men," was there an inkling of the differences, the impossibility, the endless contention. I couldn't tell her the truth because I dared not look at it then, and now she won't speak to me because I hadn't told her or because I still might tell her and she is as afraid to know as I was. She's never trusted me since, rightfully. Now she irons someone's shirts and cries when she burns holes in them. My sweet daughter with your excellent mind, your lovely soul, your trusting and innocent heart, there is something hidden in your someone, something multiple, something not familiar, not family. Something dark, something murderous, something noisy and hairy, something cannibal.

"Why are you hunting me, Steven?"

"I'm not hunting you. I've sent Banks to protect you."

"There are more than two, Steven. I hear more than two. All the birds are quiet. All the frogs are quiet. I hear more than two."

"I sent only Banks. I swear."

"It's guns and buns time, isn't it? Logic is left behind. It's out of your control now. You've scented the field with guns, money, women. I hear men coming. I hear their balls clacking together with excitement like so many pairs of maracas. Four pairs, Steven, at least. And I hear the roar of an airplane landing on the shell road and a truck, two trucks pulling in, and the stroke of a canoe that is not the ghost of an Indian coming to trade. Rid the wilderness of bewitched wives and ripping beasts. Make it safe for God and Man and Cotton Mather."

"Linda, come home. We won't fight, Linda. I promise I won't fight. I love you, Linda."

"I don't think I want to be loved anymore. I want to be believed."

"Linda."

"Steven. I have to do something."

"Listen, there are only two and they are not there to harm you."

"Talk to her, John. You've got to talk to her. You need help, darling. Come home and let us help you. You know we belong together."

"You're drawn by instinct to me, Steven, but it is not a friendly instinct. It has never been."

I had to get everyone out of the swamp, away from Moses. I slipped down the tree. It was I who had to flap the broken wing of the mother bird. It was I who had to ignite the fire of sex to displace the fire of the hunt. Hadn't I done this forever? I heard clicks, no footsteps. I dashed naked toward them, through them, whoever they were. I heard intakes of breath on both sides of me.

"Deer. What the hell? Linda?"

I ran along the boardwalk. I thought I saw Moses crouched in a curve along the boardwalk. One-track minds, the deep straight track of instinct. I'd bumped them onto another track. As I rounded the chickee, Stavros leaped from it, ran toward me, stumbled, dropped. I caught a glimpse of Moses running. He had run too lightly, too smoothly. I passed the mother cypress. Moses was in his hammock. Just beyond the mother cypress, the arm I had expected for years to grab me in the darkness of my own hallway grabbed me. "Dear girl, everything's all right. I'm taking you home. If you don't come home, Steven is going to have you declared incompetent and take your True Value stores and half the principal. So . . . oh, my." John Banks slumped in my arms. He'd slumped in my arms before, but not this way. I let him fall to the boardwalk.

"It's me, Old MacDonald." Paul pulled off his gorilla head, released his laughter, slapped his gorilla knees. Paul in a gorilla suit. Oh, God. Paul had a dart gun. He was laughing. "Did you see? I ran between them. They didn't know the other guy was there. I dropped just as I got between them; they took each other out. Did you see them? I hit the ground. They shot each other. Stavros comes running down after you. Naked, son of a bitch, naked. What an idea! So then I get Stavros."

"And John Banks grabs me."

"And I get him. Who's he?"

"An old friend."

"You don't pick 'em so good, Linda."

"Curiosity is one of my fatal flaws. Who was the Cubaverra?"

"Stavros's connection. Stavros must have been selling the gorilla to him, which means I smell money." Paul stood above Stavros. "How long before Moses comes to?"

"I guess about twenty minutes, a little less."

"My babies have thirty-five minutes. Which gives you fifteen to get Moses and get out of here. Why don't you go put your clothes on?"

I'd forgotten my clothes. Paul stood over Stavros too long. He snapped Stavros's red suspenders against Stavros's belly again and again. Stavros already had the Cubaverra's money belt. Paul lifted it, handed it to me.

We sat cross-legged on the boardwalk. He left his gorilla suit on. Moses snored deeply. The birds started their noises, the frogs, the grackles. The swamp was back to normal except for the snoring men.

"You know I was Stavros's boy."

I rubbed his gorilla back.

"You *said* you weren't free."

"Not free; not brave. Hooked."

I took out piles of American dollars and gave him half the weight of the belt. "Free and brave. Unhook."

"That's a lot of coke."

"It's a lot of choices."

He flipped through the bills. "Jesus, thousands."

I stuffed my pockets.

"What did you say your name is?"

"Linda."

"Linda, my guys have twenty-seven minutes now. Your truck is out there behind a restroom about a hundred feet from the parking area. Drive around the south end of the lake toward the cane fires. Drive away from the sun in the morning, toward it after lunch. Look for signs."

A light swept over us. A man halloed, "Estevez, where the devil are you? Linda, honey?"

"Everett Everett, the savior," I whispered to Paul.

"Linda, I know you got the gorilla. I want that there gorilla." Everett Everett turned a curve in the boardwalk. "Linda, I want you to bring that there gorilla over to the truck up the end of the boardwalk."

Paul grabbed my arm. "Wait. He means me."

I giggled. Paul pulled his gorilla head on.

"Don't come any closer, Everett. I'm not dressed."

"Oh, sorry. Sorry. I'll wait. What are you-all doing not dressed?"

"Where are you taking him, Everett?"

"Mexico. He's got a ticket to a nice zoo in Mexico."

"I'm that there gorilla." Paul whispered, stuffed cash into his gorilla suit. "Do it. Turn me in."

"You dressed yet, honey? Bring the nets, guys. *Aquí. Aquí.* Hey, Señor Estevez, I got him. I got him right here. Hurry on up, Linda, honey."

"I trusted you, Everett Everett. You said you'd be my safe harbor."

"I *am*. I'm helping to get you where you-all bee-long, and that there monkey where he bee-longs."

"Right," Paul whispered. "On the beach at Acapulco. Do it, Linda. Take me to the truck."

"What if they hurt you?"

"Are you kidding? You think they're gonna open the cage to give me a tickle? You come down to Acapulco and find me. Gay, mental, has half a jaw, gives good massages, likes rain forests and exotic animals."

"Do you like to be touched, Paul?"

"Sure, don't you?"

"Get the truck ready. Open the doors. Open the cage."

As if I were reluctant, I led Paul over the boardwalk toward the chickee. "You better work on that knuckle walk," I whispered, and tucked the last one-hundred-dollar bill into his back.

Everett Everett turned his cap backward. The drivers were looking at their watches. "We gotta meet that plane, Mr. Everett."

"Hurry on up, Linda. Puhlease." Everett cupped his hands around his mouth. "Señor Estevez, we can't wait but a minute. See you in Mexico City. We gotta go. Linda, honey, you see anyone in there?"

"Not a soul, Everett Everett. Not a soul."

Paul hopped into the truck, into a cage. The two men hammered a shipping crate closed. The truck kicked sand. Everett leaned out the passenger window, waved his hat at me. "I love ya, honey. You keep in touch if you need anything. Hear?"

I stepped lightly over the sleeping men. John Banks, Estevez, Stavros, someone in a bush jacket.

Moses sat upright, chewed the bark of the strangler fig. "Time to go to your waterfall, Moses."

Moses looked at his non-watch, climbed down the fig wood girdle of the tree, stood in his awkward upright, grabbed me, sucked suddenly on a handful of T-shirt, a mouthful of T-shirt, embraced me, touched his brow to mine, opened my mouth very carefully with one hand, and with the other touched my molars.

Then, like a teenage boy on his first date, not quite knowing how to touch me, he put his arm around my back, then around my waist, very lightly. I put my arm around his shoulders. His hand rested on my waist. And that is how, linked, we walked up the boardwalk. I held that moment before me. More than the dreams, more than his lying on me, more than the gift of water, this was his gift of friendship. I would keep him with me always, the soft sweep of the long fur of his arm, the naked hand, light on my waist, the silly little naked feet next to mine, the massive body brushing against me, the majestic head, the girdle of royal gray. We walked down the boardwalk, friends, the way it might have been, perhaps still could be. "You don't think that day at the beach I went off with the wrong ape, do you, Moses? I'm going to cry over you, you big cheese." He growled softly, rumbled pleasure from deep in his throat. We walked that way, Moses and I, and between us there was a weight, a great sadness, a great and painful grief and sweetness, the weight and play of all Being between us. My burden, his burden. I will hear his ape hymn in the gurgle of waterfalls. Words are rain. The waterfall is a story. The pool beneath the waterfall is sweet and holds our stories forever.

I heard Everett Everett's plane take off, found my truck behind a small stilted building I hadn't seen when we'd arrived. Moses would beat his chest when he stood under the waterfall, grumble and grunt when the little male gorillas climbed on him, stroked him, absorbed his silvery power. I wondered how long he would live. I wondered what all the men would say to each other when they woke up in the swamp, what Paul would say when they opened the cage at the Mexican zoo. He'd say something very, very funny. I wondered what Steven would say when I came home to get Diggety.

"The last I heard, John, she had been treated in the Alliance Nacional Hospital in Santiago, Chile, and I received a bill for four million somethings or other for an item called a pretzel cushion and antibiotics. Then she disappeared into the bush and I have not heard of her since. It was two years ago. I hear from the hospital. I've never paid the bill."

"Wacko, Steve. Abysmally wacko off the wall. Had she ever been to a shrink?"

"Linda? No, not that I know."

"Gone wild, has she?"

"But I did have her paintings analyzed. She was dark and brooding, unstable and perhaps homicidal, and had difficulty expressing herself."

"Her paintings, you say?"

"Yes. Dark, brooding, unstable, hostile, paranoid, with a strong ability to compartmentalize and ignore."

"Menopause."

"It makes me uneasy."

"Yes, as if your mother's gone and she comes back barefoot and ragged and wild from New Orleans, where she'd been a hooker."

"And you're alone in the house."

"Yes, alone. Have you married, Steve?"

"I've tried. You?"

"Young ones. Yes. Yes, young ones. Won't do."

"Pretty, I'll bet."

"English girls, you know. The skin."

They chuckled, paused, remembered English girls.

"Why would she leave us?" Steven asks John.

"I daresay she's crazy."

"Crazy to leave us or just crazy?"

"Both. I daresay, both."